White Crow

White Crow

The House Of Crow Series Book 1

John W. Wood

DEDICATION

It has taken me two years to write White Crow. During that time I have, through research, come to hold the Crow Indians of The Yellowstone and the Vaqueros of Old California in high regard. The Crow had to be great warriors as everyone (Other Tribes) was more significant in population and wanted the Crow lands and their horses. The Crow were excellent horsemen, and their war ponies were coveted by the other tribes. The Vaqueros were also brave and legendary horsemen; from the Vaqueros, evolved the American Cowboy.

I respectfully dedicate this story to both.

WITH DEEP APPRECIATION TO

Mary Felix, the love of my life for her continuing support

Richard Wildbur, editor, researcher, and patient friend

Robert Muccigrosso PhD

James Spears

Len Dempsey

Michael J Schroeder

Ted Koppenaal

Jim Cook, photography

Lancaster Muzzle Loading Rifle Association

John W. Lesich

Curt Beckner, Crow research books

Henrietta Robles, Quinceañera and the wedding

Forris Hudkins

Raul Urbano

ALTA CALIFORNIA - THE BANDITS

Juan Ortiz sat astride his horse watching his prey below. Ortiz, hidden by trees, wrinkled his nose at the foul odor of rotten eggs. The smell was coming from the hot sulfur springs at the base of the hill. Overlooking the hill quilted in spring flowers, Juan counted three two-wheeled ox carts, four armed men, eight women and as many children. While the men were talking and watching the children, the women were scrubbing great heaps of white linens in the waters of the hot springs.

When Ortiz raised his hand, six men rode out through the trees and joined him. The horsemen and Ortiz wore sombreros, vests over simple white shirts and chaps over their leather trousers. They were all armed with muskets, pistols, and knives. The man next to Ortiz stood in his stirrups and looked down the slope. He eased back in his saddle and looked expectantly at Ortiz.

Ortiz told the man, "Chico, take three men and move down the hill and stay out of sight. I will take the rest and attack from here. When we start firing and have their attention, you attack from the rear. There are only four men. It should be simple and quick."

On a nearby hill, two men dressed in buckskins were watching Ortiz and his men.

"That looks like trouble," said Isaiah Crow, the larger of the two men. "Those folks at the springs won't stand a chance."

"Bandits! Those bastardos will kill the men and children, but it will be worse for the women. They will rape and abuse them. When they tire of them, they will sell them on the black market as slaves," said LeRue.

"That just doesn't sit well with me; how about you?"

"I figure we could be of some help," said LeRue matter-of-factly.

"It looks like they are going to split up. I'll follow the ridge from here so I can get a shot at the leader. If you ride fast on the backside, you can pick off some of the second bunch from behind."

With a nod, LeRue spurred his mount with his heels and began racing through the trees.

"Come on boy," Crow said to his mount, "let's make some wolf meat."

THE BATTLE OF HOT SPRINGS

At the hot springs, the women were on their knees, scrubbing the wet, heavy linens on the rocks in the hot, smelly, water. With their sun-browned hands and a rock, they rubbed and washed the fabric to a bright white. There was a sense of pride that their Don had three carts of linens. The other ranchos were envious of such wealth.

As the four-armed vaqueros smoked and talked, they appeared casual and unaware, but they had positioned themselves so they could keep an eye on their charges and the surrounding area.

The children were playing chase when the bandit leader fired the first shot. The women dropped the linens and immediately ran to the children. The men shouldered their muskets ready to meet the threat.

From the trees, five horsemen came charging down the hill. As the horse's hooves churned clods of sod into the air, Ortiz fired his musket, the heavy lead ball striking one of the guards in his leg.

Behind the bandits, Crow raised his rifle and fired. The ball hit Ortiz between the shoulders. Dead, he fell from his saddle. Crow let out a hair-raising war-whoop and charged down the hill.

Hidden by the hill, the second group of bandits, having heard the shooting, charged. From behind the bandits, LeRue aimed at the last villain in the group and pulled the trigger. His shot hit the bandit dead-center in the small of his back, knocking him from his saddle. He gripped his rifle in one hand and drew a war-hawk from his belt with the other. As he caught up with the unsuspecting bandits from behind, one by one, he began to kill them.

At first, the guards at the hot springs could not believe their eyes. The bandits were charging, chased by a wild man on horseback, a rifle in one hand an axe in the other. As he caught up with the bandits, he began to kill them with his axe. The guards, quickly regaining their senses, joined the fight. It was over in moments. Seven bandits lay dead or dying as their horses fled across the fields.

Crow and LeRue rode up to the group at the springs. The women were comforting the children, while two men tended to the wounded guard. From the group, one man, younger than the rest but better dressed, greeted their rescuers. He saw before him, two men. The tall one had broad shoulders and a full beard that enhanced his blue eyes. He wore his thick black hair in a pompadour that was caught up in a woven net at the nape of his neck. The second man was a bit smaller. His beard could not hide the smile on his face as he said in Spanish, "Hola, me llamo Jacques LeRue, y esto es Isaias Crow. ¿ Habla usted Inglés? (Hello, I am called Jacques LeRue, and this is Isaiah Crow. Do you speak English?)"

The young man, handsome with a gracious smile, replied in English, "I am Carlos Batista."

Crow stepped down from his saddle. "My compadré and I were on the hill when we saw the bandits. It looks like we got them all. How's your man? Is he going to make it?"

"Yes, I think he will have supper with his wife tonight. Thanks to you, we will all go home."

"We are going to San Diego. Is it far?" asked Crow.

"It is several days ride from here. However, first, I must take you to my father, Hernando Batista. He would never forgive me if I did not bring you home so that he could thank you for what you have done."

"That is right kind of you. We have been traveling a long way and could do with a rest. Perhaps we could buy some supplies?"

"But of course. We will finish here and return to the rancho." Carlos turned to one of his men. "Take one of the horses. Tell my father what has happened here. Tell him that we are all safe, but will be later than usual. Go now!" He called to one of the men tending to the wounded man, "José, collect the weapons from these bastardos. See if you recognize any of them."

The sun was beginning to cast shadows as the oxen plodded along pulling the three carts stacked high with the washed linen. Alongside each ox, one of the older boys would occasionally encourage the beast with a long staff. The children and most of the women sat atop the linens on the first two carts. The wounded man lay under a blanket on top of the linens in the last cart.

Later, as the procession began to climb a hill, Crow saw a man on horseback appear at the top accompanied by six armed men. Crow and LeRue immediately readied their rifles.

"It is my father! Do not shoot!" shouted Carlos.

The horsemen arrived in a cloud of dust. One man pulled up next to Carlos. Crow saw the concern mixed with anger on the face of the man. "You are all right, Carlos?"

"I am fine father, thanks to these two men." Reining his mount around, Carlos continued, "This is Isaiah Crow and his compadré Jacques LeRue. They saved our lives with great courage."

The older man, tall and lean, his dark face clean-shaven, maneuvered his mount between Crow and LeRue and offered his hand to each man. In English, he said, "I am Hernando Batista. I thank you for saving my son and my people. We will escort you back to the rancho. We will have something to eat, and we can talk." Next, Hernando greeted each of the guards, "I hear you fought bravely. You each will be rewarded." He moved to the cart and the wounded man who tried to rise. "No, no, stay still. We will take you home. Your family knows that you live, and they are waiting."

Hernando nodded at his son. Carlos raised his hand and motioning toward the hill called out, "¡Vamos a casa! (Let us go home!)"

THE RANCHO

As the horsemen and carts arrived at the rancho, a crowd of more than twenty people shouted greetings. The group was mostly vaqueros and Indian house servants. A woman and a young girl stood in front of the group. As the carts stopped and the men dismounted, everyone rushed forward to greet their friends and loved ones.

Crow and LeRue stood apart from the others. They watched as Hernando and Carlos approached them with the woman and the girl. Crow was struck by the beauty of the girl. Though she was young, she had a presence about her. Hernando said to the women, "These men are Señor Crow and Señor LeRue. They are responsible for the safe return of Carlos and the others. This is my wife, Señora Carmen Batista and our daughter, Francisca."

The woman and the girl wore bright, white dresses. Each had their hair pulled back in a bun. The woman was striking in her mature beauty. With a voice pleasant to the ear, she said in Spanish, "Welcome to our home. I am grateful to you both for saving the lives of my son and our people."

Crow, obviously uncomfortable, turned to LeRue. LeRue responded, "Estamos encantados de que podríamos estar de servicio. (We are happy that we could be of service.)"

"You speak Spanish well Señor LeRue," replied Señora Batista.

"I'm a Texican Señora and a citizen of Mexico. Isaiah speaks some Spanish, but is not fluent."

In English, she replied, "We will try to speak English until you are comfortable, Señor Crow. We are preparing a meal for you, but you will want to freshen yourselves first." The Señora motioned to one of the Indian servants who rushed over. "Take these gentlemen to the guest room." To Crow and LeRue she said, "I will send Carlos for you when the meal is ready."

As Crow and LeRue were led to the hacienda, Francisca turned to her brother. "They are interesting men."

Carlos, at first distracted, looked at the two departing men and then at his sister. "Yes, interesting, and perhaps… handsome?"

Francisca's face flushed, "I meant only in the way they dress and speak!"

Carlos, with a knowing smile that seemed to infuriate his sister more, replied "Of course, the way they dress and talk. They are fascinating."

Before Francisca could respond, her mother said, "Come, Francisca, we must see that everything is ready for our guests."

With an indignant glare at her brother, Francisca joined her mother as she walked to the hacienda.

Hernando, placing his hand on his son's shoulder asked. "Do I owe these men, Carlos?"

"Yes father, we had no idea the bandits were on the hill. Crow and his friend did not have to do what they did. Had they not stepped in, we all would have died."

"The man Crow, there is something about him, something different."

"LeRue told me on the ride back that Indians raised Crow. Do you see that shirt he wears under his coat, with the tufts of hair and the quill work? LeRue said that is a Crow Indian war-shirt, and that Crow had been what is called a Dog Soldier."

"I am looking forward to dinner. I want to learn more about these men."

Carlos, remembering Francisca's reaction to Crow thought, 'You are not the only one who wants to learn more, father.'

Carlos and his father headed to the hacienda. In one of the small white-washed cottages, the wounded vaquero lay upon his bed. His face was slowly regaining its color. His anxious wife sat, while his two teenage sons stood next to the bed. "I will be fine. The ball passed through. You must not worry."

His wife, silent tears slowly rolling down her cheeks, reached out and took his callused hand. "We could not help but to be concerned about you."

One of the boys asked, "Poppa, the two men in buckskins, they saved your lives?"

"Oh, you should have seen it!" his father replied, a spark of excitement in his eyes. "The big one, the one called Crow; he shot the bandit leader while riding on horseback! He let out a yell that made our hair stand on end. He had an axe in his hand, and he rode right into the middle of those bandits! It was something to see. He is el Guerrero (a warrior)!"

The boys were spellbound as their father told his story. Later, after their father slipped off into sleep, they met with the other young men who lived at the rancho. The story spread about the buckskin Guerreros and the one they now called 'el hombre con el hacha' ('the man with the axe').

THE STORY OF WHITE CROW

In a guest room of the hacienda, LeRue and Crow were changing their shirts. The red woolen shirts were prized possessions and were worn only for special occasions. Crow, like LeRue, wore his shirt outside his pants. He had just tied his belt around his waist and was reaching for his knife when LeRue said, "It would not be proper to go armed to dinner."

"Nothing?" asked Crow.

"Nothing!" replied LeRue. "Our rifles and knives will stay here in the room. Everything will be safe, as will we."

Reluctantly, Crow left the knife. "Should we bring a gift for our host?"

LeRue went into his pack and brought out a bundle of furs. Moving to the bed, he placed the bundle on the bed and removed the fur wrap. Inside was a jug with a cork in its spout, sealed with wax. "I figured I would give 'em a taste of corn whiskey," said LeRue.

Crow turned and went to his possibles bag and rummaged around inside it. From the bag, he removed a leather pouch, the size of his opened hand. The leather was nearly white, with a leather drawstring at its opening and decorated on both sides with colorful beadwork and geometric designs with black-and-white quills. "I will give this," said Crow.

There was a knock at the door. LeRue went to the door and opened it. Standing in the hallway was Carlos. "Ah, I see you are ready," he said to LeRue.

LeRue opened the door wider, "Please, come in."

As Carlos entered the room, Crow returned to his possibles bag and reached inside. He withdrew a knife in a highly decorated sheath. He turned to Carlos and handed the knife to him. "You fought well today and have brought us to your home. I want you to have this."

Carlos took the sheathed knife and marveled at the intricate beadwork on the scabbard. He took the stag-horn handle in his hand and withdrew the knife. The blade was thick at the top. Its honed edge slightly curved to a clip point. The point was sharpened upper and lower. Carlos positioned the guard at the side of his open palm and smiled at the balance of the knife. "This is a beautiful gift. Where did you obtain such a knife if I may ask?"

"I made the blade from an old butcher knife. The handle is from the antlers of an elk I killed. The sheath is from a buffalo hide. I did the beadwork during the winter so that I would not get cabin fever."

"I will carry this with pride! Muchas gracias, amigo. And now, let us eat! My mother and sister have had an excellent meal prepared."

Led by Carlos, Crow and LeRue entered a large room where a long table commanded the center. Crow and LeRue, more accustomed to a one-room cabin or more often, eating around a campfire, were nearly overwhelmed. Six high-backed leather-upholstered chairs lined each side of the table. There were two slightly more ornate chairs at each end.

Carmen and Francisca had changed for the occasion, wearing colorful formal gowns. Crow had to force himself not to stare at Francisca. LeRue, the jug of whiskey cradled in his hands, leaned close to Crow and said, "Are you all right my friend, you look a little flushed."

Glancing at LeRue, Crow caught the knowing smile on his friend's face. Before he could speak, LeRue stepped away.

"Gentlemen, welcome," said Hernando. LeRue moved over to Hernando and presented him the jug. "We thought you might enjoy this. It is what we call bourbon whiskey. At the last rendezvous, a man from Kentucky brought this. It is made from corn and is amazingly smooth."

Hernando took the jug, flashing a satisfied smile at LeRue. "Gracias. Perhaps we will have a taste after our meal." Hernando was placing the jug in the middle of the table when Crow stepped up to him.

"Señor Batista, I thank you for your hospitality and want you to have this." He handed the beaded leather bag to his host.

Hernando took the bag in his hands and examined it, and looked up at Crow. "This is beautiful. The beadwork is exquisite. May I ask where you acquired this?"

"I made it. The leather is from a mountain sheep. Our winters are long, it kept us busy and out of trouble," Crow said with a smile.

Carlos joined in by saying, "Look at the workmanship of this father." Carlos handed the knife Crow had given him to his father. Hernando pulled the knife from its scabbard and turned it side to side in his hand. He returned the blade to its sheath and ran his fingers lightly along the design on the leather. Looking up at Crow, he asked, "Another winter?".

Crow smiled and nodded. "Don Hernando, your son fought well today. It is something I want him to have."

Hernando handed the knife back to Carlos. He looked with pride at his son and thought, 'If this man speaks of your courage, it is a great compliment I think.'

Carmen, placing a hand on Hernando's forearm said, "Come, let us take our seats. The meal is ready."

As they began to take their seats, Crow heard the tones of silver spurs on the tiled floor. Crow looked to his left and saw a man, perhaps thirty years of age, enter the room. His black hair was combed straight back, close to his scalp ending in a queue at the back of his head. His green eyes accented by his dark, clean-shaven face; his bearing projected strength and self-importance.

Crow did not like him.

Don Hernando, who was about to sit, stood up. "Ah, Hector." Stepping around the table, he greeted Hector. Turning to Crow and LeRue, he said, "Hector, these are our guests, Isaiah Crow and Jacques LeRue. Gentlemen, this is Hector Camacho; he runs the rancho."

Hector flashed a brilliant smile full of white teeth. With a slight bow, he said, "I have heard of your courage and thank you for the saving of Carlos and the others." Turning to Hernando, he continued, "I apologize for being late. I stopped and talked to the vaqueros about the banditos. None of our men recognized any of them."

"We will talk of this later. For now, let us eat before the food becomes cold."

Crow felt a pang of jealousy when Hector took a seat next to Francisca. He was sure his full beard had hidden any facial expression he might have shown. His thoughts were interrupted by Hernando, "Here sit to my right Isaiah, and Jacque, you sit next to him."

The meal was roast beef and vegetables with a hearty wine. The glasses were never allowed to go empty. Crow quickly learned to drink slowly. LeRue, on the other hand, seemed capable of drinking unlimited quantities. LeRue told them that he and Crow were what the Americanos called Mountain Men and that they had been trappers. The wanderlust brought them to California with a man named Jedadiah Smith. When Smith had turned north, Crow and LeRue had decided to stay. That was when they had come to the hot springs and the bandits.

Near the end of the meal, Carmen announced, "It is getting late. If you will excuse us, Francisca and I will retire now."

As the two women began to get up from the table, Hernando and Hector quickly stood and helped the ladies with their chairs. Saying their goodnights, the women left the room. Hernando and Hector returned to their seats. Hernando motioned to one of the servants who immediately came to Hernando's side.

"Bring us glasses. We will drink from Señor LeRue's gift. Glasses were soon placed in front of each man, while one of the servants poured the amber liquid into the glasses. Hernando raised his glass followed by the men at the table, "Salud!" The response was in unison, "Salud!"

"Ah, that is muchas grande," said an obviously pleased Hernando. "That warms the soul."

"I am pleased that you like it," responded LeRue.

His glass in hand, Hernando leaned back in his chair and said, "Señor Crow, it has been mentioned to me that you once lived with the Indians. May I ask how that happened?"

Crow took a moment and said, "My parents were killed by Blackfoot raiders. Crow Indians found and adopted me.

It was now that he realized that the wine followed by the whiskey had hit LeRue. "Tell them, tell them the whole story. It is a fascinating account."

"Yes, please tell us," insisted Hernando. "I would like to hear it."

With a moment's hesitation, Crow began…. "My parents apparently were settlers, traveling west when…"

Eighteen years earlier, American Great Plains

Brian Pringle and his family were on the high plains of America looking for a place to settle. Brian walked alongside the oxen, guiding them with his walking-staff. His wife Elizabeth sat in the back of the covered wagon with their two-year-old son, little Brian. Brushing the hair from her face, she smiled as her son struggled to open a small wooden box. She kept her bits of "precious" in that box which included a cross Brian had given to her. It was a Celtic cross made of silver with 'E. Pringle' engraved on the back. Elizabeth reached to take the box from Brian when he managed to open it and scatter the contents.

"Brian, you must be careful! Now help pick these up."

A short distance from the wagon, hidden in a fold of land, a war-party of Blackfoot raiders watched the travelers. With a hand signal from their leader, the Raiders broke the silence with their war-cries. The pounding hooves of their war-ponies shook the ground as they charged.

Brian desperately tried to get his musket from the wagon, but it had become wedged under the seat. He heard a shot from the back of the wagon as Elizabeth protected their son and met the challenge. Unable to retrieve his musket, Brian gave a Celtic war-cry and swung his massive walking staff, knocking a rider from his mount. Another well-placed strike of the staff cracked the warrior's skull. Brian sagged, as an arrow hit him in the thigh. Regaining his footing, he struck a mighty blow with his staff to the forelegs of a passing war-pony. The war-pony stumbled, sending the rider over its head. In fear and agony, the war-pony danced around stomping on the fallen warrior.

When Elizabeth heard the war-cries, she pushed Little Brian to the floor of the wagon and grabbed her musket. A Blackfoot warrior tried jumping on the wagon. She shot his painted face. With no time to reload, she grabbed for an axe they kept in the wagon, but an arrow struck her in the back. Mortally wounded, Elizabeth fell forward, covering little Brian. The last thing she saw was her silver cross in the small hands of her son.

This was not to be a good day for the Blackfoot raiders. The raiders had lost three braves and one war-pony. Now, from nowhere, came a band of Crow, the mortal enemy of the Blackfoot. The Crow made short work of the Blackfoot raiders, who were intent on plundering the wagon.

The Crow leader, Broken Leg, clambered into the wagon where he found Elizabeth and the dead warrior in the back of the wagon. He spied the small hand of little Brian, protruding from under his dead mother, still clutching the silver cross. Roughly, he pushed Elizabeth's body aside with his foot. Little Brian, now covered in his mother's blood, stared up at the Crow warrior with his father's piercing blue eyes.

Broken Leg picked up the child and held him out at arm's length. His memory flashed to his wife and her grief at the death of their infant son. Reaching down, Broken Leg pulled at a blanket that the dead woman laid on. Pulling it free, he wrapped the baby in the blanket and stepped from the wagon onto his war-pony. One of the Crow warriors joined him. Broken Leg showed him the child, "The child will need to eat soon. I will ride ahead. You gather what you want from here." With that, he galloped away.

It was evening when Broken Leg entered the Crow encampment. He knew the child must be hungry, but it had never cried out during the long ride. Broken Leg was already developing pride for this boy who had come into his life. As he dismounted in front of his tipi, his wife, Yellow Leaf, stepped out to greet him.

"I have brought you a son. He is hungry and needs a mother." Yellow Leaf took the bundle and pulled at a corner of the blanket. A boy child of nearly two years looked at her with startling blue eyes. He reached out with both arms and smiled. Without a word, Yellow Leaf turned with the child in her arms and reentered the tipi.

Back to The present

"So these Indians took you in, and adopted you, so to speak?" Hector asked tauntingly.

Crow did not like the tone of Hector's question. Before he could say what was on his mind, LeRue reached across and squeezed the top of Crow's thigh…hard. Relaxing, Crow said, "It is not unusual for Indians to adopt a child into the tribe. Broken Leg is a war-chief and has a high standing in the tribe. He and Yellow Leaf became my parents."

Hector watched Crow for a moment. He was sure that his taunt had gotten to the Mountain Man, but to look at him now, he could not tell.

"So Señor Crow," continued Carlos, "what is a Dog Soldier? LeRue described a shirt that you wore earlier as a war-shirt. Please tell us about this."

Crow looked at LeRue, who had suddenly found something interesting on his pant leg. "You tell them LeRue," said Crow. LeRue, looking up from his pant leg reached over, picked up his glass and had a sip of whiskey. Setting his glass down, LeRue said, "A Dog Soldier is a warrior, chosen from the bravest of the tribe. They wear a red sash around their waist and carry a sacred arrow. When they fight, there is no retreat. They pick their stand and stake one end of the sash to the ground with the sacred arrow."

Hector looked at Crow with interest, 'Do not underestimate this man who lives with Indians,' he thought.

LeRue took another sip from his glass and continued. "The Dog Soldier is also the protector of widows and orphans of the tribe. When he returns from a raid, he gives away whatever he has captured so that his charges can live comfortably. He keeps nothing for himself, he lives a spiritual life. That is how Isaiah got his name. His friend, Putnam, named him after the saint of widows and orphans, Isaiah."

Hernando looked at the young man next to him and wondered, 'What kind of man stands his ground and fights, yet has the goodness of heart to help others?' Aloud, Hernando asked, "The shirt you had on, the war-shirt, is that what you wore when you were a Dog Soldier?"

This time Crow answered, "When I joined up with the Mountain Men it was a sign to the Indians we met, that I was a warrior. It helped us keep our hair."

Hernando, picked up his glass, and holding it up he said, "It is late. The day has been a long one for all of us. Let us retire for the evening. We can talk again tomorrow; Salud!"

Raising their glasses to their host, they said in unison, "Salud!"

A MOTHER'S GUESS

Francisca had just finished getting ready for bed when there was a knock at her bedroom door. A click of the latch and her mother entered. It was a ritual that the two had, brushing each other's hair. Francisca took a seat on a backless upholstered bench that was placed in front of a dressing table with an adjustable mirror. She watched in the mirror as her mother removed the combs that held her hair in place, and combed it out with her fingers.

"I envy the thickness of your hair," said Carmen, taking Francisca's hair in her hand. She straightened and smoothed it. "It is well past your waist. You have been truly blessed."

Carmen, reaching over Francisca's shoulder for a hairbrush said, "Señor Crow appears to be very much a man, but he is also very rough in his manners. Señor LeRue is much more the gentleman. It must be his French-Mexican background that makes him so."

Carmen picked up the hairbrush from the table and began brushing her daughter's hair. "So, did you find the after-dinner conversation interesting?"

Francisca's heart leaped. She stared at her mother's reflection. As Carmen brushed her daughter's hair, the corners of her mouth curled up slightly, indicating she knew she had guessed correctly. Francisca had eavesdropped, listening to the men talking.

Francisca conveniently bent her head down so her mother could better brush her hair and also so she could not see her blush. "I think they are brave men who saved my brother's life. However, they live with Indians, and they are rough men."

Carmen brushed the long black hair, keeping her eyes on the mirror. Her daughter did not look up.

AMOUR

Crow and LeRue sat on the huge bed in the guest room. Crow bounced a bit and went to his pack that lay on the floor. He pulled his bedroll out and tossed it on the floor.

"Too soft?" asked LeRue.

"Too soft," replied Crow.

As Crow spread out the bedroll, LeRue went to his possibles bag and rummaged around inside. He pulled out a straight razor and a pair of scissors. Crow watched with curiosity as LeRue went to a low chest of drawers. A water pitcher and basin sat on top of the chest with a mirror hanging over it. Pulling out a couple of drawers, LeRue found a towel and spread it out flat. He began cutting his beard with the scissors, the hair falling onto the cloth.

"What are you doing?" asked Crow.

"Why I am going to skin this wild-man. I thought I'd say 'howdy' to Francisca … when the time is right of course."

Crow was surprised by the feeling of jealousy that washed over him at what LeRue had just said. Staring at his friend's reflection in the mirror, he was sure he could see a smirk on LeRue's face, even through his beard. Acting nonchalantly, Crow returned to his pack and pulled out a pair of scissors and a straight razor. Moving up next to LeRue, Crow pointed his chin up and combed his beard from his neck to his chin with the backs of his fingers. "I figure I can take you both, one at a time or together," he said in a murmur that seemed more threatening than if he had shouted.

LeRue stopped cutting his beard, "Together? Who together?"

"Why, Hector and you. He thinks he's got the nod from Hernando for Francisca's affections. I think Hector… and you are going to be disappointed," Crow said as he began trimming his beard.

LeRue returned to cutting his beard and thought, 'I knew I saw amour in your eyes tonight my friend. There will be no competition from me. But Hector... I think you may have to kill Hector someday.'

LeRue started to hum. Picking up his razor, he began to shape his mustache.

THE STALLION

Shaved and trimmed, Crow and LeRue arose before daylight. They both dressed in their buckskin trousers and red shirts. Crow was again reluctant to leave his rifle behind. For years, it was either in his hand or within grabbing distance. LeRue said nothing when Crow slipped his sheathed Bowie knife into his belt.

Outside, they could hear the rancho awakening. Men were greeting each other, their voices mixing with the sounds of livestock. LeRue stopped what he was doing and listened. LeRue said, "Sounds like your friend Hector is going to break a horse this morning."

Crow finished adjusting his knife and said, "Let's have a look-see."

The sun was just beginning to peek over the hills as Crow and LeRue stepped outside. Tied in front of the hacienda were several saddled horses. They could hear a commotion coming from the direction of the corral. Men could be heard yelling encouragement to someone, mixed with the sounds of an enraged horse.

LeRue looked at Crow questioningly. Crow shrugged his shoulders stepped out into the yard just as the sounds of breaking timber filled the air. From the corral, a magnificent horse, a big gray, came across the yard. It stopped and reared up on its hind legs, pawing at the sky. Crow was already at a dead run when the gray decided to move. It passed close to Crow, who in one swift motion grabbed a handful of the horse's mane. Swinging his legs up, he mounted the big running stallion. LeRue watched as his friend raced off into the dim light of morning.

In Spanish, a voice said, "We had better mount up and go look after your friend. He will need help." It was Hector covered in dust, and his forehead was cut and bleeding.

"I don't think we need to follow. He'll be back. However, my friend, you should do something about that cut."

Hector, for the first time, seemed to notice that he was injured. Touching his forehead with his fingers, they came away bloody. "Yes, I will clean up," he said. Turning on his heel, Hector left. From the entrance of the hacienda, Carlos came to stand next to LeRue.

"I have never seen such a thing," he said to LeRue. "He seemed to float up onto the back of that animal."

"He's a Crow Indian at heart," replied LeRue. "They are fine horsemen."

"That horse has injured three vaqueros who tried to ride it. Hector was going to show them how to do it this morning."

As the two men stared off in the direction where Crow and the horse had disappeared, LeRue thought, 'Ah my friend, now I'm sure you will have to kill this man, Hector.'

Carlos stopped and reached out to LeRue, who turned to face him. "You have shaved your beard!"

"Crow and I figured we needed to get civilized."

Carlos thought, 'I wonder if Francisca may have inspired this need to shave?'

It was daylight when Crow rode the now docile, but still spirited, gray stallion into the yard. The vaqueros elbowed each other as man and horse approached the corral. From the gray's back, Crow dropped to the ground and rubbed his hand along the gray's neck. "You have a great heart, my friend," Crow said to the horse.

Carlos approached, "He has fought everyone who has tried to ride him."

Crow, his hand now resting on the gray's back, gave it a pat. "He has spirit. Once he knew I respected him, he respected me."

"He is yours. I do not think anyone will want to try to ride him," said Carlos with a smile. "Too many that tried are still limping around."

Crow said, "Muchas gracias, but are you sure?"

"He would have been turned loose or killed for meat if no one could break him. Horses are as plentiful as chickens. Have you noticed the horses in the fields with a rope about their necks? Anyone may take and ride them. As you travel cross country, if your horse gets tired, you just saddle another and move on. Here at the rancho, there are many mounts always with a tether. Anyone may take one. So yes my friend, he is yours."

LeRue who had joined them, commented, "He is a beautiful animal. Back home you would be the envy, and target, of every Sioux warrior."

"They would steal the horse?" asked a surprised Carlos.

"It is a requirement of many tribes, that to become a war-chief, a warrior must take an enemy's horse or horses," said Crow.

"Isaiah here was muy bueno at it. He is known for taking the war-pony of a Blackfoot warrior who had tethered it to his arm while he slept."

Carlos looked at his two new friends. 'They are amazing,' he thought. 'Life seems to be an amusement. I like them.' "Come, el desayuno (breakfast) is ready!"

In her bedroom, Francisca had just finished dressing. Pirouetting in front of her mirror, she liked what she saw. 'I think I will wear a ribbon, the red one that father bought for me,' she thought. 'Oh, I wonder whether that will be too forward? I do not care. I am going to wear it anyway.'

Going to her dressing table, she opened a wooden cedar box in the shape of a chest. The top and sides had carvings of birds and flowers. It was a gift her brother brought back from Mexico. Francisca removed the red ribbon from the box. It was carefully rolled so there would be no creases. Her fingers deftly circled the fabric around her hair-bun and tied it in a bow. Turning left then right, she looked over her shoulder in the mirror. She was proud of her black hair and flawless olive skin. The white blouse she wore was in beautiful contrast to the red ribbon. It made her feel… mischievous? 'I wonder what father will think? I do not care! I saw how you looked at me last night Señor Crow.' With one more look in the mirror, Francisca headed through the door.

As the family and guests headed into the dining room, the Indian women in the kitchen were readying breakfast. This morning the kitchen smelled of carne asada (beef), roasted on an iron rod over an open fire. Additionally, there would be chorizo sausage, mixed with spices and ground chilies, a favorite of Hernando Batista. The meat was served with eggs, onions, frijoles refritos, and tortillas. Hot chocolate would be served instead of coffee this morning.

Carmen and Hernando were already in the room when Francisca entered. Then, from a different doorway, Carlos, Crow, and LeRue came into the room. Several things began to happen at the same time:

Hernando saw the look on Francisca's face. There was a hint of a smile that had always made him wonder what she was thinking. Next, he noticed that his daughter looked especially radiant this morning. Then he saw the red ribbon.

Carmen had also seen the red ribbon, and then she saw Crow. He was clean-shaven now, which revealed perhaps one of the most handsome men Carmen had ever seen. His blue eyes and black hair accented his features. She knew immediately why her daughter wore the red ribbon.

Francisca flushed at the sight of Crow. She had not expected such a handsome man under the thick beard he had been wearing. Then she saw the looks of her mother and father.

Carmen said, "Francisca, you look lovely this morning."

LeRue saved Crow by bringing him back to reality with an elbow in the ribs. Carlos' smile nearly went to laughter at the scene unfolding before him. Much to the relief of his mother and sister, he maintained control and guided Crow and LeRue to their seats at the table. He saved the moment by saying, "Father, Señor Crow rode the gray this morning."

THE RANCHO

Hector Camacho let his sombrero hang from his neck down his back from its chin strap. His forehead was bandaged where the gray had kicked him. Crow was sitting on the gray, which was casually munching at the sweet spring grass. Hector, Carlos, Crow, and LeRue, sat astride their mounts on a hill overlooking a lush green valley. There were longhorn cattle, as far as the eye could see.

Carlos stood in his stirrups, and with a sweeping motion of an extended arm said, "The rancho is about 8,000 hectares (20,000 acres). Our main income is derived from cattle and the hide industry. We will be making a trip to San Diego soon to sell our hides and tallow. You will be able to apply for citizenship there if you wish to stay. If you do, be aware that you will have to pledge allegiance to Mexico, and join the Catholic Church. After you do this, you will be on probation for a year, but then you can apply for a land grant."

Crow looked over the valley. In his mind's eye, he saw not cattle, but horses. Crow had learned that the Mexicans, although overrun with horses, paid well for fast, well-trained ones. 'I think I see an opportunity here,' he thought. "I might like to do that," said Crow. "What do you think, LeRue?"

"I have my papers with me, showing that I'm already a citizen of Mexico and a Catholic. I too think I like this California. If you stay Isaiah, I will stay too."

Unseen by the three, Hector's green eyes, blazing with hatred, thought, 'I think maybe these gringos should be dealt with as soon as possible.'

Carlos, settling onto his saddle, said, "Come, we will check on el lugar de los cráneos."

Crow looked questioningly at LeRue.

LeRue said, "The place of the skulls."

THE PLACE OF THE SKULLS

As Crow and LeRue rode side by side with Carlos and Hector, their horses made visible paths through the California spring flowers and lush grass. Looking at the position of the sun, Crow knew it was already late morning.

Crow smelled it long before he saw it. It was the odor of blood and decaying flesh. On the rolling hills, they began to see dozens of rotting carcasses of skinned cattle. The cattle hides were stretched out in the sun to dry. In the distance, they could hear the bawling of cattle.

Cresting a hill, the three men stopped. From their vantage point, they saw a corral with restless longhorn cattle. Surrounding the corral were mountains of horned skulls, bleached white by the sun. Near the entrance, were the severed heads of butchered longhorns.

Inside the corral were two vaqueros on horseback. One had his braided rawhide lariat looped around the rear legs of a Longhorn while the other vaquero controlled the front legs with his. A third man moved in and slit the throat of the struggling animal, and jumped back from the fountain of blood. After the animal died, the vaqueros shook out their lariats and coiled them as they rode, chasing after another Longhorn.

Carlos said, "This is the slaughter corral. Here the Longhorns are skinned and their hides dried. In another week, we will take the hides to San Diego and to the hide houses. The tallow is placed in bags to be rendered later in San Diego. Ships from the American East Coast and many European countries will sail up and down the California Coast, purchasing hides and tallow. The leather is used to make saddles, chaps, whips, door and window coverings, trousers, hats and so on. Even leather armor for our soldiers."

"Carlos," said Hector, "I will leave you here. I need to speak to the vaqueros at the corral. After that, I will check on the outer south camp."

"You will be back late?"

"Si, I am sure after dark."

"Viaje seguro, mi amigo y esté pendiente de bandidos (Ride safe my friend, and watch out for bandits)."

As Hector rode down the hill toward the corral, Carlos said, "Come, we will return to the rancho. By the time we return it will be time for almuerzo (noon-day meal)."

CONSPIRACY

Hector rode toward the slaughter corral. He maneuvered his mount so he could see the hill he had just left. From the corner of his eye, Hector saw the Mountain Men disappear from view behind the hill. He turned his attention to several Indians who were scraping hides. The Indians quickly looked down at their work, intimidated by el jefe's (the boss') glaring green eyes.

Hector took one more look around, then spurred his horse and rode off at a gallop toward the mountains.

As the sun peaked in the sky, Hector stopped in the shade of a tree and dismounted. He removed a canteen from his saddle and took a seat beneath the tree. Resting against the trunk, he opened his canteen and took a drink. From behind him, a voice said in Spanish, "I expected you sooner."

Without looking back, Hector said, "Carlos and Hernando have taken a liking to the gringos. I had to ride with Carlos to show them around the rancho."

The voice asked, "What happened to your head, amigo."

"A horse kicked me."

With a hint of sarcasm, the voice asked, "The gray the gringo is riding?"

Hector, scissoring his sturdy legs to stand, came to his full height and angrily faced the trees. "You could easily find yourself in the same hole as the gringos."

"I meant no offense," said the now taut voice.

Hector stared at the trees, visibly gaining control over his anger. "We will take the hides to San Diego in a week. Either on the way or before we leave, I want those two dead. Make it happen when I am not around, and if you can deal with Carlos, so much the better."

"Consider it done. I owe the gringos for the deaths of my men. We missed Carlos at the hot springs because of them. It will not happen again."

Hector, his back to the trees, mounted his horse, tied the canteen to the saddle's pommel, and without another word, rode off.

From a distant hill, two vaqueros watched as Hector rode away. One of the vaqueros, Juan, said to the other, "José that looks like el jefe."

"Si, I think you are right."

"I wonder what he is doing up here and not stopping to speak with us."

"It is certainly strange amigo."

Unknown to the vaqueros, a man was watching them from the trees. From the scabbard mounted on his saddle, he withdrew a musket. With the gun in one hand and the horse's reins in the other, he spurred his horse and moved through the trees above the two vaqueros. 'It is a shame that you are here at this time,' he thought, 'pero, lo que es, es (but, what is, is).'

HOW CROW BECAME ISAIAH

Crow, LeRue, and Carlos rode across an open field filled with spring flowers. The brilliant colors were enhanced by a bright blue sky. A multitude of birds sang and squabbled while honey bees hummed as they gather pollen.

The sun warmed their backs, and the pace was slow. Carlos, who was riding next to Crow, broke the silence. "The other night, you said that you were brought up by the Crow. How is it that you are called Isaiah?"

Carlos saw a smile on Crow's face. With a knowing nod of his head, Crow said, "That would be Yahoo Putnam who gave me my name. He was a Mountain Man who came to our village for the winter..."

The Past
The Crow Indian Village

The winter wind whistled across the smoke-hole of the tipi, rattling the hide-walls against the lodge poles. Buffalo robes covered the floor. The flickering yellow firelight cast a moving shadow of a man on the walls of the tipi. Yahoo Putnam sat cross-legged as he worked on a broken trap. The slightest bump to the trap, and it would snap shut. Putnam looked up from his work when wind, snow and a young Indian came through the entrance. The young man was handsome, with thick black hair. His hair was so long that it was kept in a net that hung down his back. Putnam eyed the rabbit held in the Indian's hand and smiled.

"What you got there?" He asked.

"White Crow gives to you," he said, handing the dressed rabbit to Putnam.

"Well set yourself down. I'll stick this critter on the fire. You'll stay and eat?"

White Crow answered with a flash of teeth in a broad smile. Dropping his buffalo robe to the floor, he squatted by the fire. His blue eyes were watching Putnam's every move as he prepared the rabbit for the cooking fire.

As Putnam worked, he watched the boy. It was his first winter with this tribe. He'd heard about the white Indian from other trappers but put it off as just another tale told around the fire.

While the rabbit cooked, Putnam again began to fiddle with the trigger of the trap. White Crow watched Putnam set the trap and placed it on the floor. Taking a stick, he poked the trap from the side. When nothing happened, he poked the trigger, and the jaws snapped shut on the stick.

"That ought to get it," he said, as he removed the stick from the jaws and handed it to White Crow. "Here, put that in that sack with the others."

White Crow took the trap and pulled the bag to him. There were now sixteen traps inside, cleaned and ready for the spring season. He pulled the drawstring tight then pushed the bag upright. That's when he saw the thick book with water stained pages. The covers had once been black, but wear and moisture had turned them a dirty gray. White Crow opened the book. On the open page, he saw a drawing of a young man dressed in a loincloth. His arm was pulled back with a sling whirling over his head. At the feet of the boy lay a pile of armor. In front of him stood a giant with a spear and a sword, dressed in full armor. White Crow looked up at Putnam questioningly.

"That's David and Goliath," said Putnam. "See the armor? The king, David's chief, gave him armor to fight the giant warrior, Goliath. But David didn't use it. David said the Great Spirit would protect him. That's a sling he's using. It can throw a rock like a bullet. He killed Goliath with it, and the enemy soldiers ran away."

"He was a Dog Soldier?" asked White Crow.

"Well no, he was a shepherd. That's a boy who protected the tribe's sheep. He had a vision that told him to fight, and that he would win a great victory and become chief."

"What are these?" asked White Crow pointing at the words.

"Those are words. They tell the story. Here let me show you. "And David went down to the river and selected five round stones and placed them in his pouch."

"They say that?"

"Yes, here." Putnam placed his finger under each word as he read.

"You will show me how this is?" asked White Crow.

"So you want me to teach you how to read, do you?"

The blue eyes fixed on Putnam's face, "Yes, teach me to read."

The Present

"Old Putnam worked with me all that winter. He had several books, even some Shakespeare. When spring came, I could get by. Later, there was many a night that we would read to each other.

"Putnam was born and raised in Virginia. His father grew cotton and tobacco. He was schooled; even had some college. It was at college where his life changed. He met a girl and fell in love. However, a local boy was jealous. He took offense to their relationship and challenged Putnam to a duel. Putnam chose pistols and shot him dead. Well, there was hell to pay. Both boys' families were wealthy and powerful. The duel was in the dead boy's town, so his family had the edge with the law and had Putnam arrested. Sometime during the night, two men who worked for Putnam's father showed up and broke him out of jail. His father met him on the road with a good horse and a bag of coin and sent him on his way. Putnam ended up in Missouri, and because he could read, write and do numbers, he got work with a fur trading company. The next year, he went out with the supply wagon to buy beaver pelts and sell supplies to the Mountain Men. Well, when he returned to Missouri, he quit his job, bought two horses, a set of traps and a Hawken rifle. He headed for the Yellowstone and never looked back."

Carlos asked, "Why did they call him Yahoo?"

"He got the name 'Yahoo' when he'd gone out with the supply train. Putnam had a voice you could hear over a stampede in a thunderstorm. When excited or angry, his voice would rise, and anything with ears could hear him for miles!"

"So you left the tribe then? You went with Putnam?"

"Yes, but it wasn't an easy thing to do. I told my father I was excited to go, but that I also felt great pain at leaving. My father, a wise man, said that I should go with the white man and learn their ways. So I went with Putnam. He taught me to read, write and do numbers. Putnam said that I would be with white men and that I should have a Christian name. He named me Isaiah Crow, after the Christian Saint, Isaiah, the protector of widows and orphans, just like a Dog Soldier.

"We'd trapped together a few seasons, then one day Yahoo started talking in a slurred voice and fell to the ground. I took him back to our camp. When he didn't get better, I built a cabin to protect him from the weather and make him comfortable. He died a short time later."

The three men rode in silence for a distance, and then Carlos asked, "So Isaiah, you can read, write and do numbers?"

"Yes, I can do that."

"Amigo, I think you may have a bright future here."

RAUL

The winded mare began to stagger. When she coughed, Raul, a boy of twelve, nearly fell off. In the bright moonlight, he saw some horses and pointed his mount toward them. Raul saw that one of the horses had a tether around its neck. He rode up, jumped from the unsaddled mare and ran to the other horse. Snatching the rope that was around the horse's neck, the boy grabbed a handful of mane as the horse bolted forward. Using the momentum of the moving horse, he swung himself up and onto its bareback.

As soon as Raul was mounted, he knew he had picked a good one. Pounding his bare heels into the horse's ribs, he yelled, "Hee-yah!" The small boy, on the large horse, raced across the shadowed, moonlit landscape. The pounding hooves muffled by the thick grass and the vast open space. The lights of the rancho were visible in the distance when the horse began to tire. Raul leaned forward onto the horse's neck and spoke to it, "¡ Vamos muchacho, sólo un poco más lejos (Come on boy, just a little farther)!"

Carlos, Crow, and LeRue were crossing the yard to the hacienda. The sound of a running horse and someone yelling got their attention. Turning and looking for the rider, they saw a small boy clutching to the mane of a hard-ridden horse.

"Jefe, jefe, bandidos!" The boy cried, "Bandidos!"

Carlos, Crow, and LeRue ran alongside the horse, helping to stop the exhausted animal as LeRue lifted Raul from its back.

"Raul, what has happened?"

"It is my papa! He and José have been shot! José is dead, but my father is alive! He is too big for me to carry. He needs help, or he will die!"

"How far?" Carlos asked.

"I rode two horses to get here. I went looking for him when he did not come home. When I found him, he said a bandit had shot him and José. He knows because the man came to check on them after he shot them. Poppa pretended to be dead, and he saw him."

A small crowd of workers began to gather around them. Then, pushing through the crowd, Hector joined them. "What has happened?"

Carlos replied, "It is Raul. His father and José were shot by bandidos. His father is alive. We must go to him as soon as possible."

Crow, placing his hand on the boy's shoulder asked, "Can you find this place in the dark? We have perhaps two more hours of moonlight left."

"Si, I can find it easy!"

Crow turned to Carlos, "With your permission, I have medicines in my possibles bag. I will need six horses, three for me and three for the boy. We will find his father, and I'll do the best I can to help him. If you get a cart and some men to follow us, they will be able to bring him here or to the hacienda."

Carlos did not hesitate, "Hector, get men and a cart readied to go. I will see to the horses."

LeRue, who was already moving, said, "I'll get our kit. You ain't leaving me behind."

"I will need twelve horses then," said Carlos, "I am going too. Hector, what are you waiting for?"

Hector, his deadpan face hiding his rage, stomped off.

SUSPICIOUS CIRCUMSTANCES

Crow, LeRue, Carlos and the boy, rode bareback. They would lose time by having to change saddles onto fresh mounts. As they raced into the night, Carlos mulled over what Raul had told them, 'Bandidos had shot them. Why would bandits want to kill two vaqueros? They were no threat to them. Perhaps they had seen something they should not have?' Something just did not seem right.

They had been on their last fresh horse and climbing a hill when Raul hauled his horse up short. He scanned a line of trees near the summit and then pointed and kicked his mount in the ribs and took off again up the hill. The others followed.

They found Raul's father, unconscious, lying next to a tree, barely alive. A few feet away lay the body of José. Crow, his possibles bag in hand, knelt next to the wounded man. Seeing blood on the man's lips, he shook his head. It bubbled with each labored breath. "LeRue, have Raul help you build a fire to signal the folks on the cart. Carlos, I will need your help to roll him over so I can see the wound."

As LeRue and the boy collected firewood for the signal fire, Carlos helped Crow. They placed the wounded man on his stomach. Crow, unceremoniously, took his Bowie knife and slit the clothing up the back and spread it away from the wound. "I'm not sure whether we will be able to save him," said Crow.

There were several flashes of sparks. Crow could smell the smoke as the fire started. Raul came over to check on his father. "Will he live Señor Crow?" Crow looked up at the boy. Raul's face was hidden in the shadows, but his voice told Crow of his fear and concern for his father.

"I don't know. The ball entered his back. If it hit his lung, I can't help him. I've dressed the wound in his back. Now we'll check his chest." Motioning to

Carlos to help, they rolled the wounded man onto his back. Because the clothing had been slit up the back, Crow removed it quickly. He began running his finger over the chest and along the ribs. His hand stopped. He started gently massaging a spot.

Crow looked up at Raul, "I think your papa is one lucky fellow." With that, Crow pulled his knife, and with one more exploration with his fingers, cut into the flesh. Blood gushed briefly, and, with a pinch of Crow's fingers over the wound, a lead ball popped out. Crow held it up for all to see. "It should have gone through his lungs, maybe even his heart. However, I think it hit a rib and went into his side. He's not out of danger, but I believe he has a good chance of making it."

Raul, who had been stoic through the entire ordeal, broke down and cried. LeRue came over and wrapped an arm around the boy's shoulders. Raul turned and wrapped his arms around the Mountain Man's waist. "Your father will be proud. If not for you, he would have died," LeRue told him.

There was the sound of horses in the dark. Crow and LeRue were instantly alert, rifles at the ready. Hector rode out of the darkness with one of the vaqueros. "We saw the fire," said Hector. "The cart and the others will be here shortly."

"I think he will live," said Crow to Hector. "I got the ball out. I need to sew him up now. By the time the cart gets here, he'll be ready to be moved."

Hector turned to Raul, "You were very brave. You are every bit your father's son." With that, he patted the boy on the shoulder. As Crow finished tending to the wounds, Hector casually looked about. 'From this hill,' he thought, 'these two had a perfect view of my meeting on the hill over there. They must have seen me. He saw them and shot them.' Hector looked again at the unconscious man. Without a word, he went to his horse and mounted up. From the saddle, he took one long look at Raul's father and then rode off into the night.

LeRue watched him go. 'I don't like that man,' he thought. 'His mouth spoke kindness, but his eyes say something else.'

A short time later the cart appeared out of the darkness. When asked, the driver said that Hector had headed back to the rancho.

MURDER AT THE RANCHO

It had been a few days since the shooting of the two vaqueros. Raul's father looked like he would survive. Crow took it upon himself to check on the man often and had just arrived at the adobe hut where he was convalescing. Pepe, Raul's father, smiled when the big Mountain Man entered the one-room cottage. "Buenos días mi amigo," Pepe greeted Crow.

Crow in halting Spanish replied, "Good morning my friend. I see that you are looking better. Do you feel as good as you look?"

"Yes, thanks to you! I do not think I will be riding for a while, but I will try walking, maybe tomorrow."

"Pepe, Raul said that you saw the bandit that shot you. Did you recognize him?" asked Crow.

"I do not know this man, but in the past, I have seen him and his men riding in the hills."

"Have you any idea why he would want to kill you?"

"I do not. José and I had just seen el jefe on the next hill. We were curious as to why he had not stopped to see us. Even so, he just rode away. Soon after he left, we were emboscaron (ambushed)."

"Pepe, I want you to keep this information to yourself. If anyone should ask, do not mention that you saw tu jefe."

Pepe studied Crow's face, and said, "I will do this."

"Gracias, amigo. I want you to know that Raul is not only brave, but he can also ride with the best of them. I would stand with him by my side any day."

Pepe's throat became tight. His eyes glistened with pride, but he could only nod his head in acknowledgment.

Crow left and headed across the yard to the hacienda. He did not see Hector slip into Pepe's hut.

"Hey Crow, espere un momento." It was LeRue. He had begun speaking to Crow in Spanish. The idea being that Crow would become more proficient in the language.

Crow waited for LeRue to catch up. Speaking in Spanish, Crow said, "I spoke with Pepe. He is much better. He told me that before they got shot, they saw Hector, but that Hector had not contacted them. You know the feeling you get when you know there is something wrong? Like when a grizzly or something is too close? I have that same feeling about Hector."

LeRue, now walking alongside his friend said, "I have had that feeling since the first time we met him. I also had the feeling that one of us was going to have to kill him."

Crow looked over at his friend. They had saved each other's lives on numerous occasions and had fought side by side against Indians. Crow had never found the man to be wanting. He trusted LeRue in all things.

"Crow, LeRue!" It was Carlos. He had a big smile on his face as he approached the two men. "My father has decided to leave for San Diego today. In a few days, we will load the hides and tallow on the wagons, and go to meet him there. He goes early to get supplies for Francisca's birthday and her Quinceañera. While we are there, it will also be a chance for you to register with the authorities for citizenship, if you wish to stay."

LeRue looked expectantly at Crow. Crow said to Carlos, "I do want to stay. I will register while we are there. You say Francisca is having a birthday?"

"Ah, it is not just a birthday. It is Francisca's Quinceañera! She will be a young woman and eligible for marriage. There will be muy grande celebrations for three days!"

LeRue noted the look on Crow's face and thought, 'Oh my friend you have it bad. I saw it as soon as he said "eligible for marriage." I think whatever comes next will be fascinating.'

There was a shout. It was Raul. "Señor Crow. My father! He needs help! Please come!" With that, Raul ran back into the hut.

The three men rushed to follow Raul inside. They found the boy standing next to the bed. Pepe lay on his back in a pool of blood, his dead eyes fixed on the ceiling. His throat had been cut.

Raul was beside himself with grief. Slowly, he felt his legs lose their strength and his knees buckled. Before Raul could fall, strong hard hands grabbed him. Crow picked the boy up as if he were a baby and held him in his arms. Raul burst into tears and wrapped his arms around the big man's neck. Crow carried him outside where a crowd was beginning to gather. The wife of the wounded vaquero from the hot springs was there. "Señora, will you care for the boy?" Crow asked her. "I will come later to see about him."

Crow eased Raul to his feet, and told him, "Go with her. I will see that your father is taken care of. I will come and get you as soon as I can." Raul stood up straight. Knuckling the tears from his eyes, he turned and left with the woman. Crow watched them walk away for a moment, and then he reentered the hut.

Carlos and LeRue were standing by the bed when Crow entered the room. "He never put up a fight. He must have known whoever killed him, or he was asleep," said LeRue.

Carlos was wrought with anger. "Pepe has been on the rancho since before I was born. He is known as a man to be trusted, and he raised his son when his wife died. "I will find who did this," said Carlos. "I will find them, and they will pay dearly."

"I don't think we can do anything more here," said Crow. "With your permission, I will take Raul and return to where they shot his father. I want to take a look around."

"Yes, that is fine. I will see to Pepe and his burial. I would go with you, but there is much to do here. There is our trip to San Diego that I must prepare for."

Crow turned to LeRue. "Will you get what we'll need? We'll stay overnight and return in the morning. While you do that, I will get Raul."

"I'll meet you by the corral."

GRIEF AND BECOMING A MAN

Crow, LeRue, and Raul rode fast. Each traveled with two horses trailing. Crow rode a black mare, his gray and another trailing. Crow wanted to keep the gray fresh. The hard ride and new mounts got them to the murder site by mid-afternoon. Dismounting, they stretched their legs while surveying their surroundings. Crow sent Raul to gather firewood, while he and LeRue moved along the tree line looking at the surrounding hills. "What are you looking for?" asked LeRue.

"Pepe told me that they had seen Hector on the next hill. Shortly after Hector left, Pepe and José were shot."

"Does the boy know this?"

"No, and don't tell him, at least not yet. We don't want to start something we can't prove."

"You think Hector shot them?"

"Pepe said he didn't know the man, but something sure doesn't smell right."

Raul approached them, his arms cradling firewood. "Raul, will you make a fire? LeRue and I want to check that hill yonder," said Crow, pointing to the hill straight across from them.

Before the boy could ask any questions, LeRue and Crow mounted up and began riding down the hill.

It took only a few minutes to get to the second hill. As Crow and LeRue got close to the tree line, Crow said, "Let's walk from here."

As they moved, Crow kept looking back at the hill where Raul was. "A horse and rider were here one or two days ago," said LeRue.

Crow walked over and saw a pile of horse droppings. After kicking at them with his foot, he moved to a tree that was slightly apart from the rest. Squatting, he ran his fingers lightly along the tree trunk. Crow sat down and leaned his back against the trunk. "Someone sat with their back against this tree. From here it gives you a good view of the trail, but you can't see the hill where Raul is."

LeRue wandered into the trees behind Crow. "Hey amigo, whoever sat there had company." Crow got up and joined LeRue.

"From the droppings and the footprints, I'd say whoever it was, they were here awhile," said LeRue.

Crow dropped to one knee and examined the ground. "He mounted here and rode over this way to leave." Crow stood and followed the track to the edge of the trees. He could clearly see Raul on the opposite hill. Examining the ground once more, Crow turned to his right and began to walk, and then he stopped. "LeRue, fetch the horses."

A short time later, Raul, who was building a fire, was startled when Crow and LeRue rode out of the tree line in front of him. "I did not see you were coming," he said to them.

The men did not answer but dismounted and tethered their horses to a tree limb. LeRue looked up at the sky. "It will be dark soon. I think we should eat now and camp cold."

"Camp cold?" asked Raul.

"Without a fire," replied Crow. "There could be Bandidos or Indians around. We don't want to show them where we are in the dark. There will still be some moonlight tonight, and it will give us an advantage if needed."

LeRue watched the boy. 'He has learned something. I can see it,' he thought. 'I like this boy. His father taught him well.'

It was dusk. The sun had dropped behind the hills. Bedrolls were brought out and arranged around the still burning fire. When they were settled, Raul asked, "I thought we were going to sleep cold?"

"If someone is watching, they'll wait, figuring we'll not go to bed-down right away. The fire will burn out. If someone wants to attack us, it will be early morning," Crow told him.

"Why do we wait so long?"

LeRue said, "Early morning is the best time. It is a time when a man is the least alert. Even after a rest, there is something about the early morning that makes a man's eyes want to close."

Crow, sitting cross-legged, opened his possibles bag. Reaching inside, he removed three thick slices of jerky. He handed one to Raul and one to LeRue. "Here's some supper, my treat."

The boy looked at the red-colored meat with suspicion. "What is this?"

"Jerky," replied Crow. "We don't want to cook tonight. It will be enough till we get back to the rancho tomorrow. Try it. You might be surprised."

Raul watched as the two men bit into their jerky. With an effort, they bit a piece off and began to chew. Taking the meat between his teeth, Raul tore a piece off and began to chew and to chew, and chew some more. The meat, spiced with pepper, soon became pliable. He found it tasted good.

As they ate, the light of day faded, and the hills became shadowed. Thoughts of his father filled Raul's head. A deep sadness came over him that was seen by Crow.

"I lost my father when I was about two years old," said Crow. "The Blackfoot Indians killed him and my mother. A man named Broken Leg, a Crow war-chief, took me in and adopted me."

"I have heard you lived with the Indians."

"I don't remember my real father as you do. It is a gift that I will have to live without. Nevertheless, I had a father in Broken Leg. He taught me, like your father taught you, how to be a man."

"Did he teach you to ride? My father taught me to ride, and to use the lariat." With a laugh, he said, "I learned to rope by roping chickens with a string!"

"I was five when my training began. I had to run a certain distance in the snow before I was allowed to eat. By the time spring came, I could run a long distance. As I got older, I could run for miles without food or water. It made me strong, and my body hard. Even so, it was the words of my father that made me a man."

"Words made you a man?"

"He told me a man could be someone who cannot walk, or see; one who may not be able to ride a horse or fight. However, if he can think, if he is kind to those in need, he can be stronger than many warriors. There are some who can be both. My father is one of those, and I think yours was too."

LeRue saw pride creep into the boy's bearing. His back straightened and his face began to lose the pain of grief.

When the fire had burned down, Crow had them move behind a pile of fallen limbs. It was a good move. They had company just as false dawn edged the eastern hills. Three shadowy shapes slipped silently into the abandoned camp, and with knives, they attacked the empty bedrolls.

The darkness became bright with the flash of two fired rifles. Two shadows fell to the ground. The third stood in silent disbelief. From out of the dark, Crow sprang onto the would-be assassin, taking him to the ground. Crow's rock-hard fist slammed into the jaw of the downed man knocking him senseless. Crow quickly rolled the man over onto his stomach and tied his hands with a length of rawhide he pulled from his belt.

Standing, Crow adjusted his belt and knife. LeRue, carrying the two rifles and followed by Raul, joined him. "Come daylight, we'll question him," said Crow.

It was not to be.

One of the rifle balls, after killing one Bandido, had passed through and struck the prisoner. He had bled out and died while they waited for daylight. There was nothing more to do. LeRue and Crow loaded the bodies onto the backs of the spare horses.

They mounted up and headed back to the rancho.

WHO WOULD PROFIT

Francisca stood looking out from her bedroom window. Beyond the yard were orchards now in full spring bloom. To the left were the gardens, also showing new growth. Many of the vegetable plants had started flowering. However, what she was most interested in was the big, handsome Mountain Man. Crow was striding across the yard to the hacienda, followed by Raul. Raul had stayed close to Crow since their return two days ago. Francisca noted that Crow didn't seem to mind. 'He appears to enjoy having him around,' she contemplated.

LeRue, on the other hand, began socializing with the vaqueros and with several of the señoritas. She smiled, thinking about how LeRue had surprised everyone when he had picked up a guitar and began to play and sing. His voice was rich and very pleasant to the ear. He was also attractive to the ladies, which did not sit well with some of the men.

Francisca saw her brother leave the courtyard and greet Crow. "Buenos días, would you like to ride out with me to check on the hides?"

"Yes, I will get my possibles bag and rifle. After I saddle the gray, I'll meet you here."

Later, Carlos and Crow rode side by side. The hills and fields were full of life; birds, flowers, even an occasional deer. "My father is opening doors for you in San Diego," said Carlos. "He likes you and hopes that you will stay."

"That is high praise coming from your father. I want very much to stay here. I understand that I too must become a Catholic."

"Si, we will see the priest when we return. The Don, my father, has already spoken to the priest. Once you are registered, he can begin teaching you."

"Carlos, while we are alone, I think you have a serious problem. I think bandits are hiding out on your land. When I spoke with Pepe before his death, he told me that he had seen the man who shot him riding through the hills. I also think you may have some of them working for you, and that one of them killed Pepe to keep his mouth shut."

Carlos reined his horse in and stopped. Crow pulled up next to him. "We have had very little trouble in the past. There were two attacks a few weeks before you and LeRue arrived."

"Tell me, when these attacks happened, were either you or your father present?"

"I was at one, and we were together at the other. We were on our way to a fiesta at our neighbor's rancho. The bandits fired at us from the trees as we passed. Our brave vaqueros charged and ran them off."

"Who would profit from the death of you and your father?"

Carlos' face showed a trace of anger. His black eyes stared hard at Crow.

"I meant no offense," said Crow. "But these attacks appear to me to be aimed at you and your father. No theft has occurred. Is there any cause for revenge against your family?"

Carlos saw that Crow was concerned and that his question had logic. His temper cooling, he began to think. "I had a run-in with a couple of Indian vaqueros last year. They had stolen two muskets and some money. I caught one and beat him rather severely. He threatened to kill me. I never took it seriously. As to who would profit from the death of my father and me, only my mother and sister."

"I think we can eliminate your mother and sister," Crow said with a hint of a smile. "But we should look at these vaqueros who threatened you. By the way, how long has Hector worked for your father?"

"Five years, I believe. Hector came up from Mexico and hired on as a vaquero. He is a hard worker and smart. About a year after his arrival, the foreman was snake bit and died. Father promoted Hector. It was a move he has never regretted. Why do you ask?"

"Just curious. Hector seems to be quite interested in Francisca."

Now Carlos smiled. "It has always been thought that they would marry. That is until you came along."

Crow felt a twinge in his chest, "What do you mean?"

"I think my sister has grown interested in a Mountain Man." Crow began to ask another question but was left hanging when Carlos spurred his horse into a gallop.

LIKE PLUCKING A THORN

Hector Camacho rode in the moonlight. The trail he followed cut through a deep, narrow canyon. Trees lined the sides of the path. Spectral jagged rocks sprang up from the mountain behind them. The warm night had patches of cold air. "Spirits," the old women called them. Hector always laughed at the old wives' tale, but deep inside they made him a bit uncomfortable.

Hector was aware of the men following him. They were his rear escorts. They would make sure no one was following him, and that he could get by the guards in the canyon. Ahead in the moonlight, he saw a man on a white horse. The horse was an impressive beast. It had to be because of the man riding it. Emiliano Diaz was himself a magnificent animal. Hector knew Diaz had remarkable strength. He'd seen Diaz beat three men to death in a fight in Mexico. The fight and the killings were one of the reasons he and Diaz were now in California. They both had a price on their heads in Mexico. The two men met with a short greeting. Then together, they continued deeper into the canyon, followed by the escort.

An outcropping of rock forced the trail to jog to the right, forming a second, narrow entrance to the canyon. Behind this natural wall was the well-hidden camp of Emiliano Diaz, the bandit leader of twenty-four men. There had been more, but Crow and LeRue had killed nine.

The camp was well organized and had apparently been in use for some time. A natural overhang of rocks and a cave made up the housing. There was a corral for horses and a communal fire pit. There was a sound of running water, its source hidden by the trees.

The riders dismounted. Diaz led Hector to the cave. As they entered, two women and a young girl greeted them. There was a table with roughly made chairs and benches around it. The air smelled of wood smoke, tortillas, and

45

frijoles refritos. Diaz and Hector took seats facing each other. There had never been an argument between them about leadership. Diaz had always felt on equal terms with Hector. Although Hector knew he was the smarter of the two, he was careful not to be pushy or domineering. He chose, as he thought of it, to guide Diaz in his thinking.

"Are you hungry?" Diaz asked.

"No, I ate earlier."

"Perhaps a drink?" without waiting for an answer, Diaz turned to one of the women. "Bring us tequila!"

As the woman brought glasses and a bottle to the table, Hector said, "We have an opportunity to end this. The day after tomorrow, Carlos will take the hides and tallow to San Diego. They will be there for several days, as they plan to register the two gringos with the authorities. If we play this right, we can eliminate Hernando and Carlos."

Diaz picked up the bottle and filled two glasses with tequila. "Why not the gringos also?"

"I think it would be too much at one time. Besides, the gringos are of no importance to our plan. But later, you can pluck that thorn from our side, and no one will care."

"The men tire of waiting. I tire of waiting. We have been at this for nearly three years, and you are the only one to profit."

Hector's hot temper began to surface. With concealed effort, he replied evenly, "I have worked hard every day to place us in an advantage. It is a given that I am to marry Hernando's daughter. With the father and the son out of the way, it will be easy work to get rid of the mother. We have a plan that we agreed to. We would have been further along if the gringos had not stepped in and saved Carlos. However, we now have another opportunity in San Diego. You and your men will not have to live here much longer."

Diaz sat back, his chair creaking with his shifting bulk. Slowly turning his glass with his thick fingers, he silently stared at the amber liquid. Instinctively, Hector went on guard. But Diaz looked up and said, "I will leave for San Diego in the morning with a few of my best men. We will make plans to deal with Hernando and his son when they arrive."

Relaxing, Hector said, "I leave it in your hands. I will remain at the rancho. I do not want any questions as to why I did not interfere when you deal with them."

Diaz, showing no emotions, stared at Hector, again putting him on guard. But Diaz picked up his glass, and said, "Salud!"

Hector, with his drink, held high, responded, "Salud!"

SAN DIEGO REUNION

Hernando Batista sat near the back of the whaleboat, out of the way of the sailors rowing it. He enjoyed the smell of the ocean and the sounds of the gulls. The gulls had found a school of fish and were noisily arguing with some pelicans over feeding rights. The ship, **The Boston Queen**, had arrived from the East Coast to deliver goods and pick up hides and tallow. Ships from America and Europe often traveled up and down the Coast of California for up to two years, picking up hides and tallow, before returning to the East Coast. **The Boston Queen's** captain, Jason King, had made the trip twice before. He and Hernando had become friends. Hernando adjusted the package that he had placed between his feet. He was pleased with himself. The wine was made from grapes from his vineyard. It was a gift for his friend, Captain King.

The Boston Queen sat a cable's length offshore in the calm San Diego waters. When they arrived, Captain King, a short man with bull-like proportions, was waiting. A crew member lowered a basket over the side. Hernando placed his gift in the basket. Both Hernando and the basket arrived on deck at the same time.

With his feet firmly planted, Hernando took the steel-like handshake of his friend, followed by a crushing bear hug. "Welcome aboard, my friend! Come, we'll go to my cabin."

In the captain's cabin below deck, the two friends sat at a small table. King removed the wicker covered bottle from the packaging and placed it at the center of the table. "What do we have here?" He asked.

"That is a red wine made from grapes from my vineyards. It was a near perfect harvest. The wine, I think, is superb."

King went to a cabinet and retrieved two glasses. He brought them back to the table and took a seat across from Hernando. Hernando stood and removed the seal and the cork from the mouth of the bottle. Carefully, he picked up the bottle and filled a glass half full. After he set the bottle down, he handed the glass to King. King smelled the wine, took a sip, savored the flavor and swallowed. Smacking his lips, he looked up at Hernando and declared, "This is delicious! You are a true friend! Please, fill our glasses, and let us drink to our reunion!"

A short time later, after a couple more glasses of the wine, King stood up. He went to a wooden sea chest and opened it. Removing a large package, the captain brought it to the table. Moving the bottle of wine and the glasses to one side, he placed the box on the table. "I think you will be pleased with this. My Mrs. had it made, using the dress you sent for size."

Hernando carefully opened the package. The silk fabric of the dress appeared like a white mist. Embroidered over the surface were small flowers made of fine red and green thread. "It is wonderful. Francisca will be pleased."

King went back to the chest and returned with a smaller package. "This is a gift from the Mrs. and me. It is a gift for your daughter on this special occasion. I picked up the silk in China, and the Mrs. did the needlework."

Taking the package, Hernando opened it to find a square, velvet-covered box with a gold latch. Slipping the lock, he opened it. Neatly layered were several silk handkerchiefs of different colors. Flowers and white doves were uniquely embroidered on each. Hernando fought the emotions that constricted his chest. Closing the box and slipping the latch closed, he said, "You have done so much, how can I ever repay you?"

"There is one thing which I desire."

"Name it, and it is yours."

"My ship will be here for several weeks. I wish to join you in your celebration."

"It is done! We will celebrate together! My wife and daughter will be so pleased to thank you personally."

"Let us have another drink, and then you can catch the next boat going to shore."

SAN DIEGO - HIDES AND KNIVES

The well-traveled La Playa trail to Pueblo (Old San Diego), had taken several days to traverse. Carlos had time to become close friends with Crow and LeRue. Twenty wagons, each pulled by eight-ox teams, were stacked high with hides and barrels of tallow. The three men were happy when they crested the hill and saw the city and the ships anchored in the harbor.

"My father is to meet us at the hide houses on the beach."

"I hope they have a place to drink there. I have a lot of dust to clear from my throat," declared LeRue.

"You always have a lot of dust to clear from your throat. I think you eat it so that you can wash it down," laughed Crow.

"There is a cantina close to the shore. Once we deliver the wagons to the hide houses, I will take you there."

The hide houses were located along the beach close to the docks. There were also buildings for rendering the tallow. The smell and the flies were hard to take. Crow watched the sailors. Some wore woolen caps to cushion the weight of the hides on their heads. They fought the breeze and the surf as they carried the hides to the whaleboats. The hides had the hair side folded in. Heavy, most were a full two arm's length wide and acted like wings in the breeze. A gust of wind could knock a man off his feet. The sailors wore blue shirts and canvas pants, rolled up to their knees. They carried the hides out to whaleboats, held in place by other sailors who gripped the sides. Once a boat was filled, the sailors would get in and row out to the ship. There, they unloaded the hides. After watching for a time, Crow came to appreciate their hard work.

"There he is!" Shouted Carlos, "There is my father!"

Crow and LeRue looked in the direction Carlos was pointing and saw Hernando in a whaleboat, waving his hat.

The boat with Hernando in it was brought up to the beach, so Hernando did not have to walk through the surf. After jumping down to the beach, he was handed his belongings. The sailors pushed the boat back out into the ocean and began loading it with hides.

Hernando, with his packages in his arms, walked over to one of the vaqueros, a handsome young man of some twenty years. "I want you to take these to the house. We will be along shortly."

After watching the young man ride away, Hernando turned to his son. "Where is Hector?"

"He felt that with the bandits in the area, he should stay at the rancho, just in case something happened."

Hernando thought about that for a moment, and without another word, went to the horse that had been brought for him, and mounted up. "We must go to the authorities now and get Isaiah registered. Señor LeRue, you have brought your papers?"

"Yes Don Hernando, I have brought my papers with me," replied LeRue.

"Good, then let us go."

The office of the alcade (mayor) was immaculate. The mayor was a man so thin, that his tailored uniform appeared to be too large for him. Crow and LeRue entered the room first. They were met with an air of hostile suspicion. That was until Don Hernando came in. The change in the official's demeanor was instantaneous. "Ah, Don Hernando, welcome! I see you have your son with you. Buenas tardes (good afternoon), Señor Batista. These are the men you wish to register?"

Hernando stepped forward, ending up quite close to the mayor, who was apparently cowed by the larger man. "Yes, these are Señors Crow and LeRue. Señor LeRue is already a citizen of Mexico, having been born in Texas."

LeRue stepped forward and handed the officer his papers. The mayor looked at them and then nodding his head said, "These are all in order. I will make a notation to make it all official. Now, Señor Crow, do you have any papers for me?"

Before Crow could answer, Hernando said, "Isaiah's father is… was a good friend of mine for many years. He and his wife were killed by Indians down Mexico way. Like Señor LeRue, they too were born in Texas. Because they were burned out, and Isaiah was kidnapped by the Indians, his papers are gone. I will atestiguar (vouch) for him."

Uneasiness filled the room. Surprised by Hernando's blatant lie, LeRue and Carlos looked at each other while Crow, showing no emotion, stood deadpan. The official stared at Hernando for a moment and then turned to Crow. "These statements are all true, Señor Crow?"

"Yes sir, factual they are."

Hernando continued saying, "My daughter will have her Quinceañera soon. I hope you and your wife will be able to attend."

Again, there was an immediate change in the mayor's demeanor. "It would be with great pride to attend, Don Hernando."

"Good, I will send an invitation, giving you the exact time, and because you will be bringing your wife, I will send a carriage for you."

The official was beside himself. 'Wait until I tell my wife. She will have much to say to our neighbors,' he thought. "I will take care of this Don Hernando. Welcome to California Señor Crow and Señor LeRue. I look forward to your invitation, and I wish all of you a safe journey home." As an afterthought, he asked, "Señor Crow are you a member of the Church?"

"No. I was taken at a young age and was away from the Church. But arrangements have been made for me to begin instruction and I will soon be a member of the Church."

"There is usually a one year probation period to become a citizen. But because you and Señor LeRue are already being of Mexican heritage, of course, that is waved. But Señor Crow, you will still have to wait until you are a member of the church. Perhaps when I come to the Quinceañera, you will have been confirmed. If so, at that time, I will then enter you as a citizen of California."

"That is most kind of you," said Hernando. "We will look forward to seeing you."

After their meeting, they once again stood outside by their horses. The dirt streets, filled with droppings of horses and oxen, were lined with one story mud-brick buildings. The din of men working and the ever-present livestock was constant. "Let us go to the cantina down the street. I promised LeRue he could bathe his dusty throat," Carlos told his father.

DEADLY ENCOUNTER

Diaz and two of his men sat behind a table in the back corner of the cantina. It was a busy place. Not only could you purchase something to drink, but one could also buy a meal or merchandise. The area for drinking had several tables surrounded by chairs. The bar, made of rough planking, worn smooth from years of wear, ran the length of one wall. Diaz had picked the table so he could watch the door, and protect his back.

Diaz felt a rush of adrenalin when Crow and Carlos Batista, followed by Hernando and LeRue, came through the door. His mind began racing. Here they were! All together! The very men he had come to kill! Diaz said to his man next to him, "Go and get the others. When you get back, stay on the other side of the room. Have our horses close by. We will want to leave quickly. The four men who just came in… we are going to kill them."

The bandit looked at the four men who now stood in front of the bar. Two were in buckskins while the other two he recognized as the Batista's. 'The killing of the gringos should be easy work,' he thought. 'Five of us, four of them.' The bandit got up from his chair and left the cantina.

At the bar, LeRue leaned over to Crow and in a quiet whisper said, "Have you noticed the men in the corner, dándonos el ojo (giving us the eye)?"

"Crow feigned a smile and said, "Yes, and it looks like his compadrés have just come in."

LeRue looked over to the corner of the room to see the man who had left, had returned; with two more.

Crow, in a quiet voice, said, "Carlos, do not look up, but we are about to be attacked. I think LeRue and I can handle this. Take your father out of here and wait for us. We may need his help with the officials."

Hernando was surprised when his son took him by the elbow and said, "Please do not question me father, but we must go, *now*!" The intensity of his son's voice convinced the older man to go with him.

As Carlos guided his father towards the door, the three bandits at the door moved to intercept them. Just then, LeRue placed himself between them and the Batista's. In the opposite corner, Diaz saw what was happening and jumped up, his bulk knocking over the table.

Crow's voice filled the room. Speaking in Spanish, he shouted at Diaz, "You're the son of a dog who had Pepe and José killed!" When Diaz hesitated, Crow hit him with a fist made of stone, knocking the big man back, but not down. The man with Diaz pulled a knife. Crow backhanded him to the side of his head with his closed fist. The man crumpled to the ground, his weapon falling from his hand.

Diaz, having regained his senses, charged Crow; only to find open space where Crow had once been standing. Before he could recover, Crow swept the big man's legs out from under him. Diaz hit the floor with his face.

Near the door, the three bandits had at first thought to attack LeRue. They changed their minds when LeRue drew his war-hawk and stood his ground.

Crow turned to LeRue, "It's time to go amigo."

Diaz stood up and wiped the blood from his face. "Next time I see you," he said, "I will kill you."

Crow turned and faced Diaz, "Why wait?" shouted Crow.

Before the disbelieving eyes of all but LeRue, Crow pulled his Bowie knife and plunged its twelve-inch blade into Diaz's stomach. In one continuous motion, he forced the blade upward, the tip piercing Diaz's heart. Diaz fell to the floor, trying to hold his stomach together. In the corner, the shocked bandits threw up their hands and headed for the door. LeRue allowed them to pass.

Crow wiped his blade on the shirt of the dead Diaz. Carlos and Hernando came back into the cantina followed by the mayor. The mayor was accompanied by two scruffy uniformed men, each carrying a musket.

Hernando and Carlos walked up to Crow. Hernando muttered "Madre de Dios, ¿qué ha sucedido (Mother of God, what has happened)?"

LeRue said, "He threatened to kill Crow."

"This is one of the men who killed, or had ordered to kill your vaqueros," said Crow. "They were intent on killing us all. LeRue stopped the three who were going to kill you when you were leaving."

The mayor asked Hernando, "Who are these men who you say wanted to kill you?"

Hernando looked at Crow for a moment, then said, "These men are bandits. They have attacked our rancho many times this year. Some of my people have been killed or wounded by them."

Carlos added, "Bandits attacked Señor Crow and Señor LeRue, just a few nights ago. Those bandits too lost their lives to these two men."

The mayor looked to Hernando, "You have vouched for these men already. I think this is a clear case of self-defense and was justified." Looking around the room at the gawking patrons, the mayor asked, "Does anyone disagree?" There was no response to his question. "Then that settles it. They all agree. Clearly, it was self-defense."

Outside the Cantina, the sound of running horses announced the hasty retreat of the surviving bandits.

A YOUNG WOMAN'S WISDOM

Carmen and Francisca sat at the long dining room table. They were sitting side by side with their heads close together, like a couple of conspirators. Carmen leaned back in her chair and watched her daughter. "You need not worry about your dress. You will be very pleased when you see it."

"Oh mother, I am so excited! I am only curious. What does it look like?"

With feigned exasperation, Carmen wagged her finger, "You just stop now young lady. You will find out soon enough," she said, softening it with a smile. 'Hernando said he would take care of it. I hope I have not made a mistake trusting this to a man,' she thought.

The musical sound of spurs and campanas (jingle bobs) got the women's attention. Hector entered the room just as they turned to look. "Buenos días Señora Batista y la Señorita Batista," greeted Hector.

"Good morning Hector," greeted Carmen for the two women.

"Señora, I must go to el lugar de los cráneos. One of the vaqueros has reported a theft of hides. I will return this evening. I do not think there is any danger here, but to be on the safe side, I have two armed men close by."

Carmen asked, "You ride alone? Perhaps you should take someone with you. Too many things have been happening of late."

"I may do just that Señora. Thank you for your concern." With that, Hector turned and left, his spurs chiming with each departing footstep.

Carmen noticed a frown on Francisca's face. Francisca replied to the silent question on her mother's face. "Hector has changed. I used to think of him as my caballero en brillante armadura (my knight in shining armor). I saw him as manly and handsome."

Carmen sat back in her chair, "But then a certain Hombre Montaña came along?"

"Isaiah is different. His eyes are kind, yet Carlos tells me he is a fierce fighter. Hector has beautiful green eyes, but I see something there I do not like. He is harsh with the vaqueros, who seem to fear him. However, Isaiah has their respect and speaks harshly to no one."

Carmen thought, 'Oh my dear Francisca. I believe you have grown wise very quickly. I also think that you have fallen in love.' "You know your father has thought that you and Hector would marry."

"I also believed that Hector and I would someday marry. I am unsure now. Do you think father will be angry?"

"No, disappointed maybe, but not angry. I believe your father likes your Isaiah, and your brother speaks highly of him. No, I think your father will not be angry."

BATISTA HOUSE - SAN DIEGO

The Batista house was small but comfortable. Built of adobe, it had a flat roof, several rooms, and an outside kitchen. In one of the bedrooms, Carlos and his father sat on separate beds, taking off their boots.

Carlos, with a boot in one hand, held up his foot and wiggled his toes. "Ah amigos, you are alive and well. You see, Papa. They wave in greeting to you."

"You tell your friends, they need a bath," replied Hernando, removing his boot.

"Papa, what do you think about what happened at the cantina? Crow thinks those men were there to kill us. Not just you and me, but him and LeRue also."

Hernando pulled off his other boot and sat holding it in both hands. "I have given this great thought, but I have no answers. I can think of no one that I have knowingly offended. I know our neighbors have not been attacked as we have. Pepe and José, why were they killed? It makes no sense."

"If the man Crow killed today was a bandit, perhaps the attacks will end."

"Maybe... we can only wait and see. But the killing of the bandit bothers me. I was told by one of the men in the cantina that Crow just turned and killed that man after the fight was over."

"The man said that the next time he and Crow crossed paths, he would kill him. One of the men who saw the fight told me. I think with all the attacks, he was not going to wait to see when that would happen."

"Crow is a good man. I have a lot of respect for him, but he can be a brutal man, and quick to temper."

Carlos watched as his father stood and took his vest off and thought, 'I think you had thoughts of Crow and Francisca, but now you have doubts.'

In another room, Crow and LeRue were each sitting on a bed. LeRue said, "I think I should have killed the others when I had the chance."

"If we'd been anywhere else, we might have done just that. As it is, I think Señor Batista is not happy with what happened."

"I think Don Hernando is slow on the uptake. Now, Carlos, that boy is pretty quick. He doesn't have any answers yet, but he sure is asking the right questions."

Crow sat up and rolling to the side, placed his feet on the dirt floor. "I don't know what's going on, but Hector is in on it, and in deep. Before Pepe was killed, he told me that he and José had seen Hector, but that Hector had made no effort to seek them out. Shortly after Hector left, someone ambushed them. Hector told us that he was going to check on José and Pepe when he left us that day. Hector lied to us. But, why?"

LeRue rolled onto his side to face Crow, using his hand to pillow his head. "There's something about Hector that chafes my ass. His smile and politeness don't match up with his eyes. The vaqueros fear him rather than respect him. I was talking to a couple of the Indians, and they told me that the old foreman died of a bite from a snake that had found its way under the covers of the foreman's bed."

"I think we'd better keep a closer eye on each other's back. Someone out there wants us dead, and will try again."

DIAZ IS DEAD

Hector's mind raced as he rode hard, his lathered mount frothing at the mouth. Hector had been surprised when an outrider for the cattle herd, one of Diaz's men, had whispered that Garcia needed to see him. 'Why would Diaz take a chance of discovery to send a messenger and want to meet? Had something gone wrong in San Diego? No one had come to the rancho to announce that Carlos and Hernando were dead.' The hill with a crown of chaparral and a few pines was up ahead. There, he would get his answers soon enough.

On the top of the hill, two heavily armed Mexicans sat astride their horses, watching the approaching rider. Garcia, a short, powerfully built man said to his taller companion, "It is Hector."

"You tell him," said the tall Mexican. Garcia looked at his companion, then with a shrug of his shoulders settled himself on his saddle.

Hector spotted the two men on the hill and viciously spurred his horse. His sudden arrival spooked the other horses, their riders angrily trying to regain control.

"Why have you sent for me?" demanded Hector.

"Diaz is dead!" the smaller Mexican nearly shouted. His excitement was mixed with anger over his spooked horse.

The answer struck Hector like a rock between the eyes. 'Dead? Diaz is dead?' His voice, now like ice, Hector asked, "What happened? How did he die?"

"The men who rode with Diaz came back and told us," replied the smaller Mexican. "He said that Diaz had called them to a cantina where the Batista's and the two gringos were. He said it was a chance to get them all. When they got there, the big gringo accused Diaz of trying to kill him."

Hector was surprised, "He said that?"

"Si, and then they began to fight. The big gringo knocked Diaz down. Diaz threatened to kill him the next time he saw him. The gringo, he pulled his knife and said, 'Why wait?' And he killed Diaz."

"What about the others? They did nothing?"

"The other gringo caught them off guard, and he had an axe. They said the soldiers came and they barely escaped capture!"

Hector stared off into space, 'Diaz, you big macho fool, I told you... Ah, I will miss you, my friend.' Hector said to the smaller man, "Garcia, you are in charge. You," he said to the taller man, "are witness to my orders. I will meet with you in a few days. Stay close to the camp. No one is to leave until I have met with all of you." Not waiting for an answer, he roughly reined his horse around and rode back down the hill.

Garcia said, "Come on amigo, we had better get back and tell the others."

On the flats, Hector rode at a fast gallop. Fear fueled his anger with thoughts of revenge. 'The gringos,' he thought, 'esos bastardos are ruining everything! Diaz, I cannot believe he died so easily. Isaiah Crow, no matter what happens, I will destroy you!'

CROW - THE BUSINESSMAN

It was their second day in San Diego. Carlos and Hernando had been monitoring the loading of the hides. Now it was time for the tally. It did not look as good as the Batista's thought it should be. Hernando held the ledger in his hands frowning.

Crow and LeRue were standing to one side as a company man from the ship counted the bundles of hides and logged them in a ledger. The hides were then loaded onto a whaleboat and rowed out to the mother ship. There were hundreds of these bundles which equated to thousands of hides. Crow leaned in close to LeRue and said, "Hernando does not look pleased with the count."

"I noticed that. Hernando seems confused about something."

"I've been watching the bundles. They just don't look right to me."

Carlos left his father's side and joined the two Mountain Men. "We had figured on more hides this trip. We also fell short on the tallow. We have done well for the year, but it still seems short."

"Perhaps I can help?" asked Crow.

Carlos looked at his new friend a moment, and then replied, "Si, you can take a look, but it is simple, just count and add."

The hides were stacked in bundles of two, hair sides in. Each hide weighed thirty-five to forty pounds.

Crow approached two sailors who were about to pick up two bundles of hides. Before they could put a hand on them, Crow drew his Bowie knife and slashed the cords holding the bales of hides together. The company man shouted, "Hey, what are you doing there?!"

Hernando rushed over, his face red with anger, but Carlos reached out and took him gently by his arm. "Wait a moment."

Crow and LeRue began taking the bundles apart. The company man was becoming agitated and started to protest once again. But Crow interrupted him, "This bundle has two skins, this bundle has three." Crow turned to the company man and took the ledger from him. Crow ran his finger down the rows of numbers. Crow's lips moved silently, as he counted rapidly in his head. Finished, he handed the ledger to Carlos. Moving to the whaleboat, Crow again began counting the bundles in the boat.

Crow walked back up the beach to where the Batistas were watching with curiosity. "May I have the ledger?" he said to Carlos. Carlos handed him the ledger. Crow opened the book and moved to Hernando's side. "Many of the bundles have an additional hide. The bundles with the extra hide have knots that are easily untied at the destination warehouse. They can remove the extra hide and re-tie the bundles to be the same as the others. The accounting shows that there have been twenty-four bundles loaded on the boat, there are twenty-six. The two extra bundles are probably marked somehow, so they can be removed from the rest when delivered. We have been here for two days and nights. This man is stealing from you! I think if you go aboard the ship and search his cabin, you'll find a second set of books."

The company man was now looking wildly about when LeRue stepped up next to him. "You cannot run fast enough or far enough my friend." The company man, his face pale, looked as if he might fall to the ground.

Hernando stood silent, his face red with rage, as he stared out the door at the mothership.

"I think we need to have a talk with your friend, the captain," said Carlos to his father.

"Yes, we will talk to my friend, the captain," replied Hernando. Then he turned to Crow. "Will you come with Carlos and me? I wish for you to check the books aboard the ship."

"Yes Don Hernando, I will go with you," said Crow.

THE SAN DIEGO HOUSE - FRIENDS

The evening was noisy. The sounds of people, livestock and the surf were mixed with the strumming of a guitar nearby. In Hernando Batista's San Diego house, seated in a chair at the table, was Captain Jason King. Across from him were Hernando and Carlos. Crow and LeRue sat at each end. King and Hernando were drunk. The others had been drinking but were not drunk yet. Hernando looked at King through bloodshot eyes and exclaimed, "That son of a bitch has been stealing from all of us!"

King, his head beginning to appear too heavy for his thick neck, replied, "It is not only him; his whole damned family is involved!"

Crow looked over at LeRue who winked and smiled back. It had turned out that the company man and his family had been making a tidy profit by falsifying the ledgers and stealing hides and tallow when the ship returned to the American East Coast. Multiply the theft by the number of stops the vessel made, and one could only guess at the magnitude of the loss to the company. It had taken restraint not kill or injure the thief.

Carlos, who seemed to be trying to catch up with his father, as far as drinking said, "I propose a toast... what did you say his name was?" he asked Crow.

"Yahoo Putnam," answered Crow with a smile.

"To Yahoo Putnam," shouted Carlos.

They all raised their glasses and drank.

Earlier, Hernando had asked Crow how he had noticed what was going on, in regards to the theft. "I had a teacher, Yahoo Putnam. He taught me numbers and how to read and write. At one time he worked for a fur trading company. It was common practice to try and short the trappers on their furs. He knew because he had done it to the trappers when he worked for the company. He showed me what to look for so they wouldn't steal from me."

In a moment of drunken emotion, Hernando reached out and patted his friend's hand, "I am so happy that you knew nothing of this. You have been my friend for many years."

Captain King, a bit of a tear in his eye replied, "Me too, my friend."

Carlos turned to Crow, and LeRue, "I think they have had enough," and then promptly passed out, his head striking the table.

HECTOR REMEMBERS

Hector Camacho was drunk. His two-room adobe cottage was large compared to the others on the rancho. A candle on the table was the only light, casting dancing shadows on the walls and ceiling. Next to the candle was a brown earthen jug of tequila. In Hector's hand was a glass of the amber liquid. Hector drained his drink, and then seizing the jug, splashed the empty glass full. Thumping the container back onto the table, he licked the liquid from his hand.

'Diaz,' Hector thought, 'you son of a bitch, I loved you like a brother! We were ferocious together! Like wolves you and I! The Federalizes tried to catch us, but they never could! We were brothers!' Hector's head hit the table as his full glass slipped from his hand, the amber liquid soaking into the dirt floor.

Unconscious to the outside world, Hector continued its remembrances.

Mexico Eight Years Earlier

Diaz and Hector had been riding hard. Their lathered horses were ready to give out. As they crested a hill, they saw the lights of a village. The moonlit night held a chill as Hector stood in his stirrups. From his vantage point, he could see a long distance across the open desert.

"I think we are safe, Amigo," said Hector. Diaz lifted his vast bulk out of his saddle and looked back.

"Perhaps we have time to warm ourselves and get something to eat," replied Diaz.

As the two men rode down to the village, the sound of music and singing wafted to their ears. Riding closer, they could see the light coming from a squat, flat-roofed adobe building. Light, music and the sound of singing came from an open window. It was an inviting scene to the two saddle-tired fugitives.

There were several saddled horses tied to a hitching rail in front of the cantina. Hector and Diaz dismounted and tied their horses to the hitching rail. The two men went to the heavy wooden door and entered the cantina. Inside, the music and the singing were loud. The air smelled of tobacco, sweat, and frijoles.

A look of curiosity came from the patrons of the cantina when Hector entered. But everything went silent when Diaz ducked his head under the doorframe and followed Hector in. The huge man stood behind Hector, his head swiveling on his thick neck, his black eyes taking in the room. "Buenas noches mis amigos. ¿Puede un hombre conseguir algo de comida (Good evening, my friends. Can a man get some food)?" asked a smiling Hector.

On the right side of the room was a doorway, covered by a once brightly colored blanket, now worn and dirty. A man with stooped shoulders and a balding head pushed back the curtain and stepped into the room. "Buenas noches, ¿ desea comer (Good evening, you wish to eat)?"

"Si, and something to drink," replied Hector.

"Find a seat," said the bald man, "and I will bring you something."

The guitarist began to play again as conversations at the tables resumed. There were several women in the cantina. Some sat at the tables while others wandered about, talking to the men. The blanket over a backroom door moved, and a woman stepped out. She was much prettier than the rest, dressed in a white blouse and a colorful skirt. The skirt stopped just above her ankles exposing gold bracelets and bare feet. There was something erotic about the gold and the bare feet, or maybe it was just the way she rolled her hips when she walked. She had every man's attention as she slipped up to Diaz and draped her arm around his neck. She leaned down and whispered something in his ear.

The response from Diaz was immediate and unexpected. Grabbing the woman by her arm, he swung her around as he pushed his chair back. As she landed on his lap, he slid his hand up her skirt and kissed her at the same time. Spouting profanity, the woman began kicking her legs, which only made Diaz laugh. The bald man came running out of the back room. He pushed the blanket aside with his hand that held a knife.

Hector jumped up, "Damn it, Diaz!" he shouted at his friend. The bald man rushed at Diaz's back. Diaz swung the woman around, just as the bald man thrust the knife at him. Instead of stabbing Diaz, the blade was stuck into the woman's stomach. Letting out a high pitched scream, she clutched at her profusely bleeding wound and collapsed to the floor. The place erupted in chaos. Men jumped to their feet and rushed Hector and Diaz. The bald man stood dumbfounded, staring at the bloodied knife in his hand.

Hector dodged the thrust of a knife and hit the attacker in his nose, knocking him back. Then Diaz was up. He picked one man up over his head and broke him like a stick over his knee. Tossing the man aside, he made a sound like a wounded animal and charged into the crowd. The sounds of his fists striking flesh were terrible to hear. Worse, were the screams of the injured. Diaz let out another animal sound and broke a man's neck. Now, the men who were once attacking were now looking for a way out. The door to the cantina was nearly ripped from its hinges, as men and women began to flee for their lives.

Hector watched as the room emptied. His right hand and arm were soaked in blood. The long bladed knife in his hand was held rock steady. Turning to Diaz, Hector yelled, "Come on, we need to get out of here!"

Diaz dropped the unconscious man he had in his grip. Moving to a table that was still upright, he picked up a plate of frijoles refritos and carne asada. With his fingers, Diaz scooped up the mix and stuffed it into his mouth. Chewing, he smiled and offered the plate to Hector. Hector turned on his heel and went out the door, Diaz following, eating as he went.

Back to Present

Heavy knocking at the door woke Hector up. He was dazed and not sure what was real and what was a dream. Hector grabbed his knife from his belt and stood. More knocking brought him to his senses. He went to the door and opened it.

One of the vaqueros stood at the door, "Jefe, you are alright? I was passing and heard yelling."

"I am all right, I do not know what you heard, but it was not from here." He slammed the door shut in the man's face. Going to the chair, he sat down hard, his head in his hands. 'You crazy bastard, we never would have had to leave Mexico, if it had not been for that fight.'

But it had happened. Now, Diaz was dead, and it was up to him to finish their plan. Soon he would be a rich man with a beautiful wife. Picking the glass up from the floor, Hector poured himself another drink. Taking a sip, he thought, 'With Diaz gone, there will be more for me. Perhaps I will not miss Diaz so much after all.'

HOMECOMING

Hector Camacho leaned his shoulder against the door frame of his adobe cottage. His head throbbed from his night of drinking. He watched the caravan of empty wagons and dusty riders arrive at the rancho. The two gringos rode by on horseback, their rifles in hand, the muzzles pointed skyward, the buttstocks resting on their legs. Hector's heart skipped a beat when Crow turned his head and stared him in the eye. Before Hector could respond, the procession had passed on. 'Bastardo,' Hector thought. 'It will be a pleasure to end your bravata (bravado).'

As the carts and the men continued across the yard, the Batistas and the Mountain Men dismounted in front of the hacienda. Carmen and Francisca were there to greet them.

"Welcome home!" Carmen greeted her husband and son with an affectionate hug. Francisca hugged her father and gave her brother a peck on the cheek.

"We heard you were coming and had food and drink prepared," said Carmen. "You are welcome to join us," she said to Crow and LeRue.

"Thank you, Señora, that is most kind," replied Crow.

Hector approached the group, a smile on his face. "Welcome home Don Hernando. We are pleased to see you have arrived safely."

Hernando studied Hector's face for a moment, and then replied, "Gracias. See to the animals and the supplies. We will talk later." Hector was taken aback by the quick dismissal. It was something that had not happened in the past. As he turned to leave, he found Crow, his face deadpan, once again staring at him. Hector's anger surged to the top, but Crow and LeRue had turned their backs on him and walked back to the hacienda.

Inside, Hernando and Carmen were in their bedroom. Hernando was removing his travel dusted clothing as he talked to his wife. "We, my love, have made a good profit this trip. All thanks to our friend Crow. He caught the thief in the act!"

"You are happy then with Señor Crow?" she asked.

Carmen's tone of voice drew a questioning look from Hernando, but then he continued. "Yes, he has many talents. Did you know he both reads and writes and he can also do numbers?!"

"He seems to have made many friends among the vaqueros and even the Indians in the short time he has been here. I know Carlos has come to consider him a friend," said Carmen.

Hernando sat down on a chair to pull his boots off. "He killed a man while we were in San Diego. The man said that he would kill Crow the next time he saw him. Crow then asked, 'Why wait?' and he killed the man, just like that," he finished, with a snap of his fingers.

"There was no trouble?"

"The mayor came and found that it was a justified killing. The man Crow killed was with others who were there to kill Carlos and me. Crow and LeRue spotted the trouble and sent us away. They faced the killers alone." Hernando set one boot on the floor and began pulling at the other one. "At first I was upset, but I spoke with Carlos. He pointed out that these men were probably bandits, and that Crow and LeRue had saved our lives, in the only way possible."

"Then you, ah, you like Señor Crow?"

Again, Hernando looked at his wife. This time with a frown, indicating a question on his mind. But before he could ask Carmen blurted out, "I think our Francisca has fallen in love."

"With Crow?"

"Si, she has seen something in him that she likes. She is in denial at the moment, but I see it. It is a woman's love, not something flighty."

Hernando finished struggling with his boot and placed it on the floor next to the other. Sitting back in the chair, he looked at his wife. "What do you think of this?"

"He appears to be a good man. I feel safe and respected around him. But as a mother, I want to wait before I say 'yes' or 'no.' Besides, I do not know, nor does Francisca, if he feels the same about her."

"Ah well, as I said, I talked with Carlos. We talked about many things. Our Señor Crow appears to be enamerado (smitten) with our daughter."

"What about Hector? It was thought that he and Francisca would wed."

"Hector has come into question with me. Let us observe the situation. Meanwhile, we have much to do for Francisca's Quinceañera."

A CONSPIRACY OF LOVE

Raul watched as Crow carried his rifle and his possibles bag. Crow strode across the yard to him. Inwardly, Raul marveled at the size of the man and how fluid his movements were. Crow smiled at the boy, and Raul felt a sense of pride at being the Mountain Man's friend.

"Raul, como estas (how are you)?"

"Estoy bien, bienvenido a casa (I am fine, welcome home)."

Crow approached the boy and placed his hand on his shoulder, "You have spoken to her?" he asked in Spanish.

"Si, she waits for you in her cottage. I have your horse and mine ready to go."

Moments later, the two rode side by side across the yard and eastward towards the mountains. From her window Francisca watched the two leaving. 'Where are they off to?' she wondered.

It was a pleasant ride. The sun, having passed its peak, was warm on their backs. Ahead, shaded by a large tree, was an adobe cottage that was twice the size of most Crow had seen.

Crow and the boy dismounted, just as the door opened. A Mexican with a dried apple face, dark from years in the sun, greeted them. Holding the door open for them, they entered.

Inside, the room was bright, illuminated by the light from a large window. A woman, every bit as ancient as the man, sat by the window, sewing. The room smelled of dyes and leather. The leather smell came from a stack of hides near a cobbler's bench. Crow noted that everything was neat and orderly.

Before Crow could say anything, the old woman stood and walked over to him. She walked around him, one finger to her lips, while she hummed softly to herself. Looking at the old man she spoke in rapid Spanish. He replied with a nod of his head and a toothless smile.

Crow looked questioningly at Raul. Raul smiled and replied, "She says you are damned big."

With a wave of her hand, she returned to her stool next to the table and began to sew. Meanwhile, the old man took Crow by the sleeve and pulled him to his bench.

From the bench, he brought two rectangular pieces of leather and indicated that Crow should remove his moccasins. Having shed his footwear, Crow was instructed to stand on the two pieces of leather. The old man traced around Crow's feet with a stick of charcoal. Finished, he handed Crow his moccasins.

Crow said to Raul, "You told them what I want?"

"Si, they understand. They make the clothes for the Don and Carlos. They are good at what they do."

Crow took his possibles bag from his shoulder and opened it. He reached inside and brought his hand out. Crow opened his hand and showed it to the old man. The cobbler's raised eyebrows were the only sign he was impressed with what he saw.

In Crow's hand was a pile of American five dollar gold pieces.

Crow indicated that the cobbler should take what he needed.

The old man, slowly and carefully, picked up four gold pieces, one at a time. He looked up at Crow.

Crow looked at the man's face then over to the woman, sewing with crooked fingers that could still run a straight seam.

Crow shook his head no, and the old man, nodding his head prepared to bargain. But Crow took four more coins and placed them in cobbler's calloused hand. Then, with his hand, he closed the old man's fingers over the gold.

"I have seen Don Hernando's clothes and his boots," Crow said in broken Spanish. "I think this is a fair price."

The cobbler stood straighter, and his smile was broad, "Gracias."

A BANDIT'S PROMISE

Hector stood before a bonfire that snapped and crackled, sending sparks into the night sky. With his clenched fists on his hips, Hector looked down at the seated men gathered around the fire. With his green eyes flashing and the silver conchos reflecting the firelight, Hector began to speak:

"We have lost a good man in Diaz, but we have not forgotten why we came here. In a few weeks, you will be living in your adobes. You will no longer have to live the lives of bandits but as vaqueros! In the meantime, you will need to eat and drink. So, you may once again make raids on the ranchos. Except... except for the Batista's. Stay away, no matter how tempting it might be. Think of it as your bank where you are keeping your money."

The seated bandits laughed at the thought of the Batista's being their bank.

Hector, his head down as if in thought, stepped to the left and then to the right, never removing his fists from his hips. He stopped and silently stared at the gathered men. In a loud voice, he said, "You are the best men I have ever ridden with! I trust each and every one of you with my life, and you can trust me with yours!"

A murmur ran through the crowd.

"¡ Estoy orgulloso de cabalgar contigo (I am proud to ride with you)!"

The men jumped to their feet, "¡ Hurra por Hector (Hooray for Hector)!"

Hector watched as the men, relieved to know that the wait would be over soon, laughed and slapped each other on the back. They had come to ride with Hector and Diaz with the promise of land and a better life. When they heard Diaz was dead, they were fearful that the dream was lost. Hector had just assured them that all was well, and they were prepared to follow him wherever he led them.

Hector watched the men, thinking, 'By attacking the other ranchos, they will draw attention away from the Batista's. I will be free to court Francisca and perhaps even show Hernando what bufónes (buffoons) the gringos are.'

A GRIZZLY COMES-A-DANCING

With the Don and his son having returned home, it was a grand excuse to celebrate. It was evening, and the air was filled with the smells of wood smoke, cooking meat, and flowers that bloomed in the gardens. Bursts of laughter were mixed with music from several guitars. The food was laid out on tables where one might take his or her choice of meats, fruits, and frijoles refritos. Visitors had come from the surrounding ranchos and had brought more food and drink to add to the festivities.

Crow and LeRue sat with Raul near the bonfire. To their right, sitting in chairs, were the Batista's and their guests from the other ranchos. The guitar players had just finished, when someone called out, "Jefe, dance the Baile Mexicano del Sombrero (Mexican Hat Dance)."

From behind the chairs, where the Batista's were sitting, Hector stepped into the firelight. He wore black trousers and a matching jacket. Silver conchos were on the seams of his trouser legs, on his shoulders and on his black sombrero that hung from a lanyard around his neck. He turned to Hernando Batista and asked, "With your permission, may I dance with Francisca?"

Hernando turned to Francisca, who nodded her head yes and stood. Hector offered her his hand as he led her to an open space near the fire. As they passed Crow, Hector looked down at the Mountain Man and smiled. Crow smiled back, but his eyes told Hector what he was thinking.

Francisca took her place next to Hector, and they waited for the music to start. The guitars hit the first cord, and the audience shouted their approval. Hector, had placed his sombrero at a rakish tilt on his head. His back was straight, his eyes never leaving Francisca.

Francisca was as light on her feet as a bird in flight. Her black hair glistened in the firelight as her skirt flared with her movements. The crowd cheered them on as Crow joined in with his voice, but not his heart.

The dance ended to shouts of appreciation for a well-done performance. Hector passed by Crow as he escorted Francisca back to her seat. He stopped in front of Crow and said with a smirk, "Perhaps the Mountain Man can dance?"

Crow felt the vice-like grip of LeRue's hand on his forearm. "Why, we'd be pleased to show you a bit of mountain dancing." With that, LeRue stood up and went to one of the Mexican guitar players and asked to use his instrument. With a smile, the man handed LeRue his guitar.

"Come on Isaiah, let's give 'em a little mountain music." Crow stood and dusted the seat of his buckskins off. With slow and feigned uncertainty, he went to the dance area. Francisca took her seat and watched as Crow, appearing reluctant, stepped into the open space she had just left. Behind her, Hector smirked at the clumsy buffoon before him.

LeRue strummed the strings of the guitar, and then his fingers began to pick at the strings, slowly, creating a melody. Crow began to shuffle his feet. LeRue's fingers began to move faster on the strings, playing an Irish jig. Crow's head came up, and his back became straight. With his head held high, he clasped his hands behind his back. His feet flew in rhythm with the strings of the guitar. Then Crow smiled with the joy of the music and the dance. The crowd cheered enthusiastically. Francisca marveled at the gracefulness, of a man so big.

Hector was gone, and no one noticed.

Crow's dance ended with much applause and cheers. He walked over to LeRue. "Perhaps my friend will sing for us?"

LeRue began to sing a Mexican love song. His tenor voice smooth and powerful filled the air and silenced the crowd. The only other sound was the crackling of the fire. Francisca changed her gaze from LeRue to Crow who smiled at her. Her heart skipped a beat, and she smiled back at him.

Someone started shouting, "¡Hay un oso, corre, corre (There is a bear, run, run)!"

Everyone began to move. Crow watched as several men ran and mounted their horses. They pulled their lariats from their saddle horns just as a grizzly entered the firelight. Then the horsemen began to cast their lariats at the bear. The bear stood up on his hind legs but was pulled down into the fire. The tension on the lariats knocked over the tables of food. The smell of burning fur filled the air. The men, shouting with glee, rode off, dragging the fighting, enraged bear behind them.

Carlos approached the Mountain Men, laughing. "That often happens. The bears smell the food, or they are just on their way to the slaughter corrals to feed on the carcasses. The vaqueros will tire him and place him in a cage. Later, we will fight him against one of our bulls."

"You fight them?" Crow asked.

"Yes, there is much wagering as to who will win, the bear or the bull. But I think our party is over for the night," said Carlos, looking at all of the overturned tables.

Crow and LeRue headed back to their room as the rest of the guests started to retire for the evening. It was later, when everyone was asleep, that Crow slipped silently out of his room and into the night.

The next morning there would be much talk about how the grizzly had escaped. There would be no wagering on a fight between the grizzly and a bull.

A SHORTCUT TO HEAVEN

The mission was not one of the originals built by the Spanish. It was constructed by the five Dons of the local ranchos because of the long distance to the nearest mission in San Diego. It was built on a beautiful spot, surrounded by several hundred hectares for cattle and farming.

Father Lopez, a man of fifty years, had been educated in Spain. Unknown to all but Hernando, his wife, and their son, Father Lopez was Hernando Batista's cousin. So, when Father Lopez saw Hernando Batista riding to the mission in the company of three men, he was pleased. Hernando had rescued him from a minor position in Mexico and brought him to California to build the **Mission Santa Maria**.

"Buenos días Padré, it is a pleasure to see you," greeted Hernando.

"Buenos días Don Hernando, what brings you out so early?"

Hernando, Carlos, Crow, and LeRue dismounted and stood before the priest. Hernando said, "I need to speak with you in private. But first, let me introduce you to our dear friends, this is Isaiah Crow and Jacques LeRue."

Father Lopez was intrigued by the two men dressed in buckskins. The man named Crow had startling blue eyes and wore his hair long. He had a presence about him that could make one feel secure or intimidated; while LeRue seemed to emanate a cavalier attitude. Father Lopez immediately had a good feeling about these men.

"Welcome to **Mission Santa Maria**," said Father Lopez. "Hernando, please come with me, and we shall talk." With a smile, he turned to the others and said, "Carlos, you and your friends may go to the kitchen. I think you know the way."

As Father Lopez and Hernando headed to the mission, Carlos led the Mountain Men to a building set apart from the others. Crow was impressed with the beautiful gardens and the large trees that shaded the buildings. Although they were out of sight, he could hear cattle lowing. Tending to the gardens were perhaps twenty Indians, dressed in white shirts and trousers.

As the three men approached the building, the scent of flowers became mixed with the fragrant aroma of freshly baked bread. Crow felt his mouth water. He turned to LeRue and winked. LeRue, grinning, nodded his head.

Carlos led them into a large kitchen. Ten Indians were busy tending to two ovens. There was a huge hearth with large, cast iron pots hanging over the fire. The smell of fresh baked bread and cooking meats and vegetables filled the room. A Mexican woman, nearly as broad as she was tall, beamed at the sight of Carlos.

"Carlos, dulce hombre (you sweet man), how happy I am to see you!" With that, she smiled a smile that made everyone feel welcome.

"Lucia, estos son mis amigos, Isaías y Jacques (these are my friends Isaiah and Jacques). The Don is with the Padré, and we have come to see you."

"You are too kind, but I think you smell the bread! You go in back and wait. I will be right out."

The three men went out through a door in the back of the kitchen. There, they found a wooden table with long benches on both sides. The branches of an old oak tree formed an umbrella over the table. A light breeze caressed the leaves of the tree, making a rustling sound. As the three men sat down, Lucia and an Indian girl came out to the table. Lucia carried a pitcher in one hand and three mugs in the other. The Indian girl had a bundle in her hands wrapped in a linen cloth. Lucia placed the pitcher and cups on the table as the girl put the bundle in front of the men. As Lucia poured wine from the pitcher into the mugs, the girl removed a hot loaf of bread from the linen wrap.

Carlos picked up the loaf of bread, tore off a piece and handed the loaf to Crow. Crow tore off a piece of bread and passed the loaf to LeRue. Lucia was happy to see the smiles as the men ate the warm bread. The Indian girl returned with a platter of carne asada and frijoles refritos. Without hesitation, Carlos led the way by taking a piece of bread, scooping up some beans and meat with it and stuffing it into his mouth. Crow and LeRue followed suit.

Father Lopez and Hernando sat at a table in Lopez's private room. On the table were pewter plates and silver flatware. Fresh bread, meat, and beans were in dishes, with fresh fruit from the mission orchard in a bowl. The Padré poured the wine into a glass and handed it to Hernando. He poured one for himself, raised his glass and said, "Salud." Hernando lifted his glass, nodded his head, and they each took a sip of their wine.

"So what brings you to the mission?" asked the Padré.

"I have a favor to ask of you. I want my friend Isaiah baptized and made a member of the church."

"That can be arranged."

"I want it done today."

Father Lopez nearly spit his wine out. "Today! Why I do not even know this man! Has he attended catechism? Who will be his el padrino (godfather)?"

"He has not, but I know him. He is a good man who wants to be a citizen of Mexico. The mayor from San Diego will be here for Francisca's Quinceañera. He will bring the papers to make Crow a citizen. But first, you must baptize him and register him in the Church. As to his compadré, my son Carlos will be his el padrino."

"I do not know. This is most irregular, I…"

Hernando interrupted, "If he were dying and asked to be baptized, you could do it. Why not a man who is alive and wants to be baptized? This man and his compadré saved my life and my son's life. Not once but twice. While we were in San Diego, he saved me a considerable amount of money from a cunning thief. I also believe he is in love with my daughter and she with him. I like him, and I want him to stay."

Father Lopez sat slouched forlornly in his chair, thinking. Slowly pulling himself upright in his chair, he leaned forward with his elbows on the table. "I will do this under one condition: If he marries, he must attend classes before he weds."

"I do not see a problem with that."

"Let us eat! Then we will go and welcome a new member of the Church into the fold."

CITIZEN CROW

The guests began to arrive two days before Francisca's birthday. Rancheros and their families came by horseback, carriage and ox cart. Don Hernando had several small but pleasant adobe cottages built for the occasion, while the extra rooms in the hacienda were for the visiting Dons and their immediate families.

Crow and LeRue had moved from the hacienda and into one of the small vaquero dwellings. Francisca had mooned about for a day, but soon the preparations for her birthday demanded her attention.

In their cottage, LeRue sat on a sleeping rack, smoking his pipe in the corner of the one-room building. Across from him, Crow sat at a wooden table. By the light of a lantern, Crow held a threaded needle in one hand as he strung small glass trading-beads onto it with the other. On the table, near the lamp, was a leather bag made of white elk hide. The sides of the bag were covered in beadwork that glistened as it caught the lamplight. LeRue smiled at the sight of his friend laboring. The tip of Crow's tongue protruded from the corner of his mouth.

Crow pinched the last strung bead to secure it and cut the thread with his teeth. "This is the last string. It is finished." With his calloused fingers, he nimbly tied a small knot at the end of the thread and held it up for LeRue to see. LeRue got up off the bed and came over to the table. He saw in the lamplight an exquisitely made bag. The leather was nearly linen white. The seams were so tight, they were invisible to the eye. The glass beads were of varying colors yet they all blended in to form an intricate design that held the eye. The bag was not an item for trade. It was from the heart.

Taking a quick puff of his pipe, LeRue placed his hand on his friend's shoulder. Crow looked up at LeRue. "She will know what is in your heart when she sees this," said LeRue. Crow took the bag and turned it over. On the backside was an "F" made with light blue and dusty pink, called "Crow Rose," beads. "You have the 'F' off center," said LeRue.

"I will leave it unfinished until I can place a 'C' there," replied Crow.

"You are taking a big chance, my friend. She may be offended. Or perhaps it may offend her father?"

"I've heard that suitors are allowed to present gifts at the Quinceañera. I will speak to both Carlos and Hernando beforehand."

LeRue placed his pipe between his lips. Clenching the stem with his teeth, he examined the beadwork. He carefully placed the bag back on the table. "I'm sure that she will receive it in the same manner as it is given."

Outside the cottage, the loud sound of voices prompted the two Mountain Men to grab their rifles and head out the door. Outside, they found a carriage surrounded by four armed men. Crow and LeRue recognized the armed men as working for Batista. One of the passengers was the Mayor of San Diego. Next to him sat a large woman who looked quite pleased with their reception.

Don Hernando, Carmen, Carlos, and Francisca were all there to greet their guests. There were introductions all around then the group headed to the hacienda. Crow noticed Hernando stop and whisper something to Carlos. Carlos excused himself and left the group and headed toward Crow and LeRue. 'I wonder what this is about?' wondered Crow.

"Isaiah, my father wishes to speak with you. Can you come now?"

"Yes, I'll just put my rifle away and be right over."

Carlos turned and walked toward the courtyard. "What is that all about?" asked LeRue.

"I think it's about becoming a citizen of Mexico," replied Crow. "I'll go see and meet you back here later."

"Si, I will meet you here."

Crow entered the hacienda and was greeted by Carlos. "They are waiting for you in the dining area."

In the dining room, Hernando and the mayor from San Diego were sitting at the table. The two men stood as Crow entered. "Ah, Isaiah, welcome! You know the mayor from San Diego."

"Yes sir, a pleasure to see you again."

"And it is a pleasure to see you, Isaiah; and under much more pleasant circumstances."

Hernando pointed to the chair next to the mayor. "Please, be seated. I think you will be pleased with what he has to tell you."

Crow sat down while Carlos sat next to his father.

The mayor picked up a leather satchel from the floor next to his chair and opened it. He withdrew a stack of documents and placed them on the table. Briefly sorting through the papers, he took two and put them in front of Crow.

Hernando, from his chair, looked over his shoulder and snapped his fingers. An Indian girl appeared with an inkpot and a pen. She placed them on the table in front of the mayor. The mayor dipped the pen into the pot and handed the pen to Crow. "I see from the documents that you are now a member of the Church. That satisfies all of the requirements for you to become a citizen. These are your citizenship papers. One is a copy for you to keep and the other is for the official files. If you will sign here, and here, please."

Crow took the pen and in a bold hand, signed the documents. The mayor blotted the ink then passed the papers to Hernando. "If you and your son will sign here as witnesses," he said. Indicating where to sign, he handed the pen to Hernando.

Hernando and Carlos both signed the documents and handed them back to the mayor. The official took one of the papers and placed it in front of Crow. "You are now a citizen of Mexico, Señor Crow. Now, I have something more for you. As a citizen of Mexico, you are allowed a league of land. That I believe is equal to 1,800 hectares (4,448 acres) as you measure land. The grant is a gift from the Mexican Government. I have the requirements for registering the property when you are ready to do so."

Crow was silent for a moment. He had not known about the land grant. "I am grateful to each of you, and the Government of Mexico. I've never owned property before, though it has been something I wished to do."

As if on que a servant appeared with a tray of glasses and a bottle of wine. The glasses were filled and placed in front of the men. Hernando picked up his glass followed by the others. "To our new citizen, and our friend, Isaiah Crow. We welcome you!" The four men drank from their glasses.

The sound of silver spurs echoed in the hallway. Hector entered the room. He appeared to be surprised to see the gathering. "Hector, you are just in time. Meet our new citizen of Mexico, Señor Isaiah Crow."

The news visibly shook Hector, but he recovered quickly and approached Crow offering his hand. "Congratulations and welcome." Crow took the offered hand and allowed Hector to squeeze it. He slowly applied pressure breaking Hector's grasp, and smiling said, "Thank you, Hector, I appreciate that."

Hector, his hand at his side, opening and closing it, said to Hernando, "The last of the supplies for the Quinceañera has arrived, and the cooking pits are ready. The fires are started and should be ready for the cooks in about four hours."

Hernando replied, "Thank you, Hector. I want you to post guards to watch for bears. I do not want any uninvited guests."

"I will see to it." With a side glance at Crow, Hector left the room.

After Hector had left, Hernando turned to Crow and said, "Do I detect... how do you say... animosity, between you and Hector?"

Crow smiled, "Oh, it is only friendly competition between two men."

Carlos smiled, 'Competition yes, but not so friendly.'

CROW, A MAN OF MEANS

Crow, the Mountain Man, the warrior, stood in front of the mirror with butter-flies in his stomach. He once again checked his hair and his freshly cleaned red shirt. He nearly jumped out of his skin, when the unseen LeRue asked, "What are you doing?"

Crow spun around, "I'm...I'm"

LeRue, a smirk on his face said, "Yes, come on you can say it."

Crow turned back to the mirror, cleared his throat and said, "I'm going to ask Hernando's permission to call on Francisca."

"Ah, amigo that is a big step. Is it because of the Quinceañera?"

"Yes, I want to give her my gift as a suitor. I had to wait to see if I would be allowed into the church and to become a citizen. Now, I have also been given a land grant. I feel I have something to offer."

"I think you have nothing to worry about, my friend. You have already proven yourself to the family."

"I hope you are right."

Crow found Hernando alone, sitting at the big table in the dining room. Papers were spread out before him; an inkpot and pen, close at hand. He looked up and smiled when he saw Crow enter, "Buenos días!"

"Buenos días, Don Hernando," he replied.

"Isaiah, why so formal? Come sit. Would you like some chocolate?"

"Thank you, but not right now. I have a question to ask you."

Hernando's face became serious. He frowned, making Crow nervous. "What is it that you wish to ask?"

"I'd like permission to call on your daughter Francisca!" Crow blurted it out loudly.

Trying to keep a straight face, Hernando asked, "This is not to be taken lightly. What have you to offer my daughter in marriage?"

Crow drew himself up straight and said, "I am now a citizen of Mexico and a member of the church. I have a grant for 1,800 hectares of land where I plan to raise and train the finest horses in California. I am also a man of means having over $1,000 in American gold coin."

Hernando was surprised by the mention of the gold coin. Few people in California had hard currency, relying on notes of promise against goods and bartering. The number of cattle a man owned told of his wealth. Hernando called out loudly, "Trae dos chocolates, rápidamente."

Moments later one of the Indian girls appeared with two cups of steaming chocolate and placed them on the table. Hernando again indicated with his hand for Crow to take a seat. Crow pulled out the chair and sat down.

"You should know others seek my daughter's hand in marriage. There are strict rules for courting."

"I understand. I will not cause you, your family or your daughter any embarrassment."

Just then Carlos entered the room. "Carlos," said Hernando, "Isaiah has asked permission to call on Francisca."

Carlos walked up to his friend and placing a hand on Crow's shoulder said, "Of course you told him 'no.' "

Crow's stomach roiled as he looked up at Carlos. Hernando replied, "I have decided to grant him permission. I will need to speak with Carlotta. I will place her in charge of this."

Carlos took mercy on Crow and said, "This is a good thing, I think. But I must warn you, Carlotta is very strict."

Crow pushed back his chair and stood. He offered his hand to Hernando. "Thank you, Don Hernando."

Hernando stood and took Crow's hand in both of his. "I welcome your interest in my Francisca. You may call on her after her Quinceañera."

QUINCEAÑERA

The celebration of a girl's fifteenth birthday and her transition from childhood to adulthood

The Mass was a thing of beauty. The church was decorated throughout with fresh flowers. It was packed with family and guests, dressed in their finest. Francisca wore the white gown her father had commissioned to be made in America. The long sleeved, white silk dress was exquisitely embroidered with small flowers made of fine red and green thread. The many petticoats beneath the gown made it flare so full that she appeared to float across the floor as she approached the altar. A white silk pillow was placed at the altar for her to kneel on as she received communion.

Carlos stood by Francisca's side, as her chambelan de honor, to symbolize her first male companion. Francisca offered a bouquet of fifteen perfect white roses to the Virgin Mary. Each rose, from their own garden, had been carefully selected by her mother.

After communion, Francisca was led by the priest to her throne, an ornate high-backed chair upholstered in red velvet. Her parents stood beside the throne. In her left hand, Francisca held a Bible and a rosary. The rosary came from the Holy Land, a gift from her cousin, Father Lopez. The Bible belonged to her father, given to him when he was a young boy. Father Lopez slipped a simple gold ring on her finger, to remind her of the unconditional love of God. A tiara, denoting Francisca as a princess before God and the world, was placed upon her head by her mother. The tiara was her mother's, who had received it from her mother, at her own Quinceañera. Her father, Hernando, presented her with her scepter, representing her taking responsibility for her own life.

At the end of the mass, Francisca exited the church like a bride, on the arm of her brother. They were followed by her court of fourteen young ladies and then the guests. Horses, with saddles decorated with silver trim that reflected the sun, stood next to the carriages and ox carts. All were decorated with colorful flowers and ribbons. They silently awaited the guests, to take them in a procession, back to the rancho and the celebration.

As Francisca and Carlos exited the church, Francisca noticed a man who stood head and shoulders taller than the rest. It took her a moment to realize it was Isaiah. He was wearing a splendid suit of black cloth, heavily embroidered with silver thread. Silver conchos were sewn down the seams of the trouser legs. Francisca's heart skipped a beat when she realized what Crow had done to honor her.

Outside the entrance of the church, Crow watched as Francisca stepped into the daylight. Her dress was a blaze of white. Her black hair, fixed in a bun, shimmered in the sunlight. The tiara, stuck in the bun of her hair, sparkled blindingly as she turned her head in greeting. 'She is a princess,' thought Crow. When she saw him looking, she smiled. Crow thought at that moment, 'You are the most beautiful woman I have ever seen.'

The entourage passed by the applauding crowd and they were assisted into the carriages. The festive mood began to build. Laughter and loud greetings filled the air. In one of the ox carts, several men picked up instruments and started to play. As the procession began to move back to the rancho, many began to sing.

Crow felt a hand on his shoulder. Turning, he saw LeRue, his eyes bright with excitement. "She is lovely my friend. Come, let's join them. Besides, I want to see the look on Hector's face when you surprise the Princess."

Crow turned to LeRue and asked, "Surprise?"

With a grin, LeRue replied, "I know of your secret lessons, and I can hardly wait to see you dance."

"You have said nothing of this?"

"No, I have said nothing. But come, we must join the others."

THE CELEBRATION

When the procession was seen approaching, the musicians at the hacienda were alerted. They began to play as Francisca's carriage entered the yard.

Holes had been dug and decorated posts erected on the perimeter of the party area. Ropes were strung from post to post, circling the yard, supporting lanterns and strands of flowers.

Sides of beef roasted over three cooking pits; the fat dripping onto the coals, producing bursts of flame and puffs of smoke. Nearby, the rancho dogs lay on their bellies, watching with bright, hungry eyes. Boys with willow switches kept them at bay.

A space, located near the hacienda, had several chairs placed in a line behind a long table that was covered with a beautiful, white linen cloth. Francisca was to hold court there. She would be in the center chair, flanked by her mother and father. Carlotta and her husband, who were Francisca's Godparents, would be seated beside her parents.

It took a while for everyone to arrive, but soon everybody was settled. There was a blare from a trumpet to get the guest's attention. Hernando, with Francisca on his arm, stepped out into the open area in front of their table. Father and daughter faced each other. Hernando gently took his daughter in his arms, and the music began. It was a waltz. The two glided across the yard. Hernando, straight and proud, smiled at his beautiful daughter. Francisca looked at her father with adoring eyes. When the dance ended, a great cheer went up, accompanied by applause.

The music changed. Francisca and her court of fourteen young ladies entered the dance area. As the music played, the girls danced the traditional waltz they had practiced together for days. The crowd cheered and applauded their moves, making the girls smile. When the music ended, the men entered the dance area, and everyone began to dance.

Crow had hesitated to respond, and Hector, dressed in a well-tailored suit of tan cloth with many silver conchos, reached Francisca first. Crow watched for a moment, and then went over to the musicians. The man with the trumpet was resting as the others played. Crow said to him, "I wish a favor amigo." As the trumpet player bent his head to hear Crow. Crow handed him an American five dollar gold piece. The musician's eyes went wide, and he listened intently to what Crow had to say.

Hector Camacho danced smoothly and with grace. He guided Francisca as if they had been dancing together for years. Others stopped and watched the two. When the music finished, Hector bowed to Francisca and escorted her back to her throne, accompanied by applause from the guests.

Francisca had just taken her seat and was having a sip of wine when Crow stepped from the crowd. He now wore a black sombrero, heavily decorated with silver that matched his perfectly fitted suit of clothes. His confident stride and beautiful clothing caught the eye of most everyone. Crow stopped in front of Hernando, removed his hat and bowed. "Don Hernando, with your permission, I request to dance the Danza de Cortejo with your daughter, Francisca.

A murmur spread through the crowd. LeRue asked a man next to him what was happening. The man said, "The gringo has invited the Don's daughter to dance the Danza de Cortejo, the dance of courtship."

At the table, Hernando was surprised at the request. "Isaiah, the dance is very complicated. Are you sure you wish to do this?"

"Yes, Don Hernando, with your permission."

Hernando turned to his daughter, "Francisca, do you wish to do this?"

"Yes, father, he dares to ask, I will dance with him."

In the crowd, Hector watched. His jealousy burned in his stomach, turning to hate for the gringo. But he calmed a bit when he thought, 'This time you have gone too far. Fancy clothes will not hide the fact you do not know our dance.'

Crow stepped in front of Francisca. Bowing, he offered her his hand. Francisca, taking his hand, stood. Crow escorted her to the dance floor. The music had been good, but the incentive of the five dollar gold piece, produced flawless tones that were noticed by all. The trumpet player played his heart out.

Francisca, playing her part, began simulating the rejection of her partner's advances, as his dance tried to entice her into intimate affection. As they danced, Crow's moves became more complicated and persistent. Francisca's dance showed signs that she was warming to his advances. Soon, the two were whirling, showing definite signs of giddiness. Their eyes were locked on each other. Crow removed his hat and dropped it on the ground between them. They began to hop and kick and dance around the sombrero. Suddenly, Francisca bent to pick up the hat. The timing was perfect, as Crow kicked his leg over her head. The crowd cheered. Francisca raised the hat to hide their faces and kissed Crow on the lips. Parting quickly, they turned to face her parents, and together they bowed.

Hernando was clapping as he stood. 'Isaiah Crow you never cease to amaze me!' he thought.

Francisca held Crow's hand as he escorted her back to her seat.

LeRue, standing near the edge of the crowd, watched as Hector Camacho took a long drink from a bottle.

AMBUSH

The celebration of Francisca's Quinceañera was beginning to slow in the wee hours of the morning. Many had retired for the evening, and the musicians had quit hours ago. Crow and Francisca had danced several dances together and now sat talking. She sat on her throne while Crow sat in a chair next to her. Behind them sat Carlotta, Francisca's Godmother, and now, her chaperon.

Carlotta got up from her seat and said, "Francisca, it is past time for you to retire. Señor Crow, this was her special day, and I have been lenient, this will not happen again."

Crow stood and faced Carlotta, "I thank you for this evening. I understand and will not take advantage of the privilege of calling on Francisca."

Francisca turned to Carlotta, "May he walk me to the entry?"

Carlotta, with a feigned sigh of exasperation, replied, "Yes, I suppose."

Crow, desperately wanting to take Francisca's hand, walked beside her, his hands clasped behind his back, his head bent down so he could listen to Francisca.

Francisca clutched the beaded bag that Crow had made for her. She was thrilled with the gift, and the "F" on the back with the blank space she understood immediately. "I had a beautiful night, Isaiah. Thank you for the lovely gift. Siempre lo aprecio (I shall always cherish it)."

As the couple, followed by Carlotta, passed by a shadowed area of the yard, Hector Camacho watched. In his hand he held his knife, alcohol clouded his reasoning. 'I will wait, and when you return, I will end this,' he thought. 'I have worked too long and too hard for you to ruin this for me now.'

At the entry, Carlotta did not allow the young lovers to linger, insisting Francisca enter the hacienda, while she stayed outside with Crow. Francisca turned to Crow, "Good night Isaiah." Her smile made Crow's heart ache. He did not want her to go.

Carlotta opened the door for Francisca and closed it behind her. She turned to Crow. "You will come to me when you wish to visit with Francisca. I will set the time and the place. You are not to converse with her without my presence, do you understand?"

"Yes, I will do as you say. I thank you for allowing us this evening." With that Crow turned and began to walk back across the yard.

As Carlotta watched Crow leave, she thought, 'Francisca, I think you are most fortunate.' She turned and entered the hacienda.

As Crow crossed the yard, something put him on alert. Then he saw it. In the shadows was the toe of a man's boot, pointing straight up. Crow moved quickly to the fallen man. It was Hector, lying flat on his back. His sombrero lay in the dust next to him. There was a knife next to his hand. Crow knelt next to Hector and found he was alive. Crow saw blood and turned the body over. He saw a large bump on the back of Hector's head that had split. Blood from the wound was beginning to coagulate in his hair. In the dim light, Crow saw a chunk of cut wood that might have come from one of the fire pits. There were footprints. They appeared to have been made by someone wearing moccasins. "LeRue," Crow said aloud.

Crow stood and looked down at Hector, 'I should kill you now,' he thought. 'But that would ruin Francisca's celebration. Our time will come, and it will be man to man and not from ambush.' Crow raised his foot and slowly crushed Hector's beautiful sombrero, and walked away.

A few hours later, dawn was breaking and so was Hector's head. As he rolled onto his side, he saw his sombrero, the crown crushed flat. Pulling his legs up he went to his knees and became instantly dizzy, the back of his head feeling like it would explode.

"Jefe, what has happened?" It was Raul. The boy rushed to Hector and taking him by the arm, helped him to his feet. As Hector stood, swaying on uncertain legs, Raul bent down and picked up the knife from the ground. "Here jefe, you must have dropped this."

Hector looked at the knife with a look of bewilderment. His memory began to clear. He had been waiting for Crow when someone must have struck him from behind.

"Raul, help me to my cottage, and bring my sombrero."

Raul walked beside Hector, allowing him to grip his shoulder for support. As they walked, the boy eyed the sombrero; a dusty bootprint could be plainly seen in the center of the crown. 'Oh, el jefe hizo enojar a alguien (made someone angry),' he thought to himself.

Raul opened the door and walked with Hector to the bed. Hector sat down slowly on the edge of the bed and held his head in his hands. Looking around the room, Raul saw a pitcher and a basin. The pitcher had water in it, and there was a towel next to it. After filling the bowl, he took it to the bed and placed it on the floor next to Hector. Wetting the cloth, he began to clean the blood from Hector's wound.

Across the way in another cottage, LeRue watched through a window. After the door closed behind Hector and Raul, he turned to Crow, who was sitting on the side of his bed. "Looks like your friend Hector had a little too much to drink last night. Raul had to help him home."

Crow looked up at his friend, a slight smile on his face. "Was he waiting for me?" he asked LeRue.

LeRue shrugged his shoulders, "He drank beaucoup tequila last night, probably fell on his head," said LeRue turning back to the window, smiling.

Crow stood up, stretching, "Thank you, amigo."

LeRue, looking out the window, again shrugged his shoulders, "No era nada (It was nothing)."

GOOD MORNING PRINCESS

Francisca, still in her bed, rolled onto her side. On a table near the bed, she could see the beaded bag that Crow had given her. Slipping out bed, Francisca went to the table and picked up the bag. She returned to the bed and wriggled back under the covers. As she lay there, Francisca examined the bag. The leather was so white and soft; the brilliant beadwork, so smooth to the touch. Turning the bag over, she smiled at the open space next to the beaded 'F.' In her mind's eye she imagined the letter 'C.' 'Francisca Crow,' she thought, 'I like the sound of that.'

A soft knock at her bedroom door and the slip of the latch announced her mother. "Good morning! Do you still feel like a princess?" her mother asked.

Francisca again got out from under the covers, stood and hugged her mother. "Oh, momma, it was a beautiful Quinceañera. Yes, I still feel like a princess."

"Señor Crow was certainly a surprise. He looked magnificent in his new clothes. And his dancing! I had no idea he knew how to dance like that."

"He told me that he took lessons."

"Here?"

"Yes, one of the vaqueros and his wife taught him. He was wonderful, mother. He was a gentleman the entire evening. He treated Carlotta with respect." Francisca handed her mother the beaded bag that Crow had made for her. "He made this for me. I think his wanting to court me is sincere."

Carmen took the bag and examined it. She first ran the tips of her fingers over the beads then slipped her fingers into the bag. "The bag is so soft, and the color of the leather is white like linen."

"Look at the back."

Carmen turned the bag over. Her fingers traced the "F" on the back. "He did not finish it."

"He said he hoped to place a 'C' there."

Carmen watched her daughter, noting her eyes. If there was truly such a thing as happy eyes, Francisca had them. If this man, Isaiah Crow, was everything he appeared to be, Francisca was a very lucky girl.

BREAKFAST WITH HERNANDO

Hernando finished dressing and headed down the stairs to the dining room. Carlos and Captain King were just stepping off the bottom step. "Buenos días," Hernando greeted them.

The two men turned. Captain King responded, "Good morning!"

Hernando joined them, and they entered the dining room together. Carlos said, "I thought the mayor would be here."

"I was going to tell you," said Hernando, "He received a message early this morning. He and his wife had to return to San Diego.

"Well, let us eat then we can watch the young men show us how well they can perform."

As Captain King pulled out a chair to sit, he asked, "Perform?"

Hernando, taking his seat said, "Yes, the vaqueros and some of the young men will compete in a riding and roping competition. For prizes, I have a silver belt buckle and a pair of silver spurs for the youngsters. The top prize is a four strand, eighty-foot lariat made by a fabricante de cuerdas (rope maker) who is a master craftsman."

Carlos added, "There will be more dancing and food later. ¡Será muy divertido (It will be a great deal of fun)!"

CHARREADA (RODEO)

The cloudless morning sky was a brilliant, bright blue. The excited voices of the guests drowned out the noise coming from the horses and cattle. The guests, gathered on a hill, were shaded by large trees. From this vantage point, they had an excellent view of the open field below. Vaqueros, dressed in their finest, strutted about like proud fighting cocks. Each man was sure he would win the coveted lariat. The boys, the sons of the vaqueros, mimicked their fathers. Each one was sure he would win a silver belt buckle or a set of silver spurs.

A temporary corral now held fifty or more longhorns. Around the top rail of the corral, children and young ladies were perched like so many birds on a tree branch. They were laughing and pointing out their fathers or a favorite boy.

On the hill, tables had been set up for merienda (snacks). On the tables were fruits and pan dulce (sweet bread) of pink, yellow, brown and white colors. Hot chocolate and pitchers of milk were available for café con leche (coffee with milk), in which the guest could dunk their sweet bread.

Blankets had been spread on the ground under the shade trees. Rather than sit on the ground, most of the women chose to stay in their carriages to watch. Carmen and Francisca decided to sit with Captain King and Hernando on a blanket, near the front of the group.

Hernando stood, faced the crowd and raised his hands to get everyone's attention. Carlos and two of the Indian servants joined him, standing at his side. Carlos held a lariat while the servants each held a basket. "My dear guests, the competition will begin shortly. I urge you to partake of the food and refreshments. My son, Carlos, holds in his hand, the prize for the grand champion." Carlos held up the lariat for all to see. There was polite applause.

Hernando continued, "The first prize, for winning the riding competition by one of the young men, will be a silver belt buckle." One of the servants held up a large engraved silver buckle that caught and reflected the sunlight. "For the young man who wins the race, there is a pair of silver spurs." One of the servants held up a set of silver spurs. "There are also prizes for second and third places. Now let us begin!"

In the field next to the corral, two vaqueros sat upon their stallions, lariats in hand. One nervously pulled at the brim of his hat making sure it was on tight. On the hill, one of the servants pointed a musket into the blue sky and pulled the trigger. Several things happened at the sound of that gunshot: Two boys pulled poles from the corral fence, and a boy with a sharp stick stuck a novillo (steer) in the rump. The surprised steer lunged forward and began to run. The vaqueros, with smiles on their faces, shouted loudly, as their horses leaped forward to pursue the steer. The men on the hill stood, in their excitement, as they watched each horse and rider working as one.

The wily steer began to zigzag, but the vaqueros stayed with him. One vaquero started to whirl his lariat above his head. He let it fly. The loop of the lasso cut through the air and caught around the horns of the steer. The horse went stiff-legged, coming to an abrupt stop. The vaquero quickly sat up straight in the saddle, leaning forward slightly in anticipation of the coming jolt. The second vaquero's lariat landed just in front of the hind legs of the steer. He jerked it tight, just as the steer stepped into the open loop. The lariat went taut, throwing the steer to the ground. The audience applauded loudly, the men whistling and shouting.

As everyone settled down waiting for the next contest, Hernando asked Carlos, "Where is Hector?"

Carlos replied, "LeRue told me that Hector took a fall after the party last night. He hurt his head, and has quite a lump."

Hernando thought, 'Hector seems to have taken several falls since Crow arrived.' Then aloud, he asked, "Where are Crow and LeRue? I thought they would be here."

"They will be father; I talked them into giving us a demonstration after the contest. It is to be a surprise."

Hernando looked skeptical. He wondered, 'A surprise for me, or your sister?'

* * *

The Charreada was an exciting event. The men and the boys had put their hearts into it. The prizes had just been awarded when it was noticed that there were several young men on the field. They were sticking long poles into the ground. Behind them, vaqueros stood in their stirrups, taking head sized gourds from sacks and placing them on top of the poles. When they finished, two boys carrying two boards, six-feet in length, came out and propped them up on end. One boy, with a piece of chalk, drew a circle at the top of each board. Hernando looked at his son, Carlos, "This is the surprise?"

Carlos, without a word, nodded his head and stood up. "Honrado invitados (Honored guests), we have something extra for you! As you know, we have two visitors; one is from Texas the other from the Americas. They are what the Anglo's call Mountain Men. They have agreed to give us a demonstration of marksmanship and horsemanship. With that, Carlos extended his arm, to point out to the field.

Carmen and Francisca looked out to where Carlos had pointed. The gray stallion, a gift from Carlos to Crow, stood alone in the field, apparently without a rider. Several men in the audience laughed, "It seems the gringo has fallen off his horse!"

The gray leaped forward and raced full tilt across the field. Crow, like magic, appeared from the opposite side and swung up onto the gray's back. The Mountain Man was dressed in his buckskins. For the first time, his hair hung loose. Crow's black mane flowed out behind him. He drew his legs up, and stood up straight, on the back of the running horse. The crowd went wild. Francisca thought she would swallow her heart. 'He is magnificent!' she thought.

Crow, his arms extended straight out from his shoulders, suddenly reached down. From each side of his belted waist, he pulled a war-hawk. The gray was stretched out now and moving fast, as it charged at the two six-foot-tall planks. Crow threw first one war-hawk, then the other. The blades of the war-hawks buried themselves into the center of each chalked circle. There was a moment of silence. Then the crowd erupted in applause, whistles, and shouts.

Crow dropped down onto the back of the gray. They raced back across the field to the point where they had started. No one had noticed that LeRue had come onto the field. LeRue, dressed in his buckskins was holding a rifle in each hand, waiting for Crow. As Crow rode up alongside, LeRue gave him a rifle and a powder horn. He then gave Crow two lead balls. Crow and LeRue raised their guns and checked to see that new caps were in place. "Let's do it," said Crow. They each put the lead bullets in their mouths. The two men looked at the gourds on the poles. Crow nodded at LeRue.

The two Mountain Men raised their rifles and fired. They kicked their heels back. Their mounts jumped forward and began to run. Downrange, the first set of gourds exploded, as the lead balls struck them. Crow and LeRue, raised their rifles, placed the powder horns into the muzzles and poured in the powder. Releasing the horns, they extended the guns straight out in front of them. They set their lips over the bore opening and blew a lead ball into the muzzle. Each slipped a new cap from his belt and put it on the nipple of his rifle. By now they were nearly on top of the second set of gourds. With one hand, they fired their guns point blank at their target, blowing it apart, as they rode past. As they passed the third round of gourds, they again began reloading on the run. They slipped on a new cap, turned their mounts, and attacked the last set of gourds; once more, destroying them as they passed.

There was an extended period of silence. The audience was in total disbelief at what they had just witnessed. Hernando stood and began to applaud. Carlos and the rest began to clap and shout.

Crow and LeRue rode up to face the crowd, which was still shouting and applauding. Carlos and Hernando walked down the hill, followed by several of the men. Hernando looked up at Crow, "How were you able to get the ball into the rifle barrel like that?" he asked.

"We used a smaller ball. It rolled down the barrel to the powder. We just made sure to keep the muzzle up to keep the ball seated. That is why we fired so close to the target."

The vaquero, who had won the lariat, rode up to the group. He sat quietly with a slight smile on his face. Crow soon became aware of him. The vaquero said, "Señor, your horse is well trained, would you consider a contest?"

Crow asked, "What do you propose?"

"We will face each other on horseback. Whatever move I make with my horse, you make with yours. Then you move, and I will copy you."

Crow, tilted his head and said, "That seems too simple a test, my friend."

The vaquero dismounted and moved to the rear of his horse. He withdrew a knife from the top of his boot. The vaquero cut two strands of hair from the horse's tail. Replacing the knife into his boot, he returned to face Crow. Holding up the two hairs he said, "We will remove the reins from the bit and tie the reins to the bit with the hairs. If too much force is used to command the horse, the hair will break. It is a simple test." The vaquero smiled up at Crow.

Crow was now smiling, "And what will we wager on this contest, my friend?"

The vaquero had not thought past the challenge and was at a loss for words. Carlos spoke up, "I will donate my spurs as the prize to the winner." With that, he removed his spurs and held them high for all to see. The engraved silver spurs sparkled in the sunlight, as the crowd applauded the gesture.

Crow turned to the vaquero, "I accept your challenge."

The crowd watched as Crow and the vaquero moved out onto the open field. The vaquero unhooked the reins of his horse and tied them to the bit with the horse hairs. Crow sat on his mount watching. Finished, the vaquero looked up at Crow expectantly. With a smile, Crow leaned forward over the gray's neck and removed the bridle and bit completely; handing it to LeRue. The smile left the face of the vaquero.

On the hill, questioning whispers began to pass through the audience. "How will he control his mount? He is a fool! The vaquero is one of our finest horsemen."

Francisca, watching Crow's every move, signaled with her hand to her brother. Carlos moved over to Francisca, "Yes, what is it?"

"What is Isaiah doing?"

"The vaqueros pride themselves in commanding their horses with a light hand. If the reins are pulled too hard, the hair will break. Isaiah has taken it a step further and will use no reins."

On the field, the two men now faced each other on horseback. Crow gestured with his hand that the vaquero should start first. Crow folded his arms across his chest and waited. The crowd began to murmur once again.

The Mexican, his back straight, made a slight movement of the reins and his mount sidestepped. To his disbelief, Crow's mount copied the move. Then, Crow's horse, without any noticeable command, backed up and stopped. With a gentle movement of the reins, the Mexican's horse copied the move.

The vaquero had his mount extend its left foreleg, and curl the right foreleg back, and take a bow.

Without any visible prompts from Crow, the gray copied the move and raised his head with a snort.

Crow, his arms still crossed, moved his feet, then his knees. The gray spun around in a complete circle. It stood on its hind legs, its front hoofs pawing at the sky. He then dropped to the ground standing stock still.

The vaquero's eyes opened wide in amazement. He pulled on the reins. His horse spun around and rose up on its hind legs. The Mexican's horse brought its front legs back to the ground and stood stock still, the reins dragging on the ground. The Mexican held up the reins for all to see. In a display of respect, he removed his sombrero and saluted Crow.

Carmen looked over at her daughter. Francisca's eyes glistened as she applauded.

On the field, Crow moved up beside the vaquero and extended his hand, "Amigo mío, eres un buen caballero y has entrenado bien a tu caballo (My friend, you are a fine horseman, and you have trained your horse well)."

"Gracias, tienes un camino con los caballos. ¿Quizás más tarde podamos hablar de ello (Thank you. You also have a way with horses. Perhaps later we can talk about this)?"

Crow, replied, "I would like that. I plan to train horses soon, and I would like to talk to you about your way of training."

"I am Santiago. When you are ready amigo, we will talk." With a wave of his sombrero, the vaquero rode away.

Carlos approached Crow and handed him the spurs. But Crow held up his hand, "Thank you, but I don't use them. They will look much better on you my friend."

Carlos with a nod replied, "Gracias, we will go now to the hacienda."

"We will meet you there. LeRue and I will put away our rifles and horses and then we'll join you."

PARTNERS

The guests had left. The Indian servants were putting away the party decorations. The rancho was getting ready for a return to a normal workday. Hector stood at the window of his cottage, his left hand shading his eyes from the sunlight. His vision had returned to normal, but his eyes were sensitive to light, and he still had headaches. From his window, he saw Carlos walking across the yard. Moving away from the window, Hector went to the table in the room, pulled out a chair and sat down. There was a knock at the door.

"Adelante!" The door opened, and Carlos entered the room.

"Buenos días, Hector, I have come to see how you are."

Hector did not stand but motioned to a chair at the table. "Please, have a seat."

"I see your bandage is gone. You are healing?"

"Yes, I am doing much better. With your permission, I will return to work tomorrow."

"That is fine, but only if you are feeling well enough. You hit your head hard when you fell."

Hector thought, 'Fell, algún hijo de puta, hit me in the back of the head.' "I think I will be well enough to return to my duties tomorrow."

Carlos got up from his chair and said, "I will be gone for the day. I am taking Crow and LeRue out to look for land. They both have been awarded land grants."

Hector felt the resentment twist his insides at the mention of Crow and LeRue. "Where do you think you might look?" he asked.

"There is good pasture lands and water in the area of a box canyon. A place my father took me to when I was young. We camped there in a cave."

Hector's resentment turned into a knot of fear. That was where his men were camped. "Do not forget the area south of there. The river pools into a small lake and there are many trees for building material and shade."

Carlos, his head bent in thought, looked at Hector. "You are right. That is an excellent place to build. I will show them both areas."

Hector's stomach roiled at the announcement.

"You rest now. I will tell my father you are doing better. But I think you should not go to work tomorrow. You do not look well." With that, Carlos went to the door, opened it and left.

Hector, head in his hands, tried to get a grip on his thoughts. 'If they try to get close to the canyon his men would attack. If Carlos, Crow, and LeRue were killed, that would be good. But if one or all managed to escape, it will end my plan to take over the rancho. What can I do?' Hector's headache came back.

At the hacienda, Carlos was just coming outside after talking to his father. He saw Crow and LeRue standing with the horses by the corral. He untethered his horse from the hitching rail and headed toward them.

LeRue saw Carlos and shouted "Buenos días!"

"Buenos días!" Carlos called back, "You are ready to go?"

Crow replied, "Yes, we are anxious to see the land you described. It sounds perfect."

Carlos, replied, "I visited Hector this morning. He also suggested another location with a small lake fed by the river. There are plenty of trees for building material and shade. I will show you both."

As the three men began to mount, there was a loud, sharp bark. "Oh, you want more do you?" asked Crow.

A medium size brown dog with big floppy ears sat staring at Crow. Carlos and LeRue watched as Crow reached into his possibles bag and pulled out a short piece of jerky. The dog's back foot started to twitch and then to gently tap the ground. The dog barked again at the sight of the jerky, his mouth drooling with anticipation.

Crow broke off a piece of jerky and tossed it into the air. The dog leaped into the air, catching the dried meat in his mouth. Landing on all fours, and with his head down, he chewed on the tough meat, his tail wagging the whole time. Crow put the rest of the meat back into the bag. "Come on, let's go. He'll just keep begging for more."

Crow and LeRue followed Carlos out of the yard, with the brown dog trailing after them. If they had looked to their left, they would have seen Hector at his window, watching them ride out of the yard. Carlos spurred his horse into a gallop. LeRue and Crow heeling theirs, to keep pace.

Hector left the window and went to the door. Opening it, he called out to a vaquero that was passing by, "Amigo, will you saddle my horse and bring it here?"

"Si jefe, right away." The vaquero ran off to fetch the horse. Hector returned to his room to get his hat and guns.

It took about an hour for Carlos, Crow and LeRue to arrive at the area Hector had suggested. From the crest of a hill, the three men and the dog looked over a large field of tall, green grass. A breeze caressed the grass into flowing waves of motion, as birds flew about catching flying insects. A small lake, fed by the river, was full of noisy waterfowl. To the left of the lake were hectares of tall, ponderosa pine. LeRue settled into his saddle and said, "This is a beautiful location. There is plenty of room for horses and cattle. There are enough trees to build a whole town if a man had a mind to."

Carlos watched the men as they surveyed the land before them. Crow had the look of a well-fed man. Pleased with what he saw, Crow turned in his saddle and asked Carlos, "This land is available to us?"

"Yes," replied Carlos, "all you have to do is measure the distances and mark them with stone monuments. You then take the information to San Diego to be registered, and it is yours."

Crow smiled at the thought of owning land and raising horses. "You say there is one other location you want us to see?"

"Yes, there is a place much like this, also with water. It has a box canyon, and it would be adjacent to this land."

LeRue said, "If it is as good as this place, we could be partners. How much land would that be?"

"3,600 hectares (8,900 acres)," answered Crow.

"Let us take a look," said Carlos. "It is about an hour ride from here to the canyon."

It took them the better part of an hour to reach the top of a large hill. It overlooked another field that flowed out toward a line of rocky slopes. Trees grew in abundance. Crow already knew he liked what he saw. But something got his attention.

"Follow me, *now!*" Crow said to his companions. Heeling his mount, he abruptly rode back down the hill, quickly followed by the others. At the base of the hill, the Mountain Man led them into the trees. He led them up a nearby hill, staying hidden by the trees. Crow stopped short, inside the tree line. The others rode up beside him. "What did you see?" asked LeRue.

Crow did not answer right away but stared off in the direction of the rocky hill. He pointed and said, "See that outcropping of rocks, just above the trees? It looks kinda like a face."

LeRue and Carlos stood in their stirrups to look. "I see the face," said Carlos, "What am I looking for?"

"There it is!" said LeRue, "Someone has a glass up there."

"I see it!" said Carlos. "Who could it be?"

Without a word, Crow started his ride back down the hill. The others followed. Crow led them through the trees as if he had traveled the area many times before. Every once in a while he would call a halt. He would leave them to go up a hill, and then return. Crow would then lead them further through the trees. Crow held up his hand to silently stop the group. He dismounted, signaling the others to also dismount.

"Carlos, LeRue and I will go ahead and scout, to see who is on the hill. You stay here with the horses. LeRue and I can travel faster and quieter alone. Do you understand?"

"Si, I understand. You go, I will stay here."

Crow started to go but stopped. "Carlos, tie the horses down here. Go to the top of this hill and stay back in the trees. You watch our backs. If you see trouble, fire your musket."

Carlos smiled. He felt better knowing he had a place in the plan. As he climbed the hill, he looked back, but Crow and LeRue had disappeared.

Crow and LeRue raced silently, zigzagging through the trees, jumping logs and dodging bushes. The brown dog followed close on their heels. Soon, Crow began to slow, LeRue copying his lead. The brown dog sat and watched the two men, then got up and followed.

The ground began to rise as they approached the rock-face on the hill. Crow held up his hand signaling LeRue to stop. They sat on their haunches, their rifles resting across their thighs, listening.

Both men froze when they heard the voices. Two or more men were speaking in Spanish. Crow turned to look questioningly at LeRue. LeRue cocked his head and listened. Soon he raised his hand and held up three fingers, three men. LeRue held a hand to his eye looking like he had a spyglass in his hand and then pointed back and forth between him and Crow. Three men were searching for them.

Crow dragged his finger across his throat and held up two fingers. He then held up one finger and with his thumb and forefinger indicated talking. LeRue nodded his head. He understood.

In the rocks that looked like a face, two Mexican bandits sat on the ground, their muskets across their laps. On an outcropping of rock, lay a third bandit with a spyglass to his eye. The prone bandit had no idea anything was wrong until he heard a wet sound of escaping air. Rolling to his side to look back he nearly pissed himself when he saw the two buckskin-clad Mountain Men and a brown dog. Both Mountain Men had blood dripping from their faces and hands that held Bowie knives. Before he could react, the larger of the two men had leaped upon him and was holding his bloody knife to his throat. This time he did piss himself. Slowly, Crow brought the bandit to his feet and walked him back to where the other two bandits lay with their throats cut. The third bandit began to shake with fear. Casually, Crow wiped the big blade of his Bowie knife off on the shirt of the bandit. Crow indicated to LeRue with his head that he should talk to the bandit. "Why do you watch us?" LeRue asked in Spanish. The bandit blurted out, "We watch for anyone. Our camp is in the canyon."

"Then you didn't see us?"

"No, I did not even know you were anywhere around."

"But you know who we are."

"Si, you are the Gringos that killed Diaz in San Diego."

Crow stepped up to the bandit and grabbed him up by his shirt front, "You were there?" Crow demanded.

"Si, we were sent there to kill you and the Batista's. I held the horses outside. I had nothing to do with the attack on you."

"Why do you want to kill us? We have done nothing to you."

"Hector said you were ruining everything. It was Hector who ordered us to kill you."

"Bastardo!" LeRue plunged his knife into the bandit. Crow let go of the bandit's shirt allowing him to fall to the ground.

LeRue was wiping his blade, and then suddenly stopped. He grabbed Crow by the arm and pointed to the trail at the foot of the rocks. There below them, on horseback, was Hector.

Crow did not hesitate. He picked up his rifle, aimed and fired. Hector pitched forward in his saddle as his horse bolted forward and raced out of sight. Suddenly, shots rang out. The sound of bullets striking the rocks close to Crow and LeRue hastened the men to run back into the tree line.

On the wooded hill, Carlos felt his scalp tighten when he heard, first one, and then many shots fired in the distance. He strained to see but saw nothing. It was nearly thirty minutes after the last shot was fired that he again felt the chill of fear run up his back. "Come on amigo, time to go!"

Carlos looked at the two Mountain men. Their faces and hands were covered in dried blood. "You have been wounded?" asked Carlos.

"No," replied Crow, "but we might get killed if we don't get the hell out of here, *now*! Let's ride!"

The three men rode, hell bent for leather, across the green grasses flushing birds and small animals as they rode. They were almost to the rancho when Crow held up his hand for them to halt on a high hill. He turned his mount to look back. No one was following. "Let's rest the horses. We'll keep an eye on our backs from here."

As the men dismounted, Carlos asked, "What has happened?"

"Crow shot Hector," Said LeRue.

Carlos stood open mouth looking at the two men. "You shot Hector?"

"We were questioning one of the bandits. He told us that he and a man named Diaz were sent to San Diego to kill you, your father and us."

LeRue said, "He told us the man who sent them was Hector."

"It appears that Hector was the leader of the bandits. I'm thinking he had plans to murder you and your family. That is all except Francisca, whom he thought to marry and then take over the rancho."

"As we questioned the bandit, Hector showed up on the trail below us. Crow shot him."

Carlos removed his sombrero and sat down on the grass. His thoughts were of what he had just heard, running through his mind. He stood and faced the two Mountain men. His face showed his anger. "We must go back to the rancho and gather our men. Will you lead us, Isaiah?"

Crow reached out and took Carlos by the shoulder. "It is late amigo. We could not get back in time to scout out the canyon. We will return to the rancho. We will make a plan and leave in the morning before light."

Carlos went to his horse and mounted up. The Mountain Men joined him, and the three rode off at a distance eating gallop.

THE PLAN

Upon their return to the rancho, Carlos led Crow and LeRue into the hacienda. As they entered the living room, Carlos called out for his father, who answered from somewhere upstairs. Hernando appeared at the head of the stairs. "What is it? What has happened?" he demanded.

"It is the bandits! We have found them!" Carlos replied as he met his father halfway up the stairs. "We must talk father. We have trusted the devil himself!"

Hernando looked down to where Crow and LeRue stood. He could see both men covered in dried blood and his first thought was they had been wounded. He turned to his son and was relieved to see neither blood nor wounds. "Let us go to the dining room where we can sit, and you tell me what has happened.

Twenty minutes later, Hernando sat dumbfounded at what he had just been told. "Bastards!" Hernando suddenly shouted and hammered his closed fist on the table. "Carlos, send riders to the other ranchos and tell them what has happened. Tell them we need armed men, to gather here tonight. Tell them we will leave before dawn to raid the bandit's camp."

Carlos got up from his seat, "Father, I have asked Isaiah to lead us."

Hernando looked over to Crow, "You will do this?"

"I will do the planning for you if you wish. But I think either you or Carlos should lead the men. They all know you and will be coming at your request."

Hernando saw the wisdom in Crow's suggestion, "Then that is what we will do. Carlos, send out the riders."

In the waning light of day, four riders, each with three extra mounts in tow, raced off in four different directions to the nearby ranchos. Each rider would eventually use up the additional mounts in his race against time.

* * *

Within hours, seventy-five heavily armed men had arrived with the four Dons of the other ranchos. Carlos and Hernando had their vaqueros round up additional mounts to take on the ride. A dust cloud, illuminated by a full moon, now hung over the rancho as men and horses arrived.

From an upstairs bedroom window, Francisca and her mother watched the dust-covered faces of the crowd below. Both women were anxious about the unfolding events. Men, maybe even their own, could be killed in this raid. From across the yard, they saw Crow and LeRue. The two men each carried a rifle and wore their buckskins. Unknown to the women, both men had washed the blood from their faces and hands and changed clothes.

Hernando turned and saw the two Mountain Men. "We are close to ready."

Crow stood before Hernando and said, "This is what LeRue and I have come up with as a plan: I will need three good horses to take with me so I can scout the area. LeRue and Carlos will lead you to the hill where we first spotted the bandits. There, you will wait for me. I'll return knowing better how to advance your men."

"You will go alone?" Hernando asked.

"Yes, it is something I have done many times in the past. If I go now, I will still have the full moon to work with when I get there. The men must be warned to keep quiet when you arrive at the rendezvous point."

Hernando looked at the young man before him. "We will do this." 'He is an amazing man. We are fortunate that he found us,' he thought.

Crow offered his hand, which Hernando grasped with both his hands, "May God be with you, and keep you safe."

"Te veré luego amigo (I will meet you later my friend)."

From the upstairs window, Francisca and her mother watched as Crow walked alone into shadows by the corral. They saw Hernando walk over to LeRue. The two men talked, and Carlos joined them. "Where is Isaiah?" asked Francisca. Then some movement caught her eye. Crow rode out of the dark with three horses in tow; one was his gray stallion. Francisca thought, 'He is saving the gray for his last mount.'

Crow raised his rifle over his head signaling Hernando and the rest that he was leaving. Digging his heels into the sides of his mount, he galloped off into the night.

Francisca turned to her mother, "He has gone alone!"

Carmen circled her daughter's shoulders with her arm and gently pulled her close. "He knows what he is doing. He is a good man. God will go with him."

In the moonlit night, Crow rode bareback at full tilt across the open fields. As one horse tired, he switched to a new mount and again rode as fast as his mount would run. Crow was within a mile of the box canyon when he changed to his saddled gray. He rode toward a copse of trees and dismounted. Getting his bearings, he let the reins drop to the ground. The gray was trained to stay in place and not move. Crow checked his rifle for a new cap, then for his Bowie knife and his possibles bag. Satisfied, he began to run along the tree line into the box canyon.

THE BATTLE OF BOX CANYON

Crow found the trail leading into the canyon. It was close to the tree line and overhanging rocks, making it difficult to be seen by the casual observer. As he approached a wall of stone, he saw in the moonlight a well-worn trail. The opening was a pinch point and easily defended. Crow stood silently and listened. He could hear voices. A man was shouting orders. 'They are getting ready to leave,' surmised Crow. Reaching down, he removed his moccasins and pushed them into his possibles bag. Barefoot, he silently moved to the opening.

Inside the cave, Garcia was in a panic. Hours ago, Hector had ridden into the camp, shot in the back. Someone had killed three of his guards and managed to get away. 'Hector is one tough hombre,' thought Garcia. Hector, after having his wound attended to and bandaged, gave orders to evacuate the camp. Garcia convinced Hector to take four men, the women, and children, and leave. The rest of the band would deal with packing up the camp. They could move faster and catch up, not having to deal with the women and the wounded Hector.

Outside the bandit's hideout, Crow slipped into the rocks so he could get a better view of what was going on. It didn't take him long to figure out that he didn't have much time left. If the bandits were to be wiped out, Crow would have to return immediately. The waiting vaqueros and the Batista's would have to be ready sooner than expected. Dropping down from the rocks, the Mountain Man dug out his moccasins and put them back on. Throwing caution to the wind, he ran down the moonlit trail. He had to get to his horse and then to the vaqueros before it was too late.

LeRue was the first to realize that Crow was among them. He saw his friend was exhausted and brought him some water.

Carlos and Hernando saw the big Mountain Man leaning on his rifle with one hand while tipping a jug of water with the other. The men gathered around Crow and waited.

Crow handed LeRue the jug and said, "The bandits are breaking camp. We must ride hard, but together. Hernando, break the men into two groups I will lead one and LeRue will lead the other. The part of the trail nearest to the camp is narrow and wooded on both sides. LeRue, I will show you when we get there where to place your men. You pick off anyone that gets past my men and me. I will attack when they are out of the box canyon. That will prevent the possibility of them retreating. If possible, capture one alive, so we can question him. Carlos, Hernando, give no quarter. If they get away, we will only have to deal with them again later. Hernando and Carlos, with grim faces, nodded their agreement.

The vaqueros, besides being excellent horsemen, could also take orders. There were no stragglers when they arrived at the trail leading into the canyon. While LeRue and Hernando organized their men, Crow and Carlos moved their people to the entrance of the box canyon. As the men waited, Crow watched the moon. 'I hope the bandits run soon. We don't want to lose the light.'

In the canyon near the mouth of the cave, Garcia moved about his men checking that all was ready. Satisfied that they were prepared to leave, Garcia turned and faced them. "You all know where we are to meet. Do not delay. It will take the rancheros time to organize and to get here. I will catch up with you shortly. I want to make sure there is nothing left behind."

At the entrance of the canyon, Crow heard horse's hooves on the rocks. "They are coming," he told Carlos. "Make sure the men do not fire until I do." Carlos quickly turned and moved down the line of vaqueros reminding them not to fire until the signal shot.

Eighteen bandits on horseback moved out of the canyon at a canter. When the last man passed Crow, he shot him in the back of the head at close range. Without hesitation, the vaqueros began shooting while the panicked bandits spurred their mounts into a run. The eight surviving bandits ran into LeRue and Hernando's men. As preplanned, they held their fire until LeRue leaped upon one of the horsemen and took him to the ground. The other seven bandits died in a hail of gunfire. None escaped.

Inside, Garcia was on his knees digging in the dirt floor at the back of the cave. The bandit had just recovered a large bag of gold coins that the bandits had stolen over the last three years. Garcia's guts churned when he heard the first shots. Quickly reburying the gold coins, he smoothed the covering dirt with his foot. He placed a large rock over the treasure. Running from the cave, Garcia went to his horse, swung up into the saddle and spurred him into a run to the back of the canyon. Garcia remembered where there was an outcropping of rocks hidden by thick brush. He would hide there.

Crow and his men collected the weapons as they examined each dead bandit. The sound of an approaching horse caught their attention. It was LeRue. He had a robber, tied hand, and foot draped across the saddle in front of him. Stopping in front of Crow, LeRue unceremoniously looped his arm under the legs of the bandit and dumped him on the ground. "There you are amigo, one live bandit."

A shaft of moonlight through the trees lit the terrified bandit's face. He had hit the ground face first, and his nose was bleeding, forcing the man to breathe through his mouth. The bandit tried to push himself away as Crow advanced toward him, drawing his Bowie Knife. With the knife in one hand, Crow reached down and with one sweeping motion, cut the bandit's legs free. Grabbing the cowering man by the shirt front, Crow jerked him to his feet. In Spanish Crow asked, "Do you know who I am?" The bandit nodded his head yes. "You have heard that I am a warrior of the Crow?" The bandit again nodded his head yes. "Then you know that I have ways of making you talk, none of which are pleasant." For emphasis, Crow held up the Bowie Knife. The bandit sagged, but Crow held him up by his shirt front. Crow turned to one of the vaqueros, "Take him to that tree and tie him to it." The vaquero motioned to a second man to help, and they dragged the hapless bandit to a tree and tied him to it.

Hernando and Carlos rode up with their vaqueros and joined Crow's men. "What is happening?" asked Hernando.

LeRue still mounted, replied, "Crow is going to question the bandit."

Hernando was not sure he liked what he saw. Crow had that damned knife in his hand, the same one he had used to kill that man in San Diego. Crow walked up to the bandit who was now shaking in fear. The thief soiled himself when Crow, in one swift motion, swept the blade upward and sliced open the robber's shirt. The terrified man felt the cold steel of the blade on his stomach, not knowing that Crow had turned the knife over. When the bandit cried out, everyone, including the bandit, was sure Crow had gutted him.

Crow laid the cold steel of the blade on the neck of the bandit, "Where is Hector?"

"He left before us with the women and children!" The man blurted.

"Where did he go?"

"There is a place in the valley east of here. They are to make camp and wait for us."

"Are there any more back in this camp?"

"Garcia, he stayed behind to check the camp. I do not know if he left or not."

"Is this all of your men?"

"Si, this is all of the men except for the four that rode with Hector."

Crow stepped away and sheathed his knife. He walked over to Hernando and Carlos. LeRue prodded his mount closer to the two men so he could hear.

"Hector got away with four men, the women, and children. There may be another man inside the cave or canyon. We should place guards at the entrance and then return in the daylight to search for him. Hector will have over two days of travel time on us before we can be ready to track him, but we know where he is going."

Hernando, with a nod at the tethered Bandit, asked, "What about him?"

"He is yours. I don't think we'll get any more useful information from him."

Hernando turned to Carlos, "Hang him."

Hernando watched as three vaqueros threw a rope over a limb. They untied the bandit from the tree. The bandit wept as the rope was tightened around his neck. The three vaqueros pulled on the line, hoisting the kicking, flailing man off the ground. It was a painful and unpleasant way to die. The hanging would be talked about for years among the vaqueros, as would Crow's questioning of the bandit. Not everyone knew that he had never cut the man. But the story would add to the legend and the myth of the Mountain Man, Isaiah Crow.

* * *

The moon had just set as the glowing edge of the false dawn appeared. Garcia led his horse out of his hiding place. After three years of living in the canyon, he had no problem walking through this area in the dark. Approaching the entrance of the canyon, Garcia froze and listened. Men were talking. Garcia dropped the reins of the horse and moved closer so he could hear. There were three men, and they had built a fire. From their conversation, they were tired. Removing his sombrero, Garcia hung it from his saddle horn. He took off his spurs and placed them in his saddlebags. With his pistol in hand, he advanced toward the voices.

The three vaqueros, left to guard the entrance, had become complacent. Had they not wiped out the gang of bandits? As they grew sleepy, they convinced themselves that no one was left in the canyon. From just outside of the firelight, Garcia's eyes swept the vaqueros' camp. Satisfied with what he saw, he crawled back into the dark. When at a safe distance, he stood and walked to his horse. Removing his spurs from the saddlebags, he put them back on. He retrieved his sombrero and placed it on his head, tightening the chin strap. Again, from his saddlebags, he removed the second pistol. With his fingers, he felt for the cap in the dark. It was there. Mounting his horse, he drew his other gun from his belt. He sat for a moment, his lips moving silently in prayer. Garcia made the sign of the cross over his heart. With the reins of his horse clenched in his teeth, he spurred his mount.

Garcia's horse crashed through the guard's campfire. The startled vaqueros jumped up, their mouths hanging open. Two of the men fell dead when the bandit fired his pistols. Only one man was left standing to watch the fleeing desperado disappear down the darkened trail to freedom.

As Garcia rode, he realized that dead men, his men, lined the trail. Shots rang out and a chill coursed through his body as bullets plucked at his clothing. Stretching his body low and his head next to his horse's neck, Garcia spurred his mount and slapped the ends of the reins on its rump. The animal lunged forward, its mouth agape and frothing, carrying the bandit off into the night.

Crow, who had been in exhausted sleep, leaped to his feet rifle in hand. As he ran to his horse, Crow shouted, "LeRue!" LeRue, without hesitation, joined Crow. They mounted their horses bareback and raced off in pursuit of the fleeing bandit. The Batista's and the exhausted vaqueros, dazed by sleep, stood about; momentarily unable to grasp what was happening.

On the trail, Garcia, realizing he could not outrun his pursuers, slowed his mount, rode into the trees, and waited. Moments later, he watched as two men rode fast past his hiding place. Garcia spurred his mount and headed back to the vaquero's encampment. When he saw the light of the campfires, he moved off the trail back into the tree line. Staying in the trees, he cautiously approached the camp. There, men were mounting their horses. Led by the Batista's, they galloped out of the camp in pursuit of Crow and LeRue. Garcia joined them.

It was early morning when Batista's group caught up with Crow and LeRue. The two Mountain Men were in the middle of the trail examining the ground. Carlos dismounted and joined them. "You have lost the track?" he asked them.

Crow replied, "We lost it further back and began casting back and forth but were unable to find it. He must have doubled back or took to the trees."

"Either way, we've lost the trail," continued LeRue. "He's a clever son-of-a-bitch."

Hernando said, "Then let us return to their encampment and see what we can find. I will have the men bury the bandit dead. We have three wounded and two dead to take back to the hacienda."

As the men rode back, one vaquero slowed until he was riding next to the last man in the group. Garcia said to the man, "Debo aliviarme (I must relieve myself). I will catch up." The man nodded his understanding and rode on.

THE HACIENDA

Francisca had just started down the stairs of the hacienda when she heard the sound of many horses and the shouting of men. Moving quickly down the stairs to the door, she met her mother in the hallway. "They have returned," said Carmen to her daughter.

The two women rushed into the yard as the band of vaqueros, led by Hernando Batista, rode into sight. Francisca became anxious when she failed to see Crow or LeRue. Hernando and Carlos dismounted in front of the hacienda, as the rest of the men headed to the corral. Carmen greeted Hernando with a hug and a kiss on his now bearded, dusty cheek. Carlos seeing the concern on his sister's face said, "Crow and LeRue are trying to track one of the bandits that got away."

"They have gone alone?" Francisca asked.

Hernando responded, "They have Santiago with them. We lost two men in the fight. Carlos and I will go to their families to inform and console them, and then come back here."

"I will have food and baths prepared for your return."

It was nearly an hour before Carlos and Hernando returned to the hacienda after visiting with the families of the fallen vaqueros. They also said their goodbyes and gave their thanks to the men of the rancheros who had helped in the destruction of the bandit gang.

As the two men entered the house, the smell of food reminded them of how hungry they were. The long table was set up and ready for them. Carmen and Francisca were seated at the table. Hernando took his seat at the head of the table while Carlos sat to his right, across from his mother.

Hernando slouched in his chair, "I did not realize how tired I was until I sat down."

Carmen reached across the table and took his hand in hers, "You look exhausted. Perhaps you would rather go upstairs, bathe and then lie down. You can eat later."

Hernando rested his head against the back of the chair for a moment and then sat up. Smiling at his wife, he said, "You are right. I will go upstairs." With that, he stood, took his wife by the hand and turned to Carlos. "You should rest also."

"Yes father, but I think I will have something to drink and to eat first."

Nodding his head in answer, Hernando smiled at Carmen, and the two headed for the stairs.

"He does look exhausted," said Francisca.

"He has been up for nearly two days and in a gun battle," replied Carlos. "A man he trusted wanted him dead and planned to kill our mother, you and me. A lesser man might not have handled it as well."

"It is difficult to believe that Hector had planned this all along."

"If it had not been for Crow and LeRue, we all might be dead now."

Francisca folded her hands in her lap and hesitantly asked, "Isaiah is alright?"

Carlos saw his sister's concern. It spoke volumes of her feelings for the Mountain Man. "Yes, he is alright. Crow is a man of great stamina and courage. While I am thinking about what to do, he is already doing something. Francisca, he went alone to the bandit's camp. He climbed a rock face in the dark so he could look into the camp. When he returned to us, we... we did not even know he was with us until father saw him drinking water from a jug! He moves in the night like a ghost."

"He has gone after a bandit?"

"One of them escaped, killing two of our men. Crow lost the track and wanted to try to find it. It appears Hector escaped before we got there. Crow thinks that the bandit will meet up with Hector and Crow hopes to finish them both off."

Francisca felt a sense of pride in knowing how brave Crow was, but it was mixed with fear for the safety of the man she was falling deeply in love with.

GARCIA

The bandit, Garcia, rode the high ground. He stayed just inside a tree line of pines. The pace was slow, but he could see for a reasonable distance without being seen. It was nearly noon now, and he had not slept for two days. He had changed horses twice, picking fresh mounts from the vast herds that were allowed to run free. Stopping, he reached back to a saddlebag and removed a small brass telescope. Extending it, he stood in his stirrups. Placing it to his right eye, he checked his back-trail. That damned Mountain Man and the two that rode with him had nearly caught him earlier. In the past, Garcia had escaped capture when he was chased by federales and Apaches, but that leather clad son-of-a-bitch Crow just would not give up.

Behind him, Garcia saw only rolling hills of grass. His pursuers could be hidden by a hill, or they might have given up, but he just did not care anymore. Garcia knew he had to stop before he fell off his horse. Closing the scope, he returned it to the saddlebag. He coaxed his mount deeper into the trees. Garcia dismounted; leaving his horse saddled and tying its reins to a tree limb. Untying a canteen from the saddle horn, he took a long drink of the lukewarm water. Garcia went to his knees in front of the trunk of a large pine. He removed his knife from its sheath and hacked several small branches off the trunk to make a smooth backrest. Replacing the knife in the sheath, he sat on the ground resting his back against the trunk. Pulling his pistol, he placed it on his lap. Within seconds, he was asleep.

The incessant call of a jay woke Garcia. He instinctively grabbed his pistol but found that it was no longer there. His bowels nearly let loose when he saw the boots of a man standing before him. "You have become careless, Garcia," said Hector Camacho. Hector and two other bandits stood looking down at the exhausted man.

"I am the only one left. All of the others were killed trying to escape."

Hector stared silently at Garcia. Reaching down, he offered his hand to Garcia. Clasping Hector's hand, Garcia stood. "How did you find me?" he asked.

"Actually, you found us," replied Hector. "We have camped a short distance from here. One of the men was checking our back-trail and spotted you."

"I am being pursued... I..."

"I have sent a man on your horse to take them off your trail. Come, we must move quickly to not lose our advantage."

A GENTLE HAND

It was the morning of the third day after the battle. The sun was just cresting the horizon. The ground was still wet with dew, and there was a hint of fog hugging the low areas. The boy, Raul, looked up and saw three men approaching the hacienda on horseback. With a look of joy upon his face, he ran to the front door of the hacienda where he was met by one of the Indian servants. "They have returned!" he shouted loudly in his excitement.

Francisca was just coming down the stairs while Carlos was coming out of his room. Francisca called out, "Carlos, they are back! They are here!"

Carlos turned and went to his parent's door and knocked loudly. Calling to them he said, "Poppa, Crow and the others are back!" Not waiting for an answer Carlos rushed off down the stairs and out the door.

Raul raced across the yard to meet the horsemen. Crow, LeRue, and Santiago rode side by side. Their normally clean-shaven faces were thick with stubble, their red-rimmed eyes telling of their fatigue. Carlos and Francisca joined Raul, as others came out of their homes and gathered in the yard.

The three men dismounted, just as Hernando exited the hacienda. He rushed across the yard his hair uncombed, his shirt tucked haphazardly into his trousers. He was barefoot. Everyone stepped back opening a pathway. "Welcome home! You are unharmed?"

Crow faced him, "We are all in one piece," he said with a tired smile. "Santiago here got your bandit."

Hernando said to Santiago, "He is dead?"

"Si, I spotted him backtracking and gave chase. He shot at me, and I fired back. It was an unlucky shot. I meant to take him alive."

As the men spoke, no one noticed when Francisca, standing close to Crow, reached out and squeezed his hand then quickly let go. Crow caught off guard nearly jerked his hand away but instead, he stood with his heart tripping, acting as if he were listening. Francisca excused herself and headed to the hacienda. Crow watched her go.

Hernando continued the questioning, "Then we have no idea where Hector has gone; Crow?"

Crow, a confused look on his face asked, "What?"

"I said we have no idea where Hector has gone."

"No, we were unable to find his tracks. We only know he was with three or four men, and several women and children. I think he will head for Mexico."

* * *

The tequila that Hector Camacho was sipping from a jug did not dull the pain, and the constant discomfort was nearly driving him mad.

The bullet that Crow fired at him had been removed by one of the women back at the cave. Over the years she had become quite adept at patching up wounded bandits.

Garcia, taking charge, knew that the best avenue of escape was to head for Mexico. 'The trip to Mexico will probably kill him,' he thought. 'I think we should head north into the hills, where we can hide until he is well enough to travel.'

Hector, in his delirium, had but one thought: Revenge against Isaiah Crow, the man who had destroyed his dream. 'No matter how long it takes,' he swore, 'we will meet again, and I will kill you.'

A MOST FORTUNATE MAN

Hernando asked Crow to take over Hector's job of jefe. Crow suggested that Santiago would be a better choice. Santiago knew all of the men and had proven himself loyal to the Batista's. "I wish to begin building my own place," he explained. "You have given me permission to court Francisca, and I must build a home of my own."

And so Crow and LeRue, with the guidance of Carlos, laid out the boundaries of what would be their ranchos. Crow took the box canyon location; LeRue the area near the lake. Crow was interested in using the canyon, with its water supply and abundant sweet grass, as a natural corral for horses. As partners, he and LeRue could use LeRue's open pastures and water to run their horses.

Crow and LeRue set out the next morning with a borrowed wagon. It was filled with the tools necessary to build their houses. As the two men crested a hill, a panoramic view of the area spread out before them. The thick growth of trees near the entrance of the canyon had just become painted by the light of the morning sun. A wisp of smoke could be seen just above the trees. "Looks like you've got company," said LeRue.

"You don't suppose Hector has doubled back do you?" replied Crow.

"Let's take a look-see," replied LeRue.

Crow smelled the campfire before he saw it. He and LeRue left the wagon hidden in the trees, and with their rifles in hand, moved forward on foot. As they neared the campsite, they heard voices. Someone, a woman, was weeping. The two Mountain Men moved forward through the trees. In a clearing, they saw three men, two women and a young child of perhaps five years. They were all Indians. One of the women sat on the ground near the fire, holding a child cradled in her arms. It was this woman who was crying.

Crow and LeRue watched for a brief time; then Crow signaled to move forward. As Crow and LeRue stepped from the trees, the three Indian men stepped between them and the women. LeRue said in Spanish, "We mean you no harm, can we help the child?"

At first, the men were unsure. But then the oldest of the three stepped back. Crow moved to the woman and child and knelt next to them. The woman looked at him with pleading eyes for his help.

Slowly, gently, Crow pulled back the blanket that was wrapped around the child. The boy, his mouth open, eyes closed, was breathing in labored gasps. As Crow examined the child, he noted that his left arm, near the wrist, was at a slight angle and badly bruised. There were cuts and scrapes on his forehead. "Looks like the boy has fallen, broken his arm and banged his head on a rock," said Crow in Spanish.

The man told Crow the boy had been climbing some rocks and fell onto the boulders below. Standing, Crow said, "LeRue get the wagon. I will splint the boy's wrist while you are gone. I'm not sure about the head injury. We can only keep him warm and quiet and hope for the best."

Crow set the broken arm with the help of one of the Indians. The boy, exhausted from the pain, slept wrapped in the blanket lying on some pine boughs. His mother sat next to him, more relaxed now that something had been done to help her son. After things calmed down, Crow and LeRue began talking to the Indians. They were Chumash, from a tribe located in Northern California. It became apparent that they had not eaten for some time. The youngest of the three men was the son of the oldest man. They all had been neophytes at a mission. The younger boy fell in love with a girl at the mission and kissed her on the cheek one evening. Unfortunately, one of the priests witnessed it and had the boy flogged. The conditions at the mission were already unbearable because of the long hours of work and the severe whippings. To avoid further punishment, they decided to run away. They were pursued but managed to evade the Mexican soldiers.

Crow listened, and when the man finished his story, Crow told him, "This is my land. I plan to build my home here. If you and your family wish to stay and help me, I will give you each a plot of land to build a house and to grow a garden. You will also help LeRue build his place." There was silence. The men stared at the big man dressed in buckskin. The two women who had heard the conversation sat stone-faced, tears making streaks on their dirty cheeks. Crow, confused by the response, turned to LeRue.

"I think you have stunned them with your kindness, my friend. They are not used to being treated in this manner."

Crow turned to the men. "I think that for now, we will not tell anyone you are here. That is if you wish to stay."

The older man replied, "Señor, I am called Juan. This is my oldest son, Peter, and my youngest, Samuel. We will stay and help you build your homes."

Smiling, Crow extended his hand, "I'm called Crow, and this is my compadre' LeRue."

LeRue also extended his hand. Juan looked at the two men who addressed him as an equal. Squaring his shoulders, Juan took their hands in a firm handshake. "Gracias, we will work hard for you."

Crow and LeRue mounted up and went out onto the flats where they killed and butchered a steer. The Indians prepared the meat, and everyone celebrated their new friendship with a feast. Later, Crow and LeRue agreed that Crow's house should be built first, as he planned to marry within a year or so. LeRue's place could wait awhile.

The next morning, the men led by Crow, began to explore the area. Following the trail in the trees, they went into the box canyon. "The entrance to the canyon can be easily gated. The headwater for the river is somewhat deeper in the canyon. After we clear the rocks from the bank of the river and from under the trees, the horses will have access to shade and water. That cave over there is perfect cover should they need it."

"Where do you plan to build your house?" asked LeRue.

Crow led them out of the canyon. Stopping, he looked back at the mouth of the canyon. Crow began to walk down the trail, counting paces as he walked. Pausing once more, he looked at the rocky wall that extended from the canyon. Running water from the river, hidden by trees, could be heard. Crow, followed by the others, walked toward the sound of the water. From just inside the tree line, they stepped into a clearing. LeRue looked around at the beautiful place. It was as if the land had been prepared for a house. The flat ground sat high above the river, with soft spongy moss and grass, all green from an abundance of water. Birds sang in the surrounding trees, and the flowing water cooled the area. "Ah amigo, I think you are a most fortunate man."

Crow, his fisted hands on his hips, slowly turned, surveying the location. He headed over to the river and standing at the edge, looked down. "LeRue, do you think I need to worry about flooding?" LeRue joined him and looked at the banks. Pointing to the far side, he said, "See the line there? It says the water has never crested the banks. Of course, that's not to say that it couldn't. But I think you'd be safe building here."

"That's the way I had it figured. Juan, go fetch the wagon and bring it here."

When the wagon arrived, Crow had the tools removed. "Juan, I want you to pick a spot in the trees and build shelters for your family. LeRue and I are going to return to the hacienda. We will return tomorrow." From the wagon, Crow removed the blankets he and LeRue used the night before and handed them to Juan. "Gracias, Señor Crow."

"You stay hidden now. We don't want anyone causing you folks any trouble."

On the way back, Crow kept looking at the sky. With a snap of the reins, he sent the horses to a run. LeRue placed his hand on his head to keep his hat from falling off. "Geehossifat Crow, you trying to kill us?" Crow just smiled and snapped the reins again.

It was late afternoon when Crow and LeRue arrived at the hacienda. Francisca was in the flower garden cutting flowers for the house. She placed the flower she had just cut in the basket and began walking back to the house. Crow saw her, and a smile spread across his face. Francisca looked about, and feeling safe, smiled back. Using the basket to hide her hand, she waved at Crow. With blushing cheeks, she rushed back to the house.

Crow turned to LeRue and asked, "Will you deal with the wagon and horses?"

LeRue saw it all and understood the wild ride. "Amigo, you have something to do?" LeRue asked with a smirk on his face.

Crow reached up and pulled LeRue's fur cap over his eyes, "As a matter of fact I do, I'm gonna take a bath!"

"Gracias, amigo…" But Crow had already jumped from the wagon and was headed for their cabin.

At the hacienda, Francisca was just entering, when a voice said, "I saw that! Now you behave yourself, young lady." Carlotta stood with folded arms a stern look on her face. "Señor Crow has asked to take you for a paseo en carruaje (carriage ride) this evening. But after the display, I've just seen…" Francisca was nearly driven to tears, "Oh no, I meant nothing other than to say I was happy he was safe."

Carlotta felt a tinge of guilt at what she had done. She wrapped her arm around the girl's shoulders and said in a softer voice, "Your father is a Don, an important man. You do not want to embarrass him."

Francisca asked, "Isaiah asked you? When did he ask?"

"Before he left with LeRue, he came to me and asked. He was sure he would be back today. But he wanted me to wait to tell you, just in case he could not get back in time." Francisca turned and hugged Carlotta, "I will be good, I promise."

* * *

For Francisca, it was a magical evening. Isaiah had arrived right on time, dressed in his finest. Carlotta was impressed when Crow offered a single red rose and his arm to Francisca. Hernando and Carmen were there with Carlos. The men formally greeted and welcomed Crow into their home. After a brief conversation, they escorted the couple, trailed by Carlotta, to the carriage. Now, Francisca and Crow sat side by side in the front seat. Crow was driving to keep his hands busy and in sight of Carlotta. Crow adjusted himself in his seat; his right foot accidentally touched Francisca's. He immediately moved it away but was pleasantly surprised when he felt her move her foot back against his.

Francisca was full of questions about his plans for building his house. She was entertained by his description of the land and the river, making it possible for her to picture it in her mind. His voice was deep but clear, and his Spanish had become almost fluent. But what made her know that he was different from other men, was that he asked about her and about the things she liked. They talked and talked, both yearning desperately just to hold hands. But soon Carlotta told them that it was time to go home. Carlotta smiled inwardly knowing full well that Crow had gradually slowed the horses for the return to the hacienda.

When they arrived at the hacienda, Crow helped Francisca and Carlotta from the carriage. He walked them to the door. "I will be gone for several days. LeRue and I will be working on clearing the land and building the house. When I return, I will meet with Carlotta."

Francisca began to reach for his hands with both of hers but remembered her promise to Carlotta and stopped. "I will miss you, Isaiah," she said simply. Crow turned to Carlotta, and giving a slight bow, said, "Thank you, Carlotta, for making this possible. I will wish to speak with you when I return."

"I will make myself available when you return."

THE MAGICAL MOUNTAIN MEN

Early in the morning of the next day, Crow and LeRue returned to the box canyon site. The wagon Crow drove was full of supplies, and the brown dog was riding on top. Tied to the back of the wagon were Crow's gray and LeRue's rider. "That dog has taken a real liking to you," said LeRue.

"I'm not sure if it's me or the jerky he likes," laughed Crow.

As the wagon neared the building site, the dog sat up and growled. The dog barked just twice, and then moved forward, sticking his head between the two Mountain Men. He began to whine, staring ahead, looking at Crow and then back ahead. LeRue readied his rifle. Crow switched the reins to his left hand. With his right hand, he placed his rifle across his lap. From the woods, the two older Indian men emerged and waved. The dog barked. Smiling, Crow roughed up its head and said, "Good boy, good boy."

Crow drove the wagon onto the building site, the three Indians trotting alongside. When the wagon stopped, Crow set the brake. He, LeRue and the dog jumped down. "Buenos días," greeted Juan.

"Buenos días," replied Crow. "We have brought food and supplies. We'll need to build a place to keep these things."

"It has already been done. Come, I will show you." Juan led them into the woods. At first, LeRue and Crow didn't see it, but then the structure came into sight. The roof was chest high, made of wood bark and mud, it was hidden by live saplings that had been bent over the roof and tied in place. The door was crude, but that crudeness helped to conceal it. Juan removed the door and stepped back. Crow, adjusting his eyes to the darkness, realized that it was two steps down to the floor. From the outside light, Crow could see that a pit had been dug and lined with stones to shore up the walls. It was cool and dry; perfect for storing food goods.

"Amigo, you have done a fine job. If you and the others will unload the wagon and place the stores in here, LeRue and I will begin laying out where the foundation of the house will be."

As Crow and LeRue moved into the clearing, LeRue said, "These people are good workers. I think we are fortunate to have them."

"Yes, but I wonder where the younger son is. Have you seen him?"

"No, I haven't. That is curious. I wonder where he has gone."

It was a good day's work. The four men found they worked well together and the Indians had learned a great deal while at the mission. Juan was good with numbers, and both men had helped to build several structures at the mission.

Not a word had been mentioned by Juan or Peter about Samuel.

The women prepared a hearty meal for the working men. It was a pleasant surprise when the small boy, who had broken his arm, joined them. He went to his mother to be cuddled, but it was apparent that he had made significant progress.

Finished with their meal, the men returned to the work area. They picked up their tools and placed them in the wagon, which was now hidden in the trees. The wagon team and the riding horses were hobbled and left to graze by the river. As the men worked, LeRue asked Juan, "Where is Samuel? I haven't seen him."

Juan hung his head and replied, "He has run off. I think it is because of a girl at the mission. I am sorry, for he said he would help and he has run off."

LeRue saw how distressed the man was. He reached out and grasped him by the shoulder, "It is alright my friend. We were all young once and crazy in love. We'll hold no hard feelings against you or the others. Now let us finish here and then go smoke a pipe or two."

It was on the morning of the fifth day when the brown dog began to bark. Everyone at the work site saw them. There were two men on horseback, heading their way. The Indians quickly gathered their tools, and like ghosts disappeared into the woods.

A short time later Carlos, accompanied by Santiago, rode up. The two men sat back in their saddles, looking at the work site. Rocks, huge rocks, had been moved. But there was also lumber being cut from felled trees. Santiago stood in his stirrups to get a better look and sat back in his saddle. "You Mountain Men are like magicians. I have never seen so much accomplished by two men in such a short time!"

Carlos dismounted and walked over to the two Mountain Men. With a wave of his arm, he said, "I know you are anxious to wed my sister; but amigo, please do not kill yourself before the wedding day!"

Crow laughed and clapped Carlos on the back. "LeRue and I have nothing better to do while we're, here but work. Besides, we find it's kinda fun."

Santiago joined them, shaking hands with LeRue and then with Crow. "I am impressed with what you have done already. Obviously, you and LeRue are unfamiliar with mañana."

The three men burst into laughter, with Crow saying, "I will have to discuss that with LeRue before he runs me into the ground! But come; let me show you what I plan to do with the box canyon. Perhaps the two of you will have some suggestions."

While Crow led Carlos and Santiago to the box canyon, LeRue and the Indians cleaned up the work site and the campsite. When Crow and the others returned, a fire was going, and a pot of coffee was on. A simple meal of beef and roasted vegetables had been prepared. Again, the two visitors were surprised by the efficiency of LeRue. Deep in the woods, the Indians were enjoying the break. They chuckled among themselves about the joke the gringos were playing on their friends.

As the four men sat on a log eating, Carlos said, "I like your ideas on the canyon. You could easily corral fifty horses in there." He looked at Santiago who, with a mouth full of beef, nodded his head in agreement. "You plan to train these horses, you said?"

"I will train work and riding horses. If I can find a few good ones, I'll train them for racing. But for now, mostly workhorses; and of course, raise some cattle."

Santiago asked, "So LeRue, your land is adjacent to Crow's?"

"Yes, the two form a rough square. We are fortunate. We have the river here and the lake on my land. We plan to run our stock together. There will be plenty of grass to feed them."

"Come over by the river. I want to show you where we plan to build my house," said Crow.

Crow led them to the lush green, clearing. The sound of the rushing water of the river, and the multitude of birds chattering or singing in the trees were pleasing to the eyes and the ears. Carlos pushed his sombrero back on his head with his thumb and gazed about him. "Amigo, this is beautiful; a perfect place for a home."

Santiago kicked at a clod of dirt with his foot and then dropped to one knee. He picked up some dirt in his hand. Standing, he squeezed the soil and separated it with his fingers. "You will be able to have some fine gardens here close to the house. I think your bride will be delighted here."

Crow imagined the finished house surrounded by gardens and Francisca with her flower basket. Suddenly he wanted to get back to work. Carlos and Santiago seemed to pick up on this. Carlos said, "I think we must be headed back to the hacienda. Do you have any idea when you will revisit us? I am sure Francisca would like to know."

Crow gave it some thought and said, "I have supplies for about three more days. I will be there late morning the day after tomorrow. I hope to purchase more vegetables if possible."

"I am sure we have enough to sell you. Besides, we can always purchase more from the mission if needed. I will let my sister know that you are coming. Perhaps you will have dinner with us?"

"I would like that my friend, gracias."

* * *

That night Crow, LeRue, and the Indians were awakened when the brown dog growled from deep in his throat. Crow and LeRue got to their feet, rifles in hand. The Indian men picked up axes and hammers. Armed, they waited silently in the dark.

From the trail, a man's voice called out, "Poppa? Poppa? It is Samuel, Poppa."

Juan dropped his hammer and rushed to the sound of the voice, "It is my son! He has come back!" shouted a gleeful Juan.

Crow reached down and roughly patted Brown dog on the head, "Good boy Ponto (little brother), good boy," Crow said, praising and reassuring the dog that all was well.

A bewildered looking Juan led not only his son Samuel, but five more men and six women. They were all riding in a wagon pulled by two mules. Samuel jumped down from the wagon seat where he had been driving. He helped a plump, yet beautiful girl down from the wagon. The men in the back of the wagon began helping the other women down.

Crow looked at Juan, who appeared to be beside himself as what to do. Crow with a touch of sarcasm said, "I see your son has returned, Juan!"

Samuel stepped forward and speaking to Crow said, "Señor Crow, I returned to the mission to get Maria, as I had promised her. While I was there, these men and women heard my story of how you had helped us and of your kindness and respect. After Maria and I left the mission, they caught up to us with the wagon. I made no promises to them, but they have endured much abuse at the mission. They saw this as their only chance."

From the new group, an older man stepped forward, hat in hand and spoke to Crow. "We are workers, I am a carpenter. My wife worked in the kitchen and was the cook for the priests." Another one of the men came forward and said that he and his wife had worked in the gardens. And so it went. All knew a trade. All said they were willing to work if they could stay.

Crow, his hands on his hips, standing head and shoulders taller than the men before him, was silent. The Indians began to fidget and shuffle their feet nervously. They all flinched when Crow spoke: "Juan is el jefe. LeRue here, or I, will tell him what we want to be done. When he speaks to you, he speaks for us. Is that understood?" Everyone acknowledged that they understood, with vigorous head nodding. "For your work, LeRue and I will give to the head of each family, some land that they may call their own. This is your land for as long as you stay on and work for us. Juan will instruct you about staying out of sight when we have visitors. Now you go and get some sleep. We have much to do tomorrow."

Crow and LeRue were shaking out their blankets, getting ready to lay down, when Juan approached them. "What is it Juan?" asked Crow. Juan, with a smile on his face, said, "With your permission, I will have a garden planted. It is late in the season, but if the weather holds, we can still grow certain vegetables. We will need them. People will become suspicious if you keep buying more supplies than you can use."

"Good idea Juan, but what about seeds?"

"There seem to be some useful items in the wagon. How they got there, I do not know. But it would be a shame to let them go to waste."

LeRue let out a snicker, which made Crow look back over his shoulder and scowl at him. Speaking to Juan, Crow told him, "I think these 'items,' as you call them, had better be stored out of sight, along with those mules and the wagon. Someone is gonna be mighty upset about losing them, and will be out looking for them."

"I understand. Everything will be taken care of. I have been asked by the others to thank you for your kindness. Muchas gracias, Don Isaiah."

Crow began to protest the title, but LeRue laid a light restraining hand on Crow's arm, shaking his head. Crow looked at his friend then back to Juan.

"Tell our people that it pleases me to accept their thanks. I will be going to the Batista's hacienda in the morning and will be gone overnight. While I'm there, is there anything you or the others need?

"I will ask them, and tell you of anything needed before you leave in the morning."

When morning broke, with the dog Ponto sitting next to him, Crow was on his way to the Batista's. His head was filled with thoughts of Francisca and the excitement of telling her about how the house was coming along. Happily, he roughed up Ponto's ears and gave the reins a snap, sending the wagon team into a trot.

THE PROPOSAL

Francisca was headed to the back of the hacienda when her brother called out, "Isaiah is coming! I see him on the road." Whatever Francisca had on her mind to do, was forgotten. Grasping her dress to lift it above her shoes, she rushed to the front door to see. Like magic, Carlotta appeared and gave her the eye. Flushing, Francisca said quickly, "I promise, I will behave." Carlotta, with a hint of a smile on her face, watched her charge skip out the door.

Crow drove the wagon to the corral and brought it to a stop. Raul was there grinning, happy to see his friend.

"Raul, will you see to the team for me?"

"Si, I will take care of everything."

It pleased Raul when Crow said, "Thank you, amigo," in front of the other ranch hands.

Crow saw Carlos coming across the yard. Behind Carlos, he saw Francisca standing in the doorway behind Carlos. She was smiling, and Crow without thinking waved at her. Carlos waved back at Crow, "Buenos días, welcome back!"

Behind Carlo's back, Crow caught the hidden wave from Francisca as she turned and entered the house.

As Carlos approached Crow, he said, "My mother and father would like you to join us for dinner this evening."

Crow, knocking the dust of the road from his shirt and trousers replied, "I acccpt! Eating around a campfire has no comparison to an excellent meal from your kitchen. But I will need to clean up first and then change. I have fresh clothes in our cabin."

"How is the building coming along?" asked Carlos.

Before Crow could answer, he saw Raul. Crow waved the boy over. "Raul, I have a silver coin for you if you fill a tub with hot water so I can clean up."

"Si, Señor Crow, this I can do. It will take some time to heat the water, but I will come for you when it is ready."

"Carlos, come on over to the cabin. While I wait for the water, I've got some things to ask you."

In the cabin, Crow pulled a chair out from the table with his foot and indicated to Carlos to take a seat. As Carlos settled onto the chair, Crow went to a cupboard and began rummaging around inside. Finding what he wanted, he returned to the table with two glasses and a bottle of tequila. Placing a glass in front of Carlos, Crow opened the bottle and poured some of the amber liquid into the glass. He poured himself a drink and sat down across the table from Carlos.

Crow picked up his glass and said, "Salud." Carlos lifted his glass, a look of puzzlement on his face, "Salud!"

Crow carefully placed his glass on the table and looked at his friend. He asked, "Do you think it is too early to ask your father for his permission to marry Francisca?"

As Carlos ran the question around in his mind, he picked up the bottle and poured each of them another drink. Carlos sat back in his chair, tilted his head back and looked at the ceiling. Crow was beginning to get restless, and said, perhaps too loudly, "Carlos, are you fooling with me?"

Carlos picked up his glass and holding it up said with a smile, "Si, amigo, that is what I am doing."

Crow took his glass, drank down the tequila and slammed the glass down on the table, "Now is not the time to be fooling with me, amigo!"

Carlos, his grin exposing perfect teeth replied, "Then my friend, I think you need to speak to my father before my sister dies an old maid." He picked up his glass and downed his drink. "But I also think we need to end this discussion before we drink too much."

Crow, now looking sheepish for his outburst replied, "Should I ask before or after dinner?"

"I think I will come and get you and bring you to the house. I will advise my father you wish to speak to him in private. You can then ask him."

"I have asked to take Francisca for a carriage ride after dinner. If your father gives his blessing will it be appropriate to ask her then?"

"You must ask my father's permission to do so. Carlotta will, of course, be there and she will tell others that you followed tradition."

"Gracias, amigo, I will clean up and wait for you here."

* * *

That evening, Carlos led Crow into the hacienda and to the dining area. Crow was unaware that Carlos had already spoken to his father and explained why Crow wished to see him in private. Carlos did not know that his father had already talked to his mother about his meeting with Crow.

"Good evening father, Señor Crow wishes to speak with you before dinner, in private."

"Yes, of course. If you will excuse us, Carlos?"

Carlos left the room, and Don Hernando asked, "What can I do for you, Señor Crow?"

"Don Hernando, I have come to ask you for your daughter's hand in marriage. As you know, I am a member of the church and a citizen of Mexico. I now own land and have nearly completed a hacienda and have a staff of men and women and four vaqueros. Hernando was surprised to hear that Crow had accomplished so much in such a short time. He thought, 'This young man never ceases to amaze me.'

Hernando said to Crow, "I have watched you as a man and as one who courts my daughter. You have shown me that you are a man of honor. You have saved the lives of members of my family, and mine as well. I could not think of a better man to wed my daughter. Yes, Isaiah Crow, I permit you to ask my daughter to marry you."

"Thank you, Don Hernando. I have asked to take Francisca on a carriage ride after dinner. I would like to propose to her then, with your permission."

"I think that would be an excellent idea. When you return to the hacienda, and if Francisca has accepted your proposal, we will announce it to all."

Crows heart skipped a beat, 'If she accepts? I never thought that she might turn me down.' Doubt began to creep into the Mountain Man's mind.

The meal seemed to take forever. Crow nearly knocked over his wine glass during the meal, and when he did get up from the table, his chair made enough noise to wake the dead. Only Francisca was bewildered by Crow's unease.

Later, as Francisca and Crow rode in the front seat of the carriage, while Carlotta rode in back, Francisca became concerned that something was wrong.

Crow had hardly spoken a word. All of a sudden, he stopped the carriage and got out. He walked around to Francisca's side and offered his hand. Taking it, she looked at Carlotta and was surprised when Carlotta said nothing. Helping her to the ground, Crow walked with her a short distance away from the carriage and took both of her hands in his. "Francisca, your father has given me permission to ask you to marry me. I ask you now, will you marry me?"

Crow felt her hands tighten around his. He saw her eyes glisten in the moonlight as she said, "I love you Isaiah, and yes, I will be your wife." It was with a great deal of control that the two did not take each other in their arms. "I love you, Francisca, I have since the first day I saw you. To know you love me too makes me the happiest man in the world."

As they approached the carriage Carlotta saw the glow of excitement on the young couple's faces, 'He has asked, and she has said yes.'

"Come on you two, it is late, and we should return to the hacienda." As they rode back, Carlotta said nothing when she saw Crow place his open hand, palm, down, on his thigh; and Francisca placed her hand over his.

As the carriage approached the hacienda, Carlotta saw Carlos, Hernando, and Carmen, standing near the door. Reaching into a pocket of her bodice, she removed a lace handkerchief, and held it to her right cheek, letting the waiting family know that Francisca had said "yes." Carlos, with a grin, made a motion with his arms. From the shadows stepped three men with guitars. They began to play. When the music started, curious vaqueros and their families began to gather. When they saw Francisca and Crow, everyone knew what had happened.

Crow and Francisca were surprised. They happily realized that the celebration was for them. As the carriage pulled up in front of the hacienda, they were surrounded by well-wishers. The crowd stepped back as Don Hernando and his wife approached the carriage. The Don offered his hand to Francisca and helped her from the carriage. Crow stepped down and went to the back of the carriage and helped Carlotta down, saying to her, "Thank you, Carlotta. I will always remember you for this."

Carlotta reached up and gently patted Crow's face. "Take good care of her, she loves you dearly."

Suddenly, Carlos was there slapping him on the back. "Congratulations!"

Hernando and Carmen, with Francisca, approached them. It was Francisca's mother who spoke, "We are pleased to welcome you to our family. Please, come in so we may celebrate."

And celebrate they did. Wine and tequila were taken outside for the vaqueros and their families. Inside the hacienda, there was much toasting, to the future Señor and Señora Crow.

FEDERALES

It had been several weeks since the second group of Indians from the mission joined Crow. The hacienda was a two-story building with a wraparound porch. The roof of the porch formed the floor for the balcony on the second floor. Red roof tiles purchased from the local mission were now in place. Two large gardens were laid out near the house, one for vegetables and the other for flowers. The fertile soil was already showing results.

Samuel was driving the wagon taken from the mission with its team of mules bringing a load of fresh cut lumber to the hacienda. A shout went up, "Federales, Federales!" Ponto began barking.

Crow and LeRue, who were inside the house, ran out into the yard, each carrying his rifle. The Indians in a panic began running for the woods. Crow called out, "Stop, go back to work. LeRue and I will take care of this."

Fourteen Mexican soldiers, with an officer leading, rode up to the two Mountain Men. The officer and his men were dusty from having been on the march for several days. The officer said, "I am Lieutenant Gonzales. I am looking for a stolen wagon and a team of mules taken from a mission in Monterey by renegade Indians. Who owns this land?"

Before Crow could speak LeRue said, "Lieutenant Gonzales, this is Don Isaiah, he owns this land and I, Don Jacques own the land you just rode across. As for renegade Indians, I think you are a week or more too late. Two groups came through here over a week ago. They tried to sell us a wagon and mules; but as you can see, we already have a team and wagon."

Gonzales stared at LeRue. He looked at the wagon and mules. He began to say something when LeRue said, "Lieutenant, please, you and your men look tired and thirsty. We were about to eat. Join us for some food and drink. Rest yourselves in the shade by the river."

Crow turned, and seeing Juan by the wagon, said, "Juan, we will have company, have the women fix food and drink for our guests."

As Crow led Gonzales and his men towards the river and away from the wagon, Juan signaled LeRue that he wanted to speak with him. The two men walked up to the edge of the woods and stopped. Juan spoke in a low voice, "A priest and sometimes mission Indians ride with the soldiers to identify runaways and stolen property. These soldiers ride alone. Try to find out why. If they are not alone, signal me, and I will have the wagon and mules moved out of sight."

LeRue said, "I will remove my hat when I know they ride alone. If there is a problem, I will come to you. Now, have the women fix a fine meal for the soldiers. I want them happy."

Juan replied, "This I will do. I will continue to work around the wagon and await your signal."

The soldiers picketed their horses with a long rope tied between two trees that gave them shade. From the river, one of the Indian women retrieved two jugs of wine that had been cooling there. The soldiers got their cups from their kit and lined up for a refreshing drink. Soon the aroma of roasting beef could be smelled. Crow, LeRue, and Gonzales stood in the shade of a tree located near the river bank. Gonzales was looking at the hacienda when he said, "You have a beautiful place in the making here."

LeRue said, "Don Isaiah is going to wed soon. He is to wed Don Hernando's daughter, Francisca."

Gonzales turned his gaze to Crow and said, "You marry well, the Don has powerful friends."

Crow, nearly a head taller than the lieutenant, coldly looked him in the eye but said nothing. Gonzales became visibly uncomfortable. LeRue quickly spoke changing the subject, "Don't you usually travel with mission people when you are looking for stolen property or runaways?"

Gonzales replied, "We had a priest traveling with us and several Indians from the mission. The priest became ill, and we had to stay at one of the ranchos for a few days. Finally, the Indians returned to the mission with the priest."

LeRue removed his hat and wiped his brow on his shirt sleeve. Looking in the direction of the wagon he saw Juan climb up to the seat, pick up the reins and released the wagon's brake. Gonzales seeing the wagon being driven away started to say something but appeared to change his mind. LeRue replaced his hat on his head just as the women began to bring the food.

Later, LeRue, to the consternation of the others, invited Gonzales and his men to stay the night. But to their relief, he declined the invitation. "We are still two days from San Diego, and I wish to push on. I have family there that I have not seen for a long time."

Juan watched with great relief when the soldiers rode out of sight. Crow and LeRue who were standing next to him began to laugh. Crow bending at the knees, slapped his hands on his thighs, "Whoo-wee, that was close! We didn't buy 'em 'cause as you can see, we already have a wagon and team!"

LeRue was grinning when he said, "I thought that Gonzales was gonna run for the hills when you gave him the cold eye. I don't know if he has family in San Diego or not, but he sure didn't want to take a chance of upsetting Don Isaiah."

Juan watched the two men who had saved him, his family and friends and gave them a home. 'They enjoy life to the fullest without being cruel or mean-spirited,' he thought. 'We are fortunate to have found them. We will build him and his bride a home they can be proud of.'

* * *

Late the next morning, Ponto began to bark. Crow and Juan were on the roof of the hacienda inspecting the new chimney for the fireplace. Crow saw four horsemen riding across the field toward the house. To Juan's surprise, Crow gave out a whoop and jumped down to the balcony and then dropped to the ground. 'The man is like a... like a squirrel,' thought Juan. He looked back at the open field and saw that one of the riders rode sidesaddle and wore a bonnet. Juan smiled with understanding for Crow's excitement.

Francisca was accompanied by Hernando, Carlos, and Santiago. As they neared the hacienda, Hernando brought his horse to a halt. The others did the same. "Look at what they have done!" exclaimed Hernando. "Why, it is beautiful!"

Carlos saw a man jump from the roof to the balcony and then to the ground. The man ran across the yard and leaped onto a gray horse and began racing in their direction. Carlos turned to his sister and said, "I think your future husband is happy to see you!"

Crow raced across the field followed by Ponto. He pulled up in front of his visitors. Standing in his stirrups, he removed his hat from his head and with a sweeping gesture said, "Welcome to the Hacienda Francita."

Francisca was pleased; Francita was a nickname for Francisca. It meant kind, home-loving, hospitable and friendly. It also could also mean courageous and bold. What a perfect name for their new home.

Crow, placing his hat back on his head, invited his guests to follow him. "You are just in time to show us how you want the rooms, Francisca. I had them delay until you could come."

As Crow and his guests arrived at the hacienda, LeRue, Juan, and several Indians came forward to take the horses. Crow gave Francisca a hand down from her horse. "Come inside, I'll show you around," said Crow.

Inside, the smell of fresh cut lumber filled the unfinished house. A cooling breeze flowed through the open windows. Songbirds could be heard in the shade trees outside. In the background was the soothing sound of the river. Carlos stood in the middle of an unfinished room and looked up. Supporting beams had been carved with birds and flowers. "I have only seen such woodwork in the missions," he said. "Why it is beautiful!"

Santiago stood near a window watching several men working. "You have managed to find many workers. It appears you have also found a gardener from the looks of your flower garden."

Crow replied, "I was fortunate to find Juan. I promised him some land and told him if he brought more workers I would do the same for them. Where he found them, I didn't ask. They are good workers, and appear loyal."

Santiago thought about the soldiers that had stopped at the rancho asking if anyone had seen a group of Indians in a wagon pulled by mules. Santiago nodded his head, and with a smile on his face and a gleam in his eye said, "Yes most fortunate, most fortunate indeed."

Crow showed them around the house, asking Francisca for her preferences for each room. Juan followed making a note of her wants and suggestions. Crow led them outside and down to the river. He pointed out an area that had been leveled and paved with stones. Posts could be seen protruding from the water. Woven between the posts was a porous wall of willow branches that allowed the river's water to flow freely through. Crow went to a post that was driven into the ground. A pole was doweled to the post at shoulder height. He pulled down on the long end of the pole, and from out of the water a basket appeared on a rope with several bottles in it.

"Juan made this," said Crow. "It keeps the wine cool. We will have some with our meal."

When they returned to the house, a table had been erected under the shade trees. Rough benches lined each side. Simple tableware, part of the "useful items" that had come with the wagon and mules, was on the table. The smell of food cooking now mixed with the smell of new lumber. As the guests took their seats, the food was brought to the table by Indians who were courteous and apparently well trained. Hernando looked at his son, and with the hint of a smile, shook his head. Carlos winked at his father. They also had been there when the Federales had come asking about the runaways.

Hernando said, "You have accomplished a great deal. When do you think you will finish?

Crow replied, "Now that we have Francisca's ideas, I think in a week to ten days it should be livable."

Hernando said, "Then I think we should begin planning for the wedding. There is a great deal to do. In two days I will send Carlos here to speak with you."

MOTHER-DAUGHTER TALK

Francisca was sitting in front of her mirror when her mother knocked and entered her room. As was their custom, Carmen removed the combs from Francisca's hair and combed it out with her fingers. "So the time has come to make plans," said her mother. "Your father told me about the hacienda and that it will be finished soon."

Francisca turned on her seat to look at her mother. "You should have seen the hacienda. It is beautiful, and it's not even finished. Isaiah asked me what I wanted in each room and also for my opinion on what he was doing."

"He holds you in high regard, and he treats you as an equal. That is not often found in our culture. I am fortunate that your father has that respect for me and I am pleased to hear that you will have it also."

"He has named it The Hacienda Francita."

Carmen placed her hands on Francisca's shoulders and gently coaxed her to turn to the mirror. She picked up the hairbrush and began brushing her daughter's hair. Francisca tilted her head forward as he mother brushed. "Mother, when he saw us coming across the field, he was on the roof of the hacienda. Isaiah jumped from the roof onto the balcony and then to the ground. It was amazing to see how he moves, like... like a dancer. He leaped onto his horse and rode out to greet us. It seems he can make the most ordinary things seem... exciting!"

Carmen smiled as she brushed her daughter's long black hair thinking, 'You are truly in love, and your Isaiah is in love with you.' "We must set a date and begin making plans for your wedding. As for the dress, I would like you to wear mine. It was my mother's and I would be honored if you would keep the tradition."

Francisca slowly raised her head and once again turned to her mother. She wrapped her arms around her mother's waist and hugged her. "I would like that very much."

FINISHING TOUCHES

Crow, LeRue, and Juan stood in the yard looking at the hacienda. LeRue said, "Amigo, you have a beautiful home." Turning to Juan, he said, "You and your men have done magic here. This has to be one of the finest haciendas around." Juan's brown, age-creased face beamed from the compliment.

Crow turned to his two friends and said, "I thank you both for all you have done. A man could not ask for better friends. I look at this place I now call home and find it hard to believe that just over two years ago LeRue and I were living in a one-room cabin."

LeRue replied, "Yes, we have come a long way, but now we must begin rounding up horses and purchasing cattle. We have much to do before your wedding in the spring."

"Juan," said Crow, "How many of your men would like to be vaqueros? Can any of them ride and handle a rope?"

"Si, I have two, and my son would like to learn."

"So we have three plus LeRue and me. I think I will ask Santiago if he would loan us a couple of his vaqueros. That should be enough for us to round up some horses. What do you think LeRue, ten or fifteen to start with?"

LeRue nodded his head in agreement, "I think maybe ten will be plenty. We should train them to be working horses. Once they are trained, we can get more riders and then more stock."

Ponto began to bark. The three men looked up to see two horsemen and three wagons coming across the open field. "Who the devil is that," asked Crow aloud.

As the wagons and men drew closer, they saw that two of the men were Carlos and Santiago. Crow, LeRue, and Juan walked out to meet them.

"Buenos días," shouted Carlos.

"Buenos días," greeted Crow. Santiago rode up, brought his mount to a stop and with his thumb pushed his sombrero back on his head. "Carlos, it looks like we have arrived just in time."

Crow now curious asked, "Just in time for what?"

Carlos dismounted and shook hands with his friend, "Why amigo, your hacienda is finished, but there is no place to sit or sleep."

Crow replied, "That was to be our next step, to purchase furniture."

Carlos turned and pointed at the wagons. "You have many grateful friends in the surrounding ranchos. You destroyed the bandits and saved lives. As a gift to Don Isaiah they have sent you three wagon loads of furniture for your new home."

Crow looked at the tarp-covered wagons and then to his friends who were all grinning. Crow went to the first wagon and pulled back the tarp. Inside were chairs, and a table top. He turned back to Carlos, "They sent all of this?"

"Si, it is enough to get you started and to make your new home livable."

LeRue said, "Well come on, let's get it inside."

It didn't take them long with all the help they had, to move the furniture into the house and to assemble the table and the bed. As they worked, Crow told Juan to have food prepared for the men. By the time they had finished with the furniture, the aroma of food had filled the air. Crow started to lead everyone outside to the rough tables and benches.

Juan's wife and the other women came through the doorway carrying trays of food which they placed on the new table. One of the young boys came in carrying dishes and flatware and set the table for four. Crow said to the boy, "Set it for five, Juan will eat with us."

As the men ate, Crow said, "Carlos, I have a favor to ask of you."

"Si, what is it?"

"I would like to borrow three or four of your vaqueros. I would also like to ask Raul to come live with us."

Carlos turned to Santiago and told him, "Pick four men that are your best." Carlos turned back to Crow, "I think Raul will be pleased to come here. When we return to the hacienda, I will ask him."

Santiago said, "I will ask our blacksmith to make branding irons for you. You will need these to mark your cattle and horses. Do you have an idea for the design?"

Juan reached into his pocket and withdrew a crumpled piece of cloth. He laid it on the table and spread it out. Drawn on it in charcoal was a simple outline of a crow with outstretched wings. "I knew a brand would be needed and I drew this."

Curious, Crow picked up the cloth and examined the drawing. Crow said, "I like it, gracias Juan."

He handed it over to the others so they could see it. Santiago looked over to Juan, "It is simple and easily made. There will be no doubt as to who the owner is. If you agree," he said to Crow, "I will have several of these irons made for you."

Carlos said, "You will have about three months to oversee the stocking of the horses and cattle. Then, my friend, you will be very busy getting ready for the wedding. There will be instruction for you from the church. You and Francisca will need to decide who to invite as guests so that there is sufficient time to contact them."

Crow sat back in his chair and stretched out his legs, his arms extended and his hands on the table. "Well amigos, there is much to do." With that, he got up from his chair and with a smile said, "I figure we'd better get started!"

VAQUERO SECRETS

Three days later, LeRue stood next to the gate and watched as the vaqueros herded eight mesteños (mustangs) through the gate and into the box canyon. As soon as the horses and men had cleared the gate, LeRue closed it. He looped a piece of rope attached to the gate over a fence post securing it. He mounted his horse and rode into the canyon.

The vaqueros had herded the horses to an area near the shade trees along the river. Most of the horses went to the river to drink while the others, still nervous, milled about. Crow rode up and joined LeRue. "That makes twenty, I think we have enough to work with for now," Said Crow.

LeRue asked, "How long do you figure it'll take to break them?"

"I figure between the vaqueros and me, maybe ten of them will be ready to ride within a few days. It will be the training that will take some time. I have a lot to learn myself about training a working horse.

LeRue said, "With Juan working with you, I'll oversee the rest of the work on the hacienda."

Juan rode up to the two Mountain Men, "I think we have a good start with these. I have checked them all, and there are no brands."

"Juan," said Crow, "I want Raul and Samuel to work with the vaqueros. Raul is young but good with a rope, and I know he can ride. Samuel hasn't much experience but is willing to learn. I think he'll make a good vaquero."

"Si, they seem to get along well together, and both are good workers."

"Who do you suggest I work with to learn the ways of the vaquero?"

Juan's face lost its smile, and he looked uneasy. "What is it Juan?" asked Crow.

"Señor Crow," Juan said in a troubled voice, "Vaqueros do not teach others, it is left to a man to learn for himself. It is tradition to mantén los ojos abiertos (keep your eyes open) and mantén la boca cerrada (keep your mouth shut). They share their secrets with no one."

Crow thought about that a moment and said, "Tell Raul and Samuel that I am going to visit the Batista's tomorrow, and I want them to ride with me. We will be gone for perhaps three to four days. I'll take one of the wagons, so if you need supplies, have a list made up, and I'll purchase them while we're there."

"I will have the wagon and team ready for you in the morning."

* * *

The fog from the night before still hugged the ground and the air held a bit of a chill. A golden line of light divided the mountains from the black morning sky as Crow, Raul and Samuel rode in the wagon. Behind them, tied to the back of the wagon, were their saddled horses. Crow had given the reins to Samuel and told him to drive while he sat back smoking his pipe. The two young men were excited to have been sent with the Don.

Crow said aloud, "The three of us have a great deal to learn. I know that it is a tradition for vaqueros not to share their knowledge. Well, I don't have time for that, I need working horses and men to gather cattle and work the rancho. Raul, I want you to teach Samuel and me how to work a rope. Do you have a problem with that?"

Raul looked over at the man he respected above all others and said, "No, of course not. I will teach you what I know, but I do not own a lariat. It will take time to make just one let alone three."

"You don't worry about that. Now, you both will need to learn about horses and how to train them. I will teach you, but you must keep this a secret. I plan to have the best-damned horses in California, and the two of you and Juan are going to help me do it."

Just then the sun broke over the mountains, its light illuminating the smiling faces of Raul and Samuel.

A CABALLERO AND HIS VAQUEROS

Carlos and Santiago were out on horseback when they saw the wagon. Both men spurred their horses forward and raced out to greet Crow and the boys. "Buenos días," said Carlos as they arrived at the wagon. "Buenos días," replied Crow. "We have come for supplies and perhaps stay a few days."

"You are always welcome. Francisca will be happy to see you."

"Carlos, I need to speak with you on some matters when you have time," said Crow.

"Come with me to the hacienda. I know there is coffee and hot chocolate available. Do you mind if Santiago joins us?"

"No, I would like that. I'll have Raul and Samuel, tend to the team and wagon, and then I'll join you."

When Crow jumped down from the wagon, he said, to Raul, "Unhitch the team and water and feed them. I will be busy for perhaps an hour. I want to meet you both here with our horses. We have some things to do." Crow reached into the wagon, and from under the seat he removed a bundle of clothing and handed it to Samuel. "Bring this with you when you bring the horses." He turned and headed to the hacienda.

As Crow walked away, Samuel said, "These clothes look like my father's. I wonder why Señor Crow has them."

"There is a pair of sandals in here also," said Raul.

In the hacienda, Crow found Carlos and Santiago in the dining room sitting at the table. "Come, join us," invited Carlos. "Do you wish coffee or chocolate?"

"Coffee, sounds good," said Crow.

Carlos waved his hand at the doorway leading to the kitchen, and a young girl stepped out. "Bring us coffee," said Carlos, and then turned back to Crow. "What can we do for you?"

Crow leaned forward and addressed both men, "I need four lariats, chapes de cuero (leather chaps) and four good working saddles. I will also need four pistols, a dozen muskets, with shot and powder."

Carlos with a smirk on his face said, "Gringo, you are supposed to lasso the steer not shoot it!"

Crow laughed, "Yes, that is true, but I need to teach my men how to shoot to protect my land. Hector may be gone, but there are plenty of banditos still roaming around."

"Si, that is true. Santiago, will you see about the purchase of the munitions and I will take you to a man who makes fine lariats and saddles. I must warn you though that these items are expensive. Usually, they are made by the vaqueros themselves."

"I have gold coin to pay with. I don't have time to make these as I need them now."

"I understand," said Carlos. The girl came out of the kitchen. "Ah, here is our coffee. Tell us what you have been doing at your rancho."

An hour later, Crow found the boys waiting by the horses. "Mount up," said Crow. "Raul, take us to the cobbler and his wife. Oh, did you bring the bundle?" Samuel held the bundle up for Crow to see. "Then, let's go."

A short time later they arrived at the cobbler's home. As they were dismounting the cobbler came out to greet them, "Hola, Bienvenidos a mi casa, (hello, welcome to my house)!"

"It is good to see you again my friend. I hope we find you and your wife well."

"Si, we are well. Who are these fine looking young men?"

"This is Raul and Samuel. We have come to be fitted for boots and the clothing of the vaquero."

Raul and Samuel looked at each other, surprised at what they had just heard.

"Come in, come in. You have come at a good time. We have not had any orders other than for repairs of clothing and boots."

Inside the house, the cobbler's wife looked up from her sewing, smiled when she saw Crow and went back to her sewing. The old man said to his wife, "Madre que han venido a buscar ropa, las tres de ellos (Mother, they have come for clothes, all three of them.)"

The old lady carefully stuck her needle into the fabric and placed it on a nearby table. She shuffled over to Crow and the boys. Crow said, "We need vaquero clothing for myself, Raul and Samuel. I have brought clothing for a fourth man for you to copy."

The old women looked at her husband questioningly. He turned to Crow, "She thinks that you want clothing of a caballero for yourself. You are a gentleman, not a vaquero."

Crow nodded his head and said, "Then make two sets of clothing for me; one as a caballero and another as a vaquero. I will need both for what I wish to do."

It took nearly an hour for the measurements to be made. Crow was told that he might have to stay longer at the rancho if he wanted to wait for all of the clothing. This did not displease him in the least.

HACIENDA FRANCITA

It took over a week to get all the items together that Crow had ordered. Plus a round trip to the Hacienda Francita by Raul to let LeRue know that all was well. Raul and Samuel rode their horses, proud of their new lariats that hung from the saddle horn of their new saddles. They wore short jackets over long sleeved shirts. Their trousers were of soft leather protected by heavier leather chaps. Both Samuel and Raul had a knife tucked into the top of their new boots. On their heads, they wore new felt, low crown, wide-brimmed sombreros; all purchased by Crow.

Crow drove with the reins between the fingers of his left hand while holding his pipe with his right. As the young men rode reveling in their new clothes, Crow thought about the last few days. He and Francisca had had time together to talk and to plan. Crow learned that the two of them would have to meet with the priest about their marriage and that there were customs that he needed to follow. Like the twelve gold coins representing the twelve apostles to be presented to the bride. But the memory he went back to and dwelled on was that moment when they had mistakenly been left alone just before he left. Francisca had taken his hand and gently pulled him to her. Crow had not hesitated; he took her in his arms and kissed her full on the lips. She had eagerly responded, kissing him back. It had been brief but intense, and he would remember that moment for the rest of his life.

It was afternoon when Crow, Raul, and Samuel saw the hacienda in the distance and a rider approaching them on horseback on the dead run. As the horse and rider drew closer, Crow saw that it was one of his vaqueros on a mustang. As the rider and horse thundered past they saw a look of glee on the vaquero's face. The boys looked at Crow bewildered, "Looks like he's got him broke, but that mustang wants one more run for freedom!" They watched a bit as the horse and rider disappeared over the hill. Crow snapped the reins, and they continued on to their home.

Juan and the rest of the Indians gathered around Samuel and Raul, marveling at their new clothes and equipment. Juan appeared as proud as a new father as he admired his son. Samuel went to the wagon and removed a bundle and brought it to his father. "Señor Crow asked momma for some of your clothes and sandals. They were used as a pattern to make these." Juan held up the jacket and then the leather trousers. His hands trembled slightly as he handled the new clothing. Juan saw the boots, picked them up and pressed them to his chest. He was unashamed of the tears that rolled down his cheeks. He looked at Crow and managed to say, "Gracias."

Crow went to the wagon, and from the back, he removed the saddle he had ordered made for Juan. "This is for you Juan. I think you will find it more comfortable than the one you are using now. Juan ran his fingers over the leather saddle. He saw the new lariat looped over the saddle horn. The lariat was the most valuable possession of a vaquero. Juan took the leather rope in his hand and with the other ran his fingers along the smooth, stiff surface. Unable to speak, he looked at Crow his face pronouncing all the words of thanks that his voice couldn't.

Crow nodded his head in acknowledgment of Juan's gratitude.

LeRue walked up, "Welcome home Amigo."

Crow replied, "I brought you tobacco along with some shot and powder. There seemed to be an abundance of tequila available, so I brought some of that along too."

"We've been busy. We got eight rideable mustangs, maybe nine if the one that just rode outta here makes it back."

"I purchased some firearms, powder, and shot. I want to train our men how to use them. There's still plenty of bandits roaming around, and I want us to be ready if need be."

TREASURE

It was early morning when Crow, rifle in hand and Ponto at his heels, walked the short distance to the box canyon. Crow enjoyed early mornings. Hearing the birds greet the morning and seeing the sun inching up from behind the mountains made him feel alive.

The vaqueros had been working with the first group of horses and Crow was looking forward to seeing what progress they had made. Arriving at the mouth of the canyon, Crow opened the gate. After entering, he closed and secured the gate behind him. There were more than twenty horses in the corral now. He'd been told that all but two or three had been broken to the saddle.

A group of ten horses watched Crow and the dog, their ears thrust forward listening. "Buenos dias," said Crow to the horses. The mustangs stood and stared. Some pawed the ground with their hooves. Crow smiled and continued walking. The horses, now curious, began to follow. At first, it was only two or three, but then another and another followed the leaders. Soon eight or more horses quietly followed the Mountain Man deeper into the canyon. Crow stopped and turned. The horses stopped. The leaders snorted and tossed their heads. Crow reached down and pulled a handful of sweet grass out of the ground and held it out. The horses, their heads held high, their ears twitching, watched silently. One of the horses, sixteen hands high, brown with four white socks, slowly left the group and approached Crow. Crow stood still holding out the grass, "Come on," Crow said in a low, soft voice, "Come on." The horse stopped just short of the offered grass and stretched his neck out, his lips pulling at the grass, but Crow held firm. Cautiously, the horse took a step closer and bit down on the grass with his teeth. As Crow fed the animal with one hand, he moved his other hand to horse's muzzle and began to stroke its velvety soft nose. "I think, muchacho, I will make you my working horse."

Finished with feeding the horse, Crow and Ponto resumed walking along the trail. Soon, they came to the area the bandits had used as their camp. Crow saw the entrance to the cave. He had not been back here since the raid on the bandit's camp, and that was in the dark of night. Curious, he approached the entrance. The dog and the mustang followed him.

When Crow peered inside, it was as if the blackness of the cave ate the light of day. Near the entrance, he spotted a pile of torches. Reaching into his possibles bag, Crow brought out his flint and steel and built a small fire by the entrance. Taking a torch, he thrust it into the flames, igniting it. With the torch held high, Crow entered the cave. Just inside the entrance, he saw a table with a bench on each side and two old chairs on each end. A section of one wall was black with soot from a cooking fire. A cast iron pot lay on its side in the fire pit. Crow thought, 'We can clean this place out and use it to store feed and equipment for the horses.'

Holding the torch high and turning in a circle, he saw torches forced into cracks in the walls. Crow went from one to another lighting them. The room was illuminated enough for him to see that it could comfortably hold thirty or more men. Leaning his rifle against the wall of the cave, Crow moved the two chairs off to the side and dragged the benches over by the chairs. Crow moved a rock aside that was in the way. He lifted the massive wooden table, sliding first one end and then the other, over to one of the walls of the cave. But one leg stopped sliding. Dropping to one knee, Crow looked under the table and saw that the table leg had dug into the dirt floor. Crow stood and lifted the table higher and tried to swing it to the wall. It stopped abruptly, and the table was jerked from his hands. Once again he dropped to one knee and peered under the table. A leather bag was caught on the leg of the table. Some of its contents had spilled onto the dirt floor of the cave.

Even in the dim light of the cave, Crow recognized the shine of gold. "¡ Hijo de puta! (Son of a bitch!)," muttered Crow and this time dropped to both knees. Digging with his hands, he excavated the heavy bag from the hole in the dirt floor. Picking up the spilled coins he placed them back in the bag. Picking up the bag he carried it to the entrance of the cave and into better light. As Crow bent over the bag, a shadow came up behind him. Ponto began to growl. Before the Mountain Man could react, he was sent sprawling onto his face in the dirt. Rolling to one side, Crow jumped to his feet while at the same time drawing his Bowie knife. His attacker shook his head and curled his lips back into a horse laugh. Ponto sat to one side, his head cocked, seeming to enjoy the scene. Returning his knife to its sheath, Crow reached out and stroked the nose of the mustang. "I think I'll call you 'Bromista' ('Joker')," He said to the horse.

Crow returned to the leather bag. It would be too heavy to carry by hand back to the hacienda. Picking up the bag, he took it to where he had stacked the chairs and benches and hid the gold behind them. 'That will do until I can return,' he thought. Crow retrieved his rifle and began running toward the gate. When he got to the gate, he stopped to open it and realized the mustang had followed him. Crow, Ponto and the horse walked through the opening, and he closed and secured the gate. "Bromista, I've never seen a horse like you," said Crow.

"Let's see how far this will go." The mustang stood watching as Crow, and the dog ran down the trail. Tossing his head, Bromista took off running, caught up to Crow and ran past him. He disappeared down the trail with Ponto racing behind him. "Well, I guess that answers that question," Crow said aloud.

As the hacienda came into view so did the mustang. Bromista was standing in the middle of the trail waiting, Ponto sitting beside him. As Crow approached, he slowed to a walk and went to the horse. Running his hand along the horse's back, he said, "Well come on, I'll introduce you to the others."

Crow saw LeRue. "Whatcha, got there amigo?" asked LeRue.

"I want you to meet Bromista (Joker), he's friendly but don't turn your back on him."

LeRue reached out and stroked the horse's nose. "He's a fine looking animal," said LeRue. "He doesn't have any bite marks on him. He must have been a herd leader. He'll be hard to break. He just followed you here?"

"Yup!" Crow reached out and ran his hand gently down the length of Joker's nose. "I think we may have come to some kind of understanding, him and me. But he picked me out. I think we'll get along just fine. But let's get our horses; I want you to go to the canyon with me."

Now curious, LeRue turned to follow Crow. Two seconds later, he was sent sprawling face first into the dirt. Crow and the mustang began to laugh as LeRue angrily stood up and started brushing himself off. "You taught him to do that!" accused LeRue.

Crow, grinning from ear to ear replied, "Hell no, he did it to me back at the canyon. For a wild mustang, he sure is friendly."

"Hmm, well I think I'll just follow you two," said LeRue. "You sure named him right."

WHAT TO DO

Crow and LeRue returned to the cave after leaving Joker in the corral at the hacienda, Crow was now riding the gray. In the cave, Crow went to the chairs where he had hidden the sack of gold coins. Lifting the bag from behind the chairs, he went to the mouth of the cave with a curious LeRue following.

Crow set the bag on the ground and opened it. LeRue looked inside. Speaking in French and crossing himself, an astonished LeRue said, "Mère de Dieu, où as-tu trouvé un tel trésor? (Mother of God, where did you find such treasure?)"

Crow reached into the bag and grabbed a handful of coins. He showed them to LeRue. "I figure this was left behind by the bandits. They didn't have time to take it with them because of our attack."

LeRue, hefting several of the coins in the palm of his hand asked, "How far back does the cave go?"

Shrugging his shoulders, Crow replied, "I don't know. Let's take a look-see."

Each man took a torch from the wall and headed deeper into the cave. LeRue noted the hole near the leg of the table where Crow had found the bag of coins. Stopping, he held up his torch and began to examine the cave wall. Curious, Crow watched and moved forward to look when LeRue said, "Hmm."

With a finger, LeRue silently pointed to the wall. Crow saw it too; a mark scratched on the wall. LeRue's eyes had an unnerving glint to them in the torchlight. "I think amigo we should venture further into the cave." With that, he turned and led the way.

Crow held his torch, examining the wall of the cave on his side while LeRue did the same on his. As they moved along, the ceiling began to get lower. Soon the two men were nearly bent at the waist as they check the walls for the sign.

Crow's attention was drawn to LeRue's side when he heard a thud and then heard LeRue painfully mutter, "Shit!"

An outcropping of rock, unseen by LeRue, had caught the Mountain Man's foot throwing him to the ground. Crow, holding his torch out in front so he could see, found his friend sprawled face down on the floor of the cave, his torch sputtering a few feet away having been knocked from LeRue's hand. Crow went to pick up the torch, and then he saw it. A mark scratched on the cave wall, just above the floor.

On their hands and knees, the two men dug at the floor just under the mark on the wall. The soft earthen floor gave way to hard rock. There was nothing buried here. The two men sat on the floor with their backs to the wall. The torches were beginning to sputter. "We'd better head back before these things burn out," said LeRue.

Crow said nothing. He just sat there staring off into space. LeRue started to say something when Crow rocked forward onto his hands and knees. He moved to the other side of the cave and began to dig. LeRue crawled over to Crow. He heard the sound of gravel on something hollow; something hollow and made of wood.

The box was broad and deep, reinforced with wide iron bands. It was not locked, and Crow opened it. In the torchlight, the gold came alive. Its reflected light casting a dull golden glow on the wall and low ceiling of the cave.

LeRue picked one of the coins from the box and examined it in the light. "Amigo, I think we may have a problem. The bandits will return for this. There is too much here to just walk away from."

"I've been thinking the same thing. We need to train our men well and to warn them to be on the lookout."

"What do you plan to do with the gold?" asked LeRue.

"I figure there is no way of getting it back to the rightful owners. Let's get it back to the hacienda, and we can decide what to do with it. But amigo, we must tell no one."

"You are right on that. We'll be in for big trouble if it ever gets out you have found this. Bandits, victims of robbery and those who will see a chance at gaining wealth by claiming it is theirs will be after it."

"Let's get this back to the hacienda. We have to start rounding up cattle for branding and finish training the men."

"The wedding, don't forget the wedding," said LeRue.

Crow smiled and took LeRue by the shoulder and gently shook it. "That my friend is never far from my thoughts. It is the reason for all that I am doing."

MEXICO

Hector Camacho sat on the cold stone floor, his back against the wall. He lifted his chin, so the sun shining through the barred window fell on his beard covered face. The sun would be there for just a few minutes each day, and Hector considered basking in it a luxury. During this time he was able to block out the stink of the prison and the cries of prisoners who had lost their minds.

Garcia, like Hector, sat with his back to a wall. The sun belonged to Hector, so Garcia just relaxed, his eyes closed, thinking. 'I am not sure I can do many years in this hellish place. We should never have come back to Mexico.' Footsteps outside their cell and then a key rattling in the lock got the attention of both men. The heavy metal hinges of the cell door screeched as it opened. Hector and Garcia stood up and quickly moved to the side of the cell opposite the door. They turned and faced the wall. It had taken only one beating by the prison guards for the two bandits to learn to do this whenever the door was opened.

The prison guard, who stood in the doorway, was backed up by a second guard who held leg irons and chains in his hands. The first guard, armed with a club, entered the cell. "Place your hands flat on the wall and back up with your legs spread. If you move, I will bust your heads!

Hector and Garcia both nodded their heads yes. That won them both a painful blow to the kidneys that dropped them to their knees. Garcia pissed himself. "You hear me?"

"Yes sir," the two prisoners shouted in unison.

"Get up and place your hands on the wall and spread your legs."

"Yes sir," the two men replied as they struggled to comply.

The guard signaled to the man carrying the leg irons to come into the cell. "Chain them," said the guard as he held his fist up clenching it. The other guard smiled, nodding his head in understanding.

Kneeling behind the two prisoners, the guard tightened the heavy iron cuffs above the ankle bone of each prisoner's leg. The weight of the cuffs now rested on the ankle bone so that each future step would eventually become agony. "Turn around," said the guard. As the two men turned around the guard pointed to the open door with his club. Hector and Garcia began shuffling out the door, the iron shackles rocking painfully back and forth on their ankle bones with each step.

The sun that Hector had enjoyed in his cell now nearly blinded him when he stepped out into the light of day. The two prisoners shading their eyes with their hands looked around. A line of ten prisoners stood silently in the sun. A jab from the guard's club prodded Hector and Garcia to move to the end of the line. Across from the prisoners were two wagons harnessed to teams of mules. Guards were sitting next to the teamsters. More armed guards roamed about watching the prisoners.

The prisoners became aware that something was happening when the heads of all the guards turned and looked to their left. A tall, thin man in uniform was coming their way, and the nervousness of the guards confirmed he had power. The guard with the club greeted the uniformed man by standing at attention and clicking his heels together. "Twelve men, as you ordered, commandant."

The commandant did not answer but turned to look at the line of prisoners. The twelve men all wore filthy, once white clothing. All were gaunt with the eyes like beaten dogs. All but one, he was taller than the other prisoners. The prisoner's eyes conveyed his contempt of the prison and its personnel. The commandant walked over and stood in front of Hector. "Who is this?" he asked the guard.

"Hector Camacho. He is a bandit who tried to slip back into Mexico. He and the one next to him shot and wounded one of the Federalizes when they arrested them."

The commandant looked Hector in the eyes, neither man blinked. The commandant smiled. "Unchain him." The guard nodded to the guard with the cuff keys. Dropping to one knee the guard unlocked Hector's leg irons. Hector's heart began to beat faster. 'What's going on? Is he going to kill me here and now?'

The commandant turned to the rest of the prisoners. "This man," he said, pointing at Hector, "will be in charge of you. The guards will tell him what to do, and he will see that you do it. If you don't do as he says, well, I leave it up to him as for how to handle it."

The commandant turned to the guard. "Load them in the wagons and take them to the mine."

As the wagons bumped along the rough road, Hector and Garcia sat side by side. Garcia leaned close to Hector and said, "I think perhaps our luck is changing."

Hector shrugged his shoulders, "I think if we are to have any luck at all, we have to make it ourselves. Stay alert and trust no one."

SIX MONTHS LATER, SPRING

THE WEDDING PROCESSION

Carmen Batista was filled with joy when Francisca turned to face her. The wedding dress her daughter wore was white with white lace accents. She had kept it all of these years with her dreams of this day. It fit Francisca beautifully.

With her lips trembling and her eyes close to tears, Carmen tried to tell Francisca how beautiful she looked; but the lump in her throat prevented her from speaking. Reaching out, Carmen took her daughters hands and gently spread her arms and smiled.

Francisca, her face flushed with excitement, said, "Thank you, the dress is beautiful." Francisca slowly turned in a full circle so her mother could see how well it fit. A knock at the door drew their attention. The door latch clicked, and the door opened.

Two young ladies, Francisca's age, entered the room. They were dressed for the occasion; Francisca's wedding to Isaiah Crow. The girls stopped; their eyes wide with admiration for how beautiful their friend looked. Carmen, her emotions now under control asked, "¿No es hermosa? (Isn't she beautiful?)"

"Si, Señora Batista, ¡ Parece una princesa! (She looks like a princess!)"

Downstairs in the dining room, Hernando and Carlos were surrounded by several male guests. The room reverberated with loud and congratulatory voices. On the long table were hot drinks of both coffee and chocolate next to bottles of wine. Platters of meats and fruits were also available for the guests to enjoy while they waited.

When Isaiah Crow, accompanied by Jacques LeRue, entered the room, the din of voices softened and then went quiet. Crow wore a black, waist-length jacket over a brilliant white shirt and black trousers embroidered with patterns of silver thread. His black boots were shined to a high gloss. He stood head and shoulders above most of the men in the room. Hernando moved through the crowded room to Crow. Without reservation, Hernando embraced the man who was to become his son-in-law, and said, "Isaiah, you look magnificent, Francisca will be so proud."

"Thank you, Don Hernando."

Hernando turned to LeRue and offered his hand in welcome. "You look very apuesto (dashing) Jacques, welcome!"

Carlos joined them, shaking hands with both men. "It is a big day my friend, are you ready?"

Crow replied, "I felt surer of myself fighting that grizzly than I do right now."

Carlos, Hernando, LeRue and those close by, laughed at the remark. "Let us hope the outcome today will be more pleasant than with the bear," said Carlos.

Hernando announced to the men, "It is time. Gentlemen, it is time to mount up. The ladies should be coming down shortly."

Nothing is as grandiose as a wedding cavalcade on its way from the bride's house to the mission chapel. The horses were richly decorated; more so than for any other ceremony. Francisca's father carried her before him, she sitting sideways on the saddle with her white satin shoe in a loop of silver braid. Hernando sat on a bear-skin covered anquera behind the saddle.

Crow and his friends mingled with the bride's party. All were mounted on the best horses that could be obtained. They rode gaily from the ranch house to the mission. It was spring, and the land was covered with wild-flowers. The light-hearted troop rode along the edge of the uplands, between hill and valley, crossing the streams. Some of the young horsemen, anxious to show their skills, rode hard and fast, showing off to the young ladies in the group. As the wedding party moved along, the musicians began to play. Many of the attendees sang to the music. Even the proud stallions ridden by the men seemed to dance to the music in celebration of the coming wedding.

SEÑOR AND SEÑORA CROW

At the church, Father Lopez greeted the wedding party. After everyone had dismounted, Father Lopez led the way to the church, followed by Francisca, Crow, her father, and mother. The wedding guests followed.

In the church, Father Lopez stood waiting while Crow and Francisca knelt on pillows before him. Father Lopez wrapped a silken tasseled sash, fringed with gold, about their shoulders in a figure-eight, binding them together for the blessing of the priest. The priest turned to LeRue, who handed him an ornate wooden box. Father Lopez opened the box revealing thirteen gold coins representing Christ and his 12 apostles. Father Lopez gave the coins to Francisca who then placed them in Crow's cupped hands.

The coins were placed on a tray and handed to an altar boy, to be held until later in the ceremony. Father Lopez began the wedding ceremony.

Near the end of the service, the box and coins were given to the priest, who placed the coins in the box and handed them to Crow.

Crow poured the coins into Francisca's cupped hands and placed the box on top as a symbol of his unquestionable trust, confidence and a pledge to provide financially for them. Father Lopez then continued, with the wedding ceremony.

To Crow and Francisca it all seemed to take so long, but suddenly it was over. They heard the applause of wedding guests as they were introduced as husband and wife. Then Francisca, her hand on her husband's arm, walked back down the aisle and out of the chapel entrance.

Outside, everyone was now free of the formality of the church. They broke into boisterous cheers and showered the new couple with rice. The throwing of rice was a time-honored tradition meant to bless the new couple with prosperity, fertility and good fortune. Crow's gray stood waiting. Crow lifted his bride up onto the saddle, placing her slippered foot into a silver loop. Crow mounted up behind her sitting on a bearskin covered anquera. The crowd cheered as Crow turned the gray and he and Francisca led the wedding party back to the Batista Rancho for the reception.

THE RECEPTION AND ESCAPE

The aroma of roasting beef filled the air. Carmen was pleased with the arrangements and was sure a more perfect day could not have been planned. A long table awaited the bride and groom. They sat in the places of honor, while Hernando and Carmen took their places to their right. Because Crow had no family, Carlos and LeRue sat to their left. In front of the wedding-table was a large open space for dancing, which was encircled with tables, two deep, for the quests. Off to one side were the musicians.

The guests were finally seated. The musicians started to play as the servants began bringing the food to the tables. Hernando leaned over and spoke to Crow. "It is our tradition for the father to dance with the bride and the groom to dance with the mother of the bride. At an appropriate time, I will present Francisca to you, and you will hand Carmen to me. We will then finish the dance."

"You wish to do this now, Don Hernando?" asked Crow.

"Yes, now is a good time." Hernando stood and offered his hand to Francisca who stood and followed her father to the dance floor. Crow stood and went to Carmen. He helped her with her chair and escorted her to the dance floor. As Francisca and her father faced each other on the dance floor, Crow started to move, but Carmen placed her hand on his arm. "Let them begin dancing, then you and I will join them."

With a nod of the Don's head, the band began to play a waltz. Francisca and her father began to dance, making their way around the edge of the dance floor to the applause of the guests. They had completed one circle of the dance floor when Carmen said, "Shall we dance?"

The wedding guests applauded as the two couples danced to the waltz. When Hernando tapped Crow on the shoulder, the two men smoothly exchanged partners to the cheers of the crowd. It was the first time that Crow had held

Francisca in his arms since their stolen kiss. He wanted to stop dancing and to sweep her up and ride off with her to their new home. But they danced on.

Francisca's heart did a little leap when Crow took her in his arms. She had not been this close to him since she had kissed him and again marveled at how tall he was. Though Francisca felt his strength, he was gentle with her and so light on his feet. She wanted desperately to be alone with him; to just run off into the night with him. When the music ended, her brother Carlos was waiting to dance with her.

The festivities continued well into the evening. There was much eating, drinking and dancing. Carmen and Hernando were seated at a table with friends. Carmen had been watching Crow and Francisca dancing, but soon conversation with friends distracted her. It wasn't until much later that she realized that she couldn't see Francisca or Crow. "Hernando, where are Isaiah and Francisca?"

Hernando looked about and to his surprise could not locate them. "I have no idea."

Carmen and Hernando quickly became aware that Carlos and LeRue were missing too. "Something is not right," said Hernando. "I will go and find them."

Just as Hernando began to leave the table, Carlos and LeRue appeared out of the night. "Where have you been?" asked Hernando. "Have you seen Francisca and Crow?"

Carlos, looking for support from LeRue, realized that LeRue had disappeared. Carlos turned to face his father alone. "Ah, they have gone home," he said in a soft voice.

"Speak up Carlos, I cannot hear you!"

Clearing his throat, Carlos replied too loudly, "They have gone home, father."

Carmen turned in her chair, "Who has gone home?"

Hernando angrily turned to his wife, "It seems our daughter and Isaiah have run off!"

Carlos knew he was treading on dangerous ground when he said, "Isaiah and his wife..."

The Don looked hard at his son. He was angry, but Carlos' words had struck home. It had not been the proper thing for them to do, but Hernando understood. He was sure that Carmen would not be as understanding, though.

Carmen had heard the conversation. She thought 'I wish Hernando had been as daring when we got married.'

HOME

The gray moved swiftly through the night; the weight of two riders not tiring him. Atop the gray's back, Crow wrapped his arms around his bride. She leaned back against him. Both thought they could never be happier.

It was a long ride. At near the half-way point, Crow decided to rest the gray before moving on. When they stopped, Crow lifted Francisca down from the saddle. As her feet touched the ground, she turned in his arms. Reaching up, she cupped his face in her hands. Crow felt the caress of her hands on his skin, and it excited him. He pulled her close and kissed her.

Her lips were full and felt hot on his. Their hearts quickened as they desperately pressed their bodies together. Crow stepped back, lifted her back up onto the saddle and climbed up behind her. "Home," he managed to say, "We're going home." He put the gray into a run, and they raced across the moonlit land.

The gray was beginning to tire when they saw the lights of the Hacienda Francita. As they drew near, Ponto appeared out of the night. He did not bark but raced in circles around the gray, happy that Crow was home. Juan and the men and women of the rancho could be seen waiting in the moonlight. They had gathered at the steps leading up to the porch of the house. It was Juan who greeted them.

"Welcome home Don Isaiah and Señora Crow. You will find everything in order."

"Thank you, Juan," replied Crow. "We are tired. It has been a long day and a long ride."

"I understand. We wish you a good evening."

The couple watched as the men, women, and children drifted off into the night.

Crow turned to Francisca and effortlessly swept her up into his arms. He carried her up the stairs, across the porch, and into their new home. Inside, the scent of fresh flowers filled the house. It was a gift of thanks from Juan and the Indians to whom Crow had given a place to live.

Crow carried Francisca into the bedroom. The soft light from a lantern illuminated a decanter of wine and a bowl of fresh fruit on a table. Crow set Francisca down and wrapped his arms around her. She stepped in close, wrapping her arms around his waist and resting her face on his chest. Crow buried his face in her hair inhaling the smell of her. "I love you," Crow whispered, "I love you more than life itself."

* * *

Francisca lifted her face and Crow kissed her, their passion of new love consuming them into the early morning hours. It was then, as they lay in each other's arms that Francisca ran her hands over her husband's back, feeling the rope like scars. "The bear did this to you?" she asked.

Rolling so that he lay on his back, he asked, "Do they bother you?"

"No, I just can't imagine what you went through. The pain ..."

"I have LeRue to thank for my life. He found me, and though he was injured himself, sewed me up, doctored and fed me." Crow kissed his wife on the forehead and slipped out of her arms. He rolled over to the edge of the bed and stood up. As he stretched, Francisca watched.

Crow turned and looked down at Francisca and saw her eyes examine his body. Crow pointed at a jagged scar on his left side, "I got this on a buffalo hunt. I was knocked from my horse by a wounded buff and landed on a stick that was poking out of the ground." With his right hand, he pointed at a puckered white and pink scar near his left breast. I was shot by a Blackfoot during a raid, and this one," Crow pointed at a white scar on his stomach, "during a knife fight with Billy One Eye."

Francisca moved across the bed, she was crying. Standing, she touched each scar. "I don't want you to be hurt anymore."

Crow held her face in his hands, "That was another life. It is different now. We have our home and each other. No one will hurt you or me."

Francisca looked up at Crow, "I love you so much."

ONE YEAR LATER

Carlos was crossing the yard heading for the house when he heard shouting. He and the vaqueros working near the corral looked up to see Raul riding hell bent for leather. He was yelling and waving his hat in the air.

Carlos immediately became concerned, 'What has happened?' he wondered. 'Francisca is pregnant but not due for a while.'

Raul arrived in a cloud of dust, his horse rearing back on its hind legs, its front hooves pawing at the sky, "It's a boy!" shouted Raul. "It's a boy, and Francisca is doing well!"

The vaqueros whooped with joy as if they were the new fathers. Carlos ran up to the house just as his father and mother, accompanied by the house servants, burst out the front door. "What has happened?" shouted Hernando.

"It's a boy!" Shouted an excited Carlos, "It's a boy, and Francisca is doing well!"

Carmen walked up to Raul, who had just dismounted. "When did this happen?" she asked Raul.

"This morning Señora! Once Don Isaiah knew that both the baby and Francisca were well, he sent me to tell you."

"His name, what have they named their son?" asked Hernando.

"Jedadiah, Jedadiah Crow," responded Raul.

Hernando looked disappointed. "Jedadiah, what name is this?"

Raul saw the disappointment on the Don's face, "The name comes from a Mountain Man who Don Isaiah says saved his life while crossing the Mojave when he came here."

Hernando nodded his head and turning to Carmen said, "It is a good name; the name of a man of courage and compassion. Come we must go and welcome our grandson!"

Hernando and Carmen Batista rode in a carriage. The Don was driving at a moderate pace because of Carmen. Carlos, with Raul on a new mount, both wanted to ride like the wind but held back. Carmen surprised Hernando when she said sharply, "The child's first birthday will have come and gone by the way you are driving! ¿A qué esperas? ¡ Más rápido, más rápido! (What are you waiting for? Faster, faster!)." Hernando, with a grin on his face, snapped the reins, sending the team of horses into a ground-eating gallop, surprising Raul and Carlos who had to spur their mounts to catch up.

It was some time later when Juan, who was standing on the porch next to LeRue saw a cloud of dust on the horizon. "If I am not mistaken, Raul has delivered the good news. I think Jedadiah's grandma and grandpa will be here shortly."

LeRue, who was smoking his pipe said, "Juan, you should probably let the kitchen know there will be company for a few days."

"Si, I will go now."

Within minutes, the Batista's, accompanied by Carlos and Raul, pulled up in front of the house.

LeRue stepped down off the porch and greeted them. "Buenos días, Abuela y Abuelo de Batista. ¡ Y usted también Tío Carlos!" ("Good morning, Grandma and Grandpa Batista. And you too Uncle Carlos!").

Crow stepped out onto the porch. He looked tired, but he had a smile on his face. Crow greeted them. "Buenos días, y ¡ Bienvenida!"

Carlos dismounted and assisted his mother down from the carriage. His father stepped down and handed the reins to one of the servants. Crow came down off the porch and was embraced by both Carmen and Hernando. Carmen asked, "Francisca is well? I did not expect her to deliver for another two or three weeks."

"Both Francisca and your grandson are doing well. They are sleeping right now." Carmen and Hernando looked disappointed but smiled when Crow said, "But I think we can take a peek."

Carlos, having turned his horse over to one of the servants, went to Crow and offered his hand, "Congratulations my friend!"

Crow took the hand, but Carlos pulled Crow forward and gave him a bear hug. "You and Francisca have made us all very happy."

"Well, come on. Let's go in and have a look-see," said Crow.

Crow led Hernando, Carmen, and Carlos to the bedroom. He slowly and quietly opened the door and peered into the room. Francisca said, "Come in, we are awake." Crow opened the door wider to allow the others to enter.

Carmen went to her daughter followed by Hernando. They stood by the bed looking at their smiling daughter who held their grandson in her arms. "I want you to meet Jedadiah Hernando Crow." Hernando smiled broadly when he heard his name. Reaching down with his index finger, he moved the blanket aside so he could see his grandson better. Hernando looked at his daughter, "Thank you, I thank you both."

INTRIGUE

Hector Camacho felt healthy. He had gained weight since being in prison. His wound, where Crow had shot him, had healed. He and Garcia now lived in a room down the hall from the prison guards, instead of being locked in a cell. It had taken Hector nearly a year to gain the trust of a few guards and the commandant. It was the promise of gold that had finally won the commandant over. Gold buried in a cave in California.

In a separate building, housing his office and private quarters, the commandant sat at his desk deep in thought. He looked out the barred office window, across the empty yard to the building that housed the prisoners. 'Hector Camacho,' he thought, 'what do I do about you? You have turned my comfortable life upside down with your offer of gold. Now I think I see an opportunity; an opportunity that will turn me into a bandito like you.'

The Commandant, making a silent decision, called out, "Guard!"

The thick, reinforced door opened and a prison guard stepped into the office, "Yes sir!"

"Find Camacho and bring him here. Alone."

The guard clicked his heels together and saluted the Commandant. "Yes, sir!" The guard closed the door behind him as he left the office. A few minutes later there was a knock at the office door. The Commandant, in a loud voice, said, "Enter!"

Hector Camacho opened the door and entered the room. He walked over to the desk and centered himself. He stood silently at attention. The guard at the door closed it and returned to his post.

When the door was closed Hector relaxed his stance, but remained silent. The commandant leaned back in his chair. "Take a seat."

Hector sat in the uncomfortable straight-back chair and waited.

Finally, the commandant said, "I have received news from Mexico City. A pardon for both you and Garcia will be forthcoming." Hector experienced a shiver of excitement. "It will cost a great deal of money to do this," the Commandant continued. Hector's optimism vanished, and he felt his stomach knot at this announcement. He had no money.

The commandant sat staring at Hector, looking for some sign of excitement or fear. There was none that he could see. He continued, "I have decided to pay this sum for your pardons. I consider it an investment toward my retirement." The commandant now had Hector's full attention.

"You have talked about gold that you have buried somewhere in California and that you would share it with me. You may keep your gold. I have a different offer for you." The commandant was again disappointed when Hector's emotions remained stoic. "I have been ordered to build a strong-room to be attached to this office. It seems that we are to become the waypoint for the transfer of gold shipments destined for Mexico City. I plan that after you are pardoned, you will return and rob me of this gold. I will, of course, be reprimanded and will lose my commission. But we will have the gold." The commandant was pleased to see a smile spread across Hector's face.

"Commandant Perez," replied Hector, "I cannot express to you how grateful I am. I am sure I speak for Garcia also. With your permission, I would like to be in charge of the building of the strong-room. This will give us many opportunities to discuss plans on how to do this."

"Yes, I think that is an excellent idea. I will get things going in Mexico City." The commandant reached down and opened a desk drawer and removed some papers. "In the meantime, here are the plans for the strong-room. Look them over and make a list of the materials that you will need. I want to begin construction as soon as possible."

As Hector took the plans, he thought, 'We will be free within a year, and with enough money to recruit and outfit good men. With the gold in California, I can live like an emperor. With any luck at all, I will have the pleasure of meeting up with and killing the gringo, Isaiah Crow.'

MEXICAN GOLD

Commandant Perez watched as the last of the two strongboxes of gold was placed in the secure room for safe keeping. The Captain, who was in charge of the guard detail protecting the gold shipment, turned to Perez and handed him some documents to sign. "I am happy to pass this responsibility off to you," said the captain, "It has weighed heavily on me getting it here."

Perez took the papers and went to his desk. He signed them, keeping a copy for himself. He gave the rest back to the Captain. "There you are. Now I can worry about it until the detail from Mexico City arrives to pick it up."

A short time later, Perez stood outside his office door. He returned the salute as the Captain led his guard detachment out through the gates of the prison compound. Perez returned to his office and his desk. Calling out loudly, "Guard!" The guard outside his door rushed in and stood at attention, waiting, "Find Chief Guard Sanchez and tell him I want to speak with him."

"Yes Sir," answered the guard, and rushed off to find the chief guard.

Perez opened his desk drawer and retrieved a bottle of tequila and two glasses. He set the glasses on his desk and opened the bottle of tequila. He filled one glass a fourth full and drank it down. There was a knock at his door. "Come," Perez called out.

Sanchez, a hulking beast of a man, entered the room. "Close the door and come have a seat," said Perez. Perez watched Sanchez as he walked across the room to the chair. 'Sanchez looks clumsy and dumb as a rock, but I know better,' thought Perez.

Perez filled the two glasses on his desk as Sanchez sat down. Perez handed the big man one of the drinks. "Tonight my friend, our lives will change forever. We will live like kings or hang like banditos."

Sanchez's thick hand wrapped around the offered glass, he waited as Perez pick up his glass, "Salud," said the commandant. Both men drank down their drinks.

Perez sat back in his chair and asked, "You have your men ready for tonight?"

"Yes, I have six I trust with my life. They will remain out of sight until the gold is loaded and then they will attack. Between my men and taking them by surprise, Camacho will not stand a chance."

Perez sat back in his chair. His stomach churned with trepidation and excitement over his decision to steal the gold. He and Sanchez had already agreed to get rid of Sanchez's six men after the robbery. Poor Sanchez had no idea that he too was being eliminated afterward. 'Such is life,' thought the commandant.

TRAITORS

On a hill overlooking the prison, Hector and Garcia stood by a freight wagon hitched to a four-horse team. Their mounts were tied to the back of the wagon. Garcia thought about how they were about to steal the gold shipment. Thanks to the commandant, both he and Hector had received pardons and were free men. They could ride away and start a new life, but the thought of the riches in the strong-room below was too strong. 'I have always been a bandit,' thought Garcia, 'Why should I stop now?'

Hector, unlike Garcia, never gave a thought to not stealing the gold. His plan, he thought was a good one. No one would ever suspect him.

Hector saw the gate of the prison open. "It is time my friend." Garcia and Hector climbed up onto the wagon. Garcia picked up the reins and snapped them over the backs of the wagon team and they started down the hill to the prison.

No one challenged them as Garcia drove the wagon to the commandant's office. Pulling the wagon up to the front door, Garcia stopped the team. Sanchez opened the door and allowed Hector and Garcia to enter. Inside, Perez was surprised to see just the two men. "Just you two?" asked Perez.

"There are four of us. We do not need any more to carry only two strongboxes. Besides, this way it is only a four-way split."

Sanchez looked at the commandant and winked. Perez said, "Then we had better get started." Perez produced a key and unlocked the door to the strong-room.

The four men stepped into the strong-room. From the light of the lamps, they could see the two metal strongboxes. Hector said, "You two grab one and Garcia and I will take the other one." With a nod of his head, Perez went to one of the boxes with Sanchez. They both grabbed a ring handle at each end of the strongbox and lifted it. Hector and Garcia picked up the other box and followed the other men out to the wagon. Between the weight of the iron boxes and the weight of the gold, the boxes were all that two men could carry. At the wagon, they loaded the boxes into the back and closed the tailgate. Perez turned to Sanchez and gave him the silent signal for his men to attack. From behind Perez, Hector drew a dagger and plunged the thin blade into the base of the commandant's skull, killing him instantly. Hector said, "Quickly, load him into the wagon. Garcia, search him for the keys to the strongboxes. Sanchez, go back to the office and lock everything and then come and join us. Hurry!"

Within minutes the robbers and the wagon were out the gate and gone.

The next day it was nearly noon before anyone knew that the commandant was not there. A search of the prison could not find the chief guard. The next in command was bewildered as to what to do when the guard detachment arrived from Mexico City. Under the supervision of the officer in charge, the door to the commandant's office was kicked open, and the entrance to the gold storage forced open. It was then that the officer in charge announced that Commandant Perez and Chief Guard Sanchez had stolen the gold of the government of Mexico. It would take two days to organize a search for the two rogue Mexican officers.

One day's ride from the prison, near the base of a mountain, the robbers stopped the wagon. Hector got two shovels from the wagon and handed them to Garcia and Sanchez. "Start digging a grave for Perez and a hole to hide the strongboxes. The ground here is soft, so it should not take long. I will open one of the boxes and get enough gold for each of us until we think it is safe to come back for the rest.

Hector went to the wagon and opened one of the boxes. Inside were gold bars. Reaching inside he took out two bars and closed and locked the box. Sanchez and Garcia finished with the digging, walked up to the wagon to get the boxes and the body. As the two men picked up one of the boxes, Sanchez saw there were only two bars of gold. He quickly dropped his end of the box, backed away and went for his gun. He was too slow, Hector shot him in the chest, and the big man fell dead to the ground. To Garcia, Hector said, "Come, we need to dig the hole deeper so we can bury them both. We will deal with the gold last."

Garcia reached over and dragged the body of Perez out the back of the wagon and onto the ground. What are your plans for when we finish here," he asked.

"When we finish here, we will head for California and round up some good men. Then we will go to the cave and retrieve the gold hidden there."

Garcia stood silently for a moment and asked, "With the gold, we have now, why risk going back for the bag of gold we buried?"

Hector smiled, "Because I buried a much larger box of gold further back in the cave that you knew nothing about. Between the bag you buried, the other box of gold and what we have here, we will give up this life. We shall live like emperors."

Garcia looked admiringly at Hector and thought, 'Here is a leader. Here is a man I can trust.' The two men turned and began dragging the bodies to their graves.

FIVE YEARS LATER

Francisca Crow cut a blossom from the bush with her pruning knife. She placed it in the basket, its handle looped over her arm. Laughter caught her attention. Looking toward the river, she saw her son playing with Ponto. Closing the blade of the knife, Francisca walked between the flowering bushes to the house. As she climbed the stairs to the porch, she saw Crow, mounted on Joker, approaching the house. She watched, taking quiet pride in the fact that he was her husband.

Crow, seeing his wife, stood in his stirrups. He removed his hat and waved it over his head in greeting. Nudging Joker in the ribs, he coaxed the mustang into a gallop.

At the river, both Jed and Ponto saw Crow and began running to meet him.

Crow rode up and leaped from his horse. Leaving her flower basket on the porch, Francisca ran down the stairs. Crow swept her up and kissed her on the neck and then full on the lips. They were nearly knocked over as they were enthusiastically greeted by Jed and Ponto.

Francisca, laughing said, "Welcome home, we missed you!"

Crow picked up his son under the arms and lifted him into the air. "You are getting too big to do this," said Crow, as he set the boy back down on the ground. Jed wrapped his arms around his father's waist, "I missed you."

Crow tousled the boy's hair with his hand and said to Francisca, "We did well. We sold all of the horses."

"Come into the house. Are you hungry?"

"Now that you mention it, yes, I'm starved."

That evening, after Jed was asleep, Crow and Francisca stepped out onto the porch and sat together on a bench. Francisca took her husband's hand in hers, "I am happy that you are home. We felt so alone without you."

Crow sat back, his head and back against the wall of the house. "I used to get the wanderlust. I would need to move, just to be moving. I needed to see what was on the other side of the mountain. Whatever I was searching for, I've found here…with you. I couldn't wait to get home."

* * *

Jedadiah felt the hand on his shoulder, waking him from his sleep. He looked up to see his father, smiling down at him. "Good morning, time to get up."

Without hesitation, Jed swung his legs out of bed and stood up and stretched. Looking out the window, he could see that it was still dark. He turned to speak to his father, but he was gone. Jed dressed and went looking for his father. He found him on the porch.

Crow greeted his son with, "Come on!" Jed watched a moment as his father went down the steps and began running. Jed raced after his father.

It was a little over a mile to where high on a hill, a large rock protruded from the ground. Crow stopped there and waited for his son to catch up. Jed was winded but pushed himself to reach his father.

Crow reached down and tousled the boy's hair. "You did right well, I'm proud of you. Now, this is what I want you to do each morning: I want you to run to this rock and back to the house. Before Jed could ask or even speak, his father raced off down the hill back to the house. A moment later, Jed ran down the hill chasing after his father.

No more was said about the running. Jed just got up each morning and ran to the rock and back. On his return, he would find his father waiting for him. It was two weeks later that Jed got up and saw his father waiting for him on the porch. Without a word, Crow signaled with his hand for Jed to follow and began running to the big rock. This time, Jed stayed with his father.

Crow did not stop at the rock but kept running. Slowly Jed fell behind, but his father kept running. Eventually, Jed slowed to nearly a walk. His sides hurt and he was gasping for air. His father returned to him. "Look around you and mark where you are. I want you to run to here and back every morning."

Jed looked around him. He noted a large tree and decided to use it as his new morning goal. He looked at his father and nodded his head. Crow smiled at his son, tousled his hair and took off running back to the house.

The running continued for months. Jed's body began to change, and his endurance increased. The routine changed one morning when upon Jed's return, Crow said, "Tell me everything you saw this morning."

Jed learned to become aware of his surroundings. If he named a bird or animal wrong, his father would correct him, but he never scolded him. Crow helped him and taught him tricks of observation. Perhaps it was because his father was a big man or perhaps it was the running, but Jedadiah Crow began to grow and fill out.

VENGANZA (VENGEANCE)

Crow finished saddling Joker and walked him to the house. He went up the steps to the porch and into the house. "Francisca," he called out, "I'm leaving now." Francisca came into the room. "Please be sure to invite my parents and Carlos to come and stay with us for a while. It would be nice to have the company."

Crow removed his hat, kissed his wife and said, "I won't forget to ask them, I promise."

Jed came into the room. "I wish I were going with you."

"I will only be there overnight then come right back. We are finishing plans for our trip to San Diego to sell our hides. I want you to work with Juan. He will teach you what you'll need to know to run the rancho."

"But, I have done this so many times already."

Crow placed his hand on Jed's shoulder and smiled. He kissed his wife again and went out the door. Inside they could hear the beat of Joker's hooves as Crow rode away.

Disappointed, Jed turned to his mother and said, "I will be with Juan if you need me."

* * *

In the moonlit hills east of the hacienda, a band of men led by Hector Camacho camped. It was late evening, and Hector called Garcia over. "Get your weapons. You and I will go to the cave and retrieve the gold."

A short time later, the two bandits rode along the tree line to the trail that led to the cave. Hector felt a wave of jealousy sweep over him when he saw the hacienda that Crow had built. There were herds of cattle and horses as far as the eye could see. 'The bastard,' he thought, 'this should have been mine.'

At the entrance to the box canyon, they found the gate. Dismounting, Garcia opened the gate. Hector rode through the opening leading Garcia's mount with him. Garcia closed the gate behind them and re-mounted his horse. They rode to the cave. In the moonlight, they saw horses moving about, curious about the two strangers.

The entrance to the cave loomed darkly in the moonlight. The two bandits dismounted and walked to the opening, finding ready-made torches. Garcia struck a fire and lit two torches. Handing one to Hector, they entered the cave.

It was not as they had left it. The table and benches were gone. A large pile of hay was stacked to one side with containers of oats. There were several saddles and tack. Garcia moved to where he had buried the sack of gold. The rock he had placed over it was gone. The bandit found a shovel leaning against the wall and began to dig. It didn't take him long to figure out the gold was gone. The two men looked into the empty hole, their anger growing. "Come on, follow me," said Hector as he led the way further into the cave. The two men, bending over because of the low ceiling, extended their torches in front of them as they peered into the dark hole. The strongbox was gone, the hole never filled in.

Rage filled Hector. He nearly struck Garcia with the torch in his frustration. Garcia saw the danger, turned and quickly walked back to the entrance of the cave. It took some time, but Hector gained control of his emotions and headed to where Garcia waited nervously by the horses.

Without a word, Hector took the reins of his horse from Garcia and mounted up. Garcia was sure he could feel the hate and anger radiating from Hector. They rode silently in the moonlight.

Back at their camp, Hector startled Garcia when he said, "We will ride in the morning to the gringo's hacienda, and we will get our gold. Send a couple of scouts out see how many men he has. Then we will know better how to attack."

HUNTING

It was early the next morning when LeRue rode up to the hacienda. Jed had just returned from his morning run. When he saw LeRue, he happily ran over to greet him.

"Jed, I'm going hunting, thought maybe you and your father would like to come along."

"My father has gone over to the Batista's and won't be back 'til late today, but I'd like to go. Come inside, I need to ask my mother first."

Inside the house, Francisca listened to her son plead rather than ask to go hunting with LeRue. "Yes you can go, but tell Juan, so he'll stay close to the house in case I need him. You will be gone overnight?" she asked LeRue.

"Yes, but I plan to be back around mid-day tomorrow."

"You be careful and good hunting."

ATTACK

LeRue and Jed had been gone just a few hours. Ponto, who was napping on the porch, stood up just as Juan was about to climb the steps. Ponto let out a menacing growl from his curled lips. "Amigo, why do you growl at me?" Then Juan realized the dog was looking past him to the east. As Juan turned, the first shot was heard followed by several more.

Juan ran up the stairs and into the house shouting, "Bandits, bandits! Arm yourselves. Francisca rushed down the stairs. "Juan, what is it, what is happening?"

More shots rang out along with the sounds of many running horses, followed by war-cries and the agonizing screams of wounded men. Juan turned to Francisca, "You must go to the root cellar in the woods. Hide there until I come for you. Go, go *now!*" Francisca turned and ran out the back door of the house and headed for the woods.

Rushing outside, Juan saw riders racing towards the house. Juan saw that many of the riders, having fired their muskets, now used swords or heavy bladed machetes. The riders were ruthless as they cut down running men with the sharp blades. A shot near the side of the house caused Juan to look to his left. Samuel had just lowered his musket to reload. From behind him, Raul came running with a gun in each hand and two possibles bags over his shoulder.

Raul ran up the stairs to the porch and handed Juan his musket and possibles bag. As Juan took the weapon and bag, Raul dropped to one knee and fired his musket. A bandit with a straw hat on his head charged the porch swinging a sword over his head. Juan snapped off a shot striking the bandit in the chest, flipping the man backward out of his saddle.

Francisca raced across open ground toward the woods. Ponto came out of nowhere and was now running alongside her. Francisca and the dog ran until the coolness of the woods wrapped around them. Francisca hurried to the door of the root cellar. She gripped the edge of the massive door and struggled to get it open. Managing to open it wide enough, she and Ponto entered the dank darkness of the cellar. The smell of fruits, vegetables, and moist dirt was thick. Francisca pulled the door shut. Her body was trembling with fear, as she listened to the muffled commotion outside.

It took a moment for Francisca to realize that the noise outside had ceased. The sounds of shouts and running feet outside the door to the root cellar became louder and louder. Francisca clutched Ponto, pulling him close for comfort. A shot rang out causing Francisca to flinch. Francisca nearly cried out when something slammed against the door.

"¡Tiro bueno mi amigo! ¡Oye, mirada, hay una puerta aquí! (Good shot my friend! Hey, look, there's a door here!)"

Francisca pulled back into the darkness clutching at the growling Ponto. Her fear nearly overwhelmed her when the door was ripped open. Two men stood in the doorway holding muskets to their shoulders, ready to fire. They cried out when Ponto tore loose from Francisca's grip and attacked the two men. Instinctively, one of the men shot at Ponto, but the bullet missed and struck Francisca in the side of the head. The other man beat Ponto in the head with the butt of his musket, knocking the dog to the ground where he lay bleeding. The two men looked down at the bleeding Francisca. One said, "She is alive. The bullet grazed her head. Let us take her to Hector."

Hector Camacho was standing in front of the house. He saw two of his men approaching; one had a woman draped over his shoulder. "Hector, look what we found hiding in the woods."

Hector walked over to the men as the woman was dropped to the ground. Hector was momentarily shaken when he recognized Francisca. "What happened, why was she shot?"

"Her dog attacked us, and when I shot at it, I missed. The bullet grazed her head."

Hector, with a menacing look, ordered, "Get some water from the river. Clean her, I want to question her."

* * *

Francisca slowly became aware of the pain in her head and then became aware of the shouting and chaos going on around her. Opening her eyes, she immediately closed them, the light of day striking like a dagger to her brain. A man's voice said, "She is awake."

A familiar voice asked, "Are you able to sit up?"

Shielding her eyes with her hand, Francisca opened her eyes. Looking down at her was Hector Camacho. "A stray bullet has struck your head. I think you will live."

Francisca said nothing. Closing her eyes, she turned her head away from the bandit leader.

"I don't have time for this!" Grabbing Francisca by her hair and jerking her upright, Hector shouted, "I want to know where the gold is that Crow stole from me!"

Hector, enraged by Francisca's silence, began violently shaking her. "Tell me where the gold is hidden, and you can live!"

Confused by the question, not knowing what Hector was asking about, Francisca responded by spitting in the face of her tormentor. Hector struck Francisca across the face breaking her jaw. The unconscious woman fell to the ground. "Bipin," shouted Hector, "Where is that damned Apache?"

A dark, bowlegged man with long black hair and a scarred face pushed his way through the crowd of men. He stood silently looking at Hector. "Bipin, I want to know where the gold is. We have little time. Use whatever means to get the answer from her."

Unseen by the bandits, three men moved through the woods surrounding the house. Juan, Samuel, and Raul having survived the initial attack had run into the woods in an attempt to rescue Francisca. They found the root cellar empty and now watched as a man tied Francisca spread eagle on the ground. "She is going to die, we cannot stop it," said Juan. "But I cannot walk away. I could never face Don Isaiah without having tried to save her. You must ride for help, I will distract them."

Samuel and Raul began to protest when a shout went up from the bandits. Ponto, one ear torn from his head from the strike of the musket stock, launched himself at the Indian's throat. Juan, seeing Ponto's attack, reacted. He jumped up, clutching a pistol in one hand and a machete in the other, and charged the bandits. Raul, seeing Juan's son Samuel follow his father, jumped up yelling his war-cry and followed.

RAGE

It was afternoon when Crow, returning home, smelled wood smoke. He saw the black spiral of smoke twisting its way into the sky. At the top of the hill, he could see by the amount of smoke the fire was big, and it was coming from where he lived. Kicking Joker with his heels, Crow sent him into a hard run. It was as if the horse knew there was something wrong and he put his heart into it.

Crow's concern grew the closer he got to the hacienda. He began seeing the bodies. His vaqueros had been slaughtered. He saw that most of the dead vaqueros had weapons in their hands. The hacienda, or what was left of it, had been burned, burned to the ground. There were bodies near the house, most were Crow's men, but some were of men he had never seen before.

Near the river, he found her; Francisca. She had been staked out on the ground, tied hand and foot. Her clothing stripped from her body, she had been butchered. Near her was the mutilated body of Ponto.

Sinking to his knees next to the body of his wife, Crow cried out his anguish. Tearing his shirt open, Crow drew his knife from his boot and dragged it slowly and painfully across his chest. His blood gushed from the cut, running freely down his stomach to the ground.

Standing, Crow slowly walked to the house where he found Juan, Samuel, and Raul. All were dead. It was evident by the bodies around them they had died fighting. Crow, protecting his face from the heat of the still burning fire, moved close enough to see there were bodies in the burned ruins of the house. 'One of those bodies must be Jed,' he thought. 'My son is also dead.' Crow returned to the body of Francisca. After cutting the ropes that had bound her, Crow dug a grave and buried her remains.

Crow picked up a handful of dirt and gritting his teeth, spread it across the cut in his chest, stopping the bleeding. He went to the river and drew a bucket of water and returned to what was left of his house. Kneeling, he scooped up some ashes into his left hand. With his right hand, he scooped some water from the bucket and mixed it with the ashes. Making a thick gray paste, Crow painted his full face with the gray ash paste. He then painted his arms and chest. He then went to Joker. After removing the saddle from Joker's back, he made handprints and other markings for war on the horse. Stepping back from Joker, Crow reached up and removed the net that held his hair. His thick black hair fell down past his shoulders. Removing his knife from his boot, he hacked off clumps of his hair, as was the tradition of the Crow who had lost someone he loved.

Taking Joker to the river, Crow let him drink. When the horse had had his fill, Crow picked up his rifle, adjusted the war-hawk in his belt and looped his possibles bag over his shoulder. Riding Joker bareback, he circled until he caught the trail of the men who had killed his family.

THE RIDE FOR HELP

It was the next day when LeRue and Jed returned. They were dumbfounded by what they saw. LeRue read the sign, as he circled around the burnt building. When he saw the stakes in the ground and the cut ropes, he was sure he knew what had happened to Francisca. Urging his mount further out and circling, he found the trail of the murderers. LeRue found what he was looking for; the prints of a single horse to one side. Crow was tracking the killers. LeRue returned at a gallop to where Jed stood silently staring in shocked silence at the ruins of what yesterday had been his happy home.

"Jed, we gotta ride to the Batista's for help. Your father has gone on the warpath. If we are to save him, we must ride *now*."

Without hesitation, Jed rushed to his horse and mounted up. LeRue and Jed rode as fast as their horses could run. When their horses tired, they mounted fresh horses they found grazing. LeRue looked over at the grim-faced youngster riding next to him and thought, 'You are your father's son, ain't no doubt.'

It was late afternoon when someone at the Batista's rancho saw LeRue and Jed coming and knew something was wrong by the way they were riding. A vaquero rushed to the house to summon the Batista's. They were at the front door when Jed and LeRue arrived. LeRue said to Hernando, I bring you bad news. Crow's hacienda has been burned to the ground. Everyone has been murdered, and Crow is alone and on the warpath. We must ride if we are to save him."

"Francisca, what of my Francisca?" wailed her mother.

"I am sorry Señora, she too was killed."

Hernando, keeping his emotions in check, turned to Carlotta who was now awash with grief, "Please take Carmen into the house. I must go now, please see to her."

With her arm around Carmen's shoulders, Carlotta guided her back into the house. Men were now rushing to the house, as word spread of what had happened. As the armed men gathered, LeRue stood in his stirrups to address them. "Don Isaiah is alone and tracking the killers of his family. I ask you to follow me, I will find the track, and we will ride to help him!"

Twenty men were riding with LeRue when they headed southeast in the hope of finding the track of Crow and the bandits. Vaqueros, who were working in the fields, saw them and joined up. LeRue rode hard, intent on finding the track. He didn't notice that Jed had not stayed behind. The grim-faced youngster, Jed Crow, rode in the back, out of sight of LeRue and the Batista's.

THE LEGEND RETURNS

EL HOMBRE CON EL HACHA (THE MAN WITH THE AXE)

Crow did not waste his horse by riding fast. He knew by the sign that the killers were not running. They were confident that no one would be following. As it grew dark, a three-quarter moon produced plenty of light for Crow to follow the bandit's trail. 'I figure eighteen to twenty,' thought Crow. 'They're headed southeast, probably gonna camp by the river.'

It was several hours later when Crow knew he had figured right. He found the bandits camped by the river. The bandits built several fires, thinking no one would be hunting them. Crow, looking ghostly in the moonlight with his gray painted face, watched them. He saw that the bandits had picketed their horses on a rope tied between two trees. Two guards were posted for the horses while three guards walked along the edge of the camp. Waiting until the moon had set, Crow silently began his attack.

In the early morning, fog covered the ground. Two bandits, going to relieve the men guarding the horses, moved through the knee-deep fog. One of them tripped and fell. The fallen man jumped to his feet shouting out, his voice echoing across the fog-shrouded ground. The second man ran over to see what was wrong when he fell over another body.

From within the camp, several men awakened to find the man next to him dead, his throat cut. Another shout came again from the horse guards when they realized all of the horses were gone.

Hector stood next to Garcia, "What the hell is going on?" he yelled.

Garcia pointing said, "Look." In the early morning fog, a lone rider faced them. His gray face was frightening in the foggy morning dawn. His gray painted chest and arms were covered in blood.

Silently, the ghostlike figure raised his rifle high over his head. The apparition spoke in a loud, clear voice that echoed across the misty river.

"I am Isaiah Crow, also known as White Crow! You have killed my family and destroyed my home. I have come to kill you."

The hair on the heads of the superstitious bandits stood on end as Crow began to chant his death song. Something he had not done since he was a Crow warrior. His powerful voice filled the air.

Hector shouted, "Kill him, he is only one man, kill him!"

Garcia raised his musket and fired, but his nervousness and the distance caused him to miss.

Crow finished his song and sat silently as the bandits fired at him. Their shots missed; fear causing them to fire wildly.

Crow raised his rifle to his shoulder and shot Garcia in the head. Hector flinched as Garcia's blood and brains splashed across his face. The Bandits continued to fire at the ghostly figure.

On a nearby hill, LeRue and the men of the rancho arrived just in time to see what was happening. Jed heard his father's voice and watched as the bandits fired at him. His father never flinched.

Isaiah Crow began to sing again. The sound of his death song drifted up the hill. Jed Crow didn't understand why it affected him so profoundly. But Jed kicked his horse in the ribs and charged down the hill yelling at the top of his lungs. LeRue couldn't believe his eyes when he saw Jed charge the bandits. With a loud whoop, LeRue drove his heels into his horse's ribs and charged down the hill after the boy. The rest of the men, swept up in the excitement, shouted out their war-whoops and charged down the slope.

Crow threw down his empty rifle, pulled out his war-hawk and charged the bandits. The bandits continued to fire at him. Some rejoiced to see him apparently fall from his mount. But when Joker crashed into the bandits, like magic, Crow reappeared on Joker's back swinging his axe. In fright, some men stood still, some tried to run. They all died as the axe from hell was swung by the vengeful Isaiah Crow.

When Crow saw Hector Camacho, he knew immediately why his family had been killed. Crow turned Joker toward Hector. A bullet struck Crow in the side, doubling him over for a moment. Then one tore into his leg. Crow's anger kept him focused on Hector who had just fired his weapon. Hector was frantically trying to reload his musket when Crow rode past the bandit. He buried his war-hawk into the top of Hector's head.

Hector Camacho was dead.

Another bullet knocked the already wounded Crow from his horse. Crow hit the ground hard and didn't move.

LeRue and the vaqueros, in a flank attack, began killing the bandits. It was over in minutes. As the vaqueros rode the battlefield dispatching any living bandits, Jed found his father. Dropping down off his horse he knelt next to his father. "He's alive," Jed called out, "He's alive!"

LeRue and the rest came running. With tears in his eyes, LeRue dropped down to his knees next to his friend, "You crazy son of a bitch, of course you're alive. Ain't no one can kill Isaiah Crow! Come on, help me make a travois, so's we can get him home."

As the battle-weary procession made its way home, the vaqueros talked about Isaiah Crow. They would always remember him as 'El hombre con el hacha (The man with the axe).'

RECOVERY

Hernando stood at the window staring out at the hills. "The Indians have been out there day and night. There must be a great number of them by the fires I have seen at night."

LeRue who was in the room with him said, "They are asking for the healing of Crow."

"Why do they do this, I have never seen such a thing."

"Crow is good to them, he gives them food when they need it and for some, a place to live. But most of all, he treats them as equals." Hernando looked again out the window and turning back to LeRue asked, "What do you think LeRue, do you think Crow will make it... will he live?"

"I can't say for sure, but I think it is important that he sees Jed if he does come around. He thinks Jed was killed too."

"Well, that boy has hardly left his side since we brought his father here," said Hernando. "Speaking of Jed, I never thought that one so young would have such courage. He charged down that hill leading us!"

LeRue replied, "Jed is like his father. He sees things, and while others hesitate, he's already doing something. It's a trait that's kept his father alive. I've seen it in Jed several times. Ain't no doubt, he's his father's son."

Several days after the battle, Crow opened his eyes. The first person he saw was his son Jed. Crow reached out and grabbed his son, pulling him roughly to his chest. Without shame, Crow cried. He released his pent-up grief at the loss of his wife and rejoiced that his son was alive. Jed managed to free his arms and hug his father. "Are you going to be alright poppa?"

Crow roughed Jed's hair and said, "Yes son, I'm gonna be alright."

After paying his respects to Crow, LeRue rode out to the Indian camp and told them the good news. The next day the Indians had disappeared as silently as they had appeared.

It took weeks for Crow to recover enough to get around without a walking stick and another month to regain his strength enough to ride.

As Jed watched his father's recovery, he became aware of a change in him. 'There is sadness that just doesn't seem to go away.' Jed thought, 'When mother died, something... a spark died in my father.'

HIS FATHER'S SON

LeRue sat in the cabin looking out a window. He, Jed and Crow now lived at the Batista's Rancho. Crow had decided not to rebuild, and LeRue's house would never be finished now that Juan and his men had been killed. Through the window, LeRue watched Crow ambling across the open yard. His gait was slow and his head bent down. 'He's dying inside, a little each day.'

A familiar figure moved from the shadows of one of the buildings. LeRue saw Jed watching his father. 'That boy has grown, sure is big for his age,' LeRue observed. 'I can see he's worried about his father. I think its way past time to put a stop to this.'

* * *

It was early one morning when Crow yelled in his sleep waking Jed. Jed looked over to see his father sitting up in his bed, his arms outstretched as if reaching for something. Throwing back his blanket, Jed went to his father. Crow now had a look of bewilderment on his face. He looked at Jed, tears silently rolling down his cheeks. "It was so real," Crow said in a whisper, "I talked to her and when I went to take her hand… she was gone."

Jed laid a hand on his father's shoulder, "It was a dream, only a dream." Crow's shoulders slumped under Jed's hand.

* * *

The door burst open, and LeRue rushed into the cabin, "Get the hell out of bed Isaiah Crow and get dressed. This bullshit is over!"

Jed could see outside through the open door. Five horses were standing in the light of the dawn. Three were saddled, and the two pack-horses appeared to be loaded to the limit. "Don't just stand there Jed, get your ass dressed, we're going for a ride! Come on Crow, its daylight in the swamp, time to get a movin."

Crow started to protest when Carlos came through the door, "He giving you trouble LeRue?"

"Naw, he just ain't awake yet." With that LeRue went to the dry sink and got a pitcher filled with washing water and came back to Crow's bed. "You can ride out of here dry, or you can ride out of here wet. But by God, Crow, you are gonna ride with us!"

Jed, who held his father in awe, watched wide-eyed as LeRue raised the pitcher, Crow yelled, "I'm coming, I'm coming!"

"Did you get ahold of Santiago?" LeRue asked Carlos.

"Si, he is on his way." Crow now fully awake looked menacingly at LeRue and Carlos just as Santiago stepped through the door. "Ah, amigo," he said to Crow, "there are four of us, and you are old and worn out."

"I'd make wolf meat of the lot of you," said Crow, "but what the hell, let's go."

For the first time in a long time, Jed heard laughter. As Jed got dressed, he felt the excitement of an adventure. He remembered something his father had said in the past: "There are times when a man just needs to see what's on the other side of the mountain."

Later, the four men and young Jed rode side by side. Crow and Jed rode in the middle. Jed's position had been decided on by the men before they started. They wanted to make sure that Jed could hear and be a part of the action. Carlos had told his mother and father, "We will be back when we get back." They both understood. Crow, the indestructible Crow, had been wounded by more than bullets. As she watched Carlos ride away, Carmen promised herself to pray for Crow and their safe return.

* * *

Crow, Jed, and the others had gone northeast into the mountains. It became cooler as they climbed through the passes. The grass was thick and green, and the game was abundant. The streams ran fast and cold. Santiago took them to a place where the brush was so thick over a part of the river; they could walk out over the water. Santiago cleared an opening in the brush and dropped a fishing line through the hole into the water. "My father brought me here to this place many times. There are deep holes in the riverbed where the fish like to hide." Suddenly, his line went taut. With a quick snap of his wrist, Santiago pulled a beautiful Golden trout up out of the hole. Holding the line up proudly so all could see his catch, he said, "I have my supper. I will go clean this and prepare my meal." With a grin, Santiago negotiated his way across the brush bridge and walked back to camp. "Guess we better get fishing if we want to eat. It's plain Santiago ain't gonna share," said Crow. A short time later they joined Santiago at the camp cook fire, each with his own fish.

As the fish cooked, Jed looked about him. They were camped near the river under a large tree. On one side, the massive mountains pushed their peaks into the sky. At first, Jed felt intimidated by their size. After looking carefully at them, he soon had an urge to climb them, 'To see what was on the other side.' Jed could hear his father's words in his mind.

Jed stood up. "I need to go wash the duck's feet," he said aloud, and without waiting for an answer headed for some brush away from camp.

Moments later, walking with quick steps, Jed rejoined the others. "I saw movement yonder, near that tree line, towards that tall peak over my shoulder. Pretty sure there are two maybe three men that way."

Carlos and Santiago quickly looked around. "Three," said Crow. "They've been on our trail for the last couple of days."

LeRue said, "I think one might be an Indian, the other two are gringos. Can't be up to any good following us up this high."

"I figure you're right. If they be friendly, seems like they'd a hailed us."

"What are we going to do?" asked Carlos.

"We've given them the chance to show themselves, and they didn't. While the three of you keep busy here in camp, LeRue and I will take a look-see when it gets dark. Keep your weapons close. They might be bandits."

Jed, his blood pumping with excitement, blurted out, "I wanna go too!"

LeRue smiled at the surprised look on Crow's face. "Hell Crow, you was younger than him when you went on your first Crow raiding party. Take him. I'll stay here in camp."

Now, fear tried to creep into Jed when he realized that his request had been accepted. He really was going to go. Closing his mind to his anxiety, he started thinking about what he needed to take with him.

It was dark when Crow and Jed belly-crawled out of the camp. LeRue banked the campfire in an attempt to make it difficult to see the number of men in camp. Stealthily, LeRue and the other men stuffed their bedrolls to make them look as though someone was in them. They crawled off and took up positions, being careful they wouldn't fire on each other in the dark.

Jed and his father stood up near some brush a distance from the camp. Each carried a rifle, a pistol, and a Bowie knife. Crow signaled with his hand for Jed to follow him. Crow began to trot, in a direction Jed thought was in the wrong direction. Soon, Crow stopped and looked up at the night sky bright with stars. He then looked over at the mountains. Getting his bearings, he again started running at an angle to where Jed felt the intruders were.

A short time later, Jed nearly ran into Crow when he suddenly stopped. Crow dropped to one knee, cupped his hands to his ears and listened. Jed copied his father, listening while he used his side vision as his father had taught him, "Don't look directly at what you are watching. Practice. You'll learn whether to use the left or right side. Look from the side of your nostril. If you look back past this area, there is a blind spot." Jed found the right side was his best vision.

Jed heard faint voices at the same time as his father. There were three men, Crow signaled to move closer. Through some scrub, Jed and Crow saw a campfire. Three men were sitting cross-legged around the fire.

Crow rolled, onto his side to face Jed. Reaching out he pulled the boy to him and whispered in his ear. "We'll move up close, and then we wait. I'll tell you when to make your move." Before Jed could speak, Crow rolled back on to his stomach and began crawling in the direction of the campfire. Jed followed. They laid in the dark listening to the men talk. As Crow and Jed listened, it became obvious from their conversation that the three men meant them no harm. Jed heard his father chuckle. Jed watched as his father cupped both hands around his mouth as if to holler, but instead, the sound of a night bird passed his lips. Around the campfire the three men became silent. Suddenly, all three pulled their rifles to them and laid flat on the ground. Crow again made the night bird sound, and then he spoke in a loud voice, "You are not welcome here!"

From the camp, Jed heard someone say in a loud voice, "Who the hell are you?"

"I am White Crow! I will lift your hair and eat your liver if you don't leave!"

There was silence. A voice from the camp asked, "Isaiah? Isaiah Crow! Is that you out there?"

Crow burst out laughing and stood up, "Cassidy, I never could fool you. Come on son, they're friendly."

As Jed and Crow entered the camp, he saw three men dressed in buckskins. Their long hair hung to their shoulders and beards covered their faces. One of the men, with massive shoulders and a thick waist, walked up to Crow and wrapped his arms around him. "God love ya Crow, but I thought you be dead! Ain't no one seen you in years."

Crow returned the greeting and held the big man out at arm's length. Looking at him he said, "Cassidy its right fine to set eyes on you again, and to know that you're alive. We thought you might be banditos when we snuck up on you."

Cassidy turned to his companions, "Crow, this here is Heinz and the other is McCarthy, good men all. But who be this with you? Do I see a resemblance?"

Crow placed his arm on Jed's shoulders bringing him forward, "This is my son, Jedadiah; named after Jedediah Smith who saved my bacon when we crossed the Mojave."

The men offered their hard callused hands to the youth. Jed shook each man's hand and asked, "Are you all Mountain Men?"

Cassidy speaking up said, "We be Mountain Men at heart, but the times are changing. The plews (beaver pelts) are few, and the big companies have all but run free trappers out of business." Cassidy then said in a lower voice, "Jedadiah got kilt. Comanche's got him when he was out lookin for water."

"He was a good man," said Crow. "He taught me a lot."

McCarthy asked, "You live close by do you?"

"A few days ride south west of here," replied Crow. "We plan to be here a week or so and then head back. You are welcome to come and stay if you like."

Before anyone could answer a voice called out of the darkness, "Cassidy you damned grizzly bear, how the hell are you? I thought you must be dead by now!" LeRue stepped into the light of the campfire. "Yee-haw, LeRue, as I live and breathe! I should have guessed if Crow was here you'd be close by. Cassidy lunged forward and picked LeRue up off the ground giving him a bear hug.

LeRue, his hat knocked back on his head, fought to get out of the big man's grasp, "Put me down damn it! It just ain't right to treat a man like that."

With loud merriment from all, Cassidy set LeRue down on his feet. "I thought I'd better come to take a look-see. These two been gone a spell," said LeRue, straightening his hat on his head.

"Come on," said Crow, "move over to our camp. We'll give you a hand with your kit."

After Carlos and Santiago were introduced to the three Mountain Men, someone opened a jug of spirits. Jed watched as the men loosened up because of the drinking and the stories began to flow. It was Cassidy who iced the mood, "So Crow, you're married?"

For Crow, Jed, Carlos, and Santiago, the sharp knife of remembrance struck them in the heart. For a brief time, they had been able to forget their pain. But now it came back, in all of its ugliness.

Santiago spoke, "There was trouble several months back. Crow's wife, Jed's mother, who was also Carlos's sister, was murdered by bandits. Their home was burned to the ground."

The three Mountain Men were silent as the reality of what they had been told sunk in. Jed felt his throat tighten and tears began to well up. 'Not in front of these men,' he thought. "Mr. Cassidy," asked Jed, "did you know the man named Buford? I've heard a few stories about him."

The men looked at Crow's son with admiration. The young man had gracefully changed the subject, saving Cassidy from any more embarrassment. Cassidy grasped the moment with both hands and said, "Buford, Buford was a friend to all; but you could never turn your back on him. He was a prankster who loved to fool people. There was always someone who was mad as hell at him."

Heinz spoke up, "Remember that time he put that dead rattler coiled up on your chest while you slept?"

McCarthy was laughing when he said, "Ole Cassidy lay there scared to move, thinking that rattler was alive and would bite him any second. Luckily, we came to Cassidy's camp later in the day. Otherwise, Cassidy would probably still be laying there!"

The laughter was contagious and changed the mood. Crow looked over at his son who was laughing with the rest of the men. 'Francisca would have been so proud of you,' he thought. Depression tried to envelop Crow, but he forced it out of his thoughts saying, "Remember when Buford snuck into the Crow camp one night and slipped a polecat into one of the tipis?"

McCarthy had tears in his eyes from laughter. "When the Crow found out who done it, whoo-wee Buford had to go into hiding; but they found him one day."

Jed asked, "Did they kill him?"

"Oh hell no," said McCarthy, "Indians, have a great sense of humor, love a joke. But they were embarrassed that he had gotten into their camp without being seen. No, Buford got a taste of his own medicine when several young men of the village found his camp one day while he was out. Well, these magpies (Crow called the boys 'magpies') spent the day hunting and returned that night. While Buford slept, they crept up on him. Each boy held a polecat. When they got close, they pointed the business end of the skunk at the sleeping Buford and then roughed up the skunk. Those polecats sprayed all over Buford. He could be smelt a mile away!"

LeRue, continued, "I hear-tell even his horses shied away from him."

The drink and the time without sleep finally caught up with them. Everyone curled up in their bedrolls and went to sleep. As Crow slept, Francisca came to him in his dream. Crow reached out to her, and as she went to take his hand, she disappeared.

Crow woke with a start, looking around with a dazed look on his face. Getting up from his bedroll, he picked up his moccasins and went over to a rock, sat down and pulled them on. Standing, Crow was startled when a voice asked, "Can I go with you?"

Crow saw Jed standing, fully dressed. "Yeah, sure, let's go."

Father and son left the camp, their grief slowly ebbing as they raced together across the open fields.

Two weeks later, the two parties split up. McCarthy, Heinz, and Cassidy headed north where the British were still successfully trapping. Crow, LeRue, Jed, Carlos, and Santiago headed for home. LeRue watched the four, Crow, Jed, Santiago and Carlos as they rode. 'This was good. They look more relaxed. It'll take time, but at least they are on their feet.'

WAR!

As time passed, the pain caused by the murders of Francisca and the others at the Hacienda Francita, became more manageable. Carlos and his father appeared more able to cope and move on. Carmen, however, sometimes slipped into moments of depression over the loss of her murdered daughter. Everyone thought Crow and Jed were handling the deaths well, but no one saw them when they were alone.

In their cabin, Jed and Crow silently began to fix their evening meal. A knock at the door got Jed's attention. He went to the door and opened it to find a boy holding a cloth covered platter.

"My mother said she cooked too much and thought you might like to have this." Lifting the tray, he offered it to Jed.

Jed took the tray and said, "Tell your mother 'mucho gracias." With a shy smile, the boy turned and ran off.

"The widow lady sent us another tray of food," Jed said to his father as he set the tray on the table. Crow lifted the cloth and looked at the food. In a soft voice, Crow said, "Right nice of her. You go ahead and eat; I think I'm gonna wait a bit, maybe lay down first."

Jed watched as his father went to his bed. Crow sat down and began pulling off his boots. 'He's getting thin,' Jed thought. 'He hardly eats, and though he's tired, I know he hates to sleep because of the dreams.'

Just as Jed decided to try and convince his father to eat something, he heard people shouting outside. Then someone was hammering on the door. Jed rushed to the door and pulled it open. Carlos was standing there, "It is war!" he said, "We are at war with America!"

Crow got to his feet and came to the door, "Carlos, what are you saying?"

"Mexico and America are at war," said Carlos, stepping into the room. "There is much fighting."

"Come, sit at the table and tell us what you have heard."

Just as Jed was closing the door, LeRue showed up and came in, "What the hell is going on?"

"There is war between Mexico and America," replied Jed.

Carlos said, "The courier told us that Mexican soldiers attacked American soldiers, killing some of them. The trouble seems to be over the Americans deciding to accept Texas into the union."

Crow asked, "How will all of this affect us here?"

Carlos, with a look of concern on his face, replied, "I don't know my friend, we are a long way from the troubles, I would think we are safe."

THE COST of WAR

The change came fast to California and the ranchos. The American settlers revolted in California against Mexico, raising the Bear Flag and proclaiming independence. But that didn't last long. A small invasion force of American soldiers sailed into Monterey Bay and raised the American Flag, claiming California for America.

There was some resistance, but in a short time, California became a territory of the United States. Just months before California was granted admission into the Union, gold was discovered.

California and its inhabitants would be forever changed. Soon, the rancheros had to prove to the American government that they owned their land.

Hernando Batista sat at the table in the dining room holding his head in his hands. Stacks of papers lay on the table. Carmen came into the room. Seeing the state her husband was in, she went to him. "What is wrong?" She asked.

Hernando, hearing her voice sat up and smiled. "I have been notified by the new government to show proof of ownership of our land. I have spoken to the other rancheros, and they too must do the same."

Carmen sat down next to her husband. "We have the land grants from the Mexican government proving the land is ours."

"Yes that is true, but the Americans want detailed measurements of the land. They say that they will honor the grants but need proof. I have sent Carlos and Santiago out to find the landmarks. Crow and Jed are with them. In the meantime, I must hire a surveyor to come and officially record the boundaries of the land. My problem is we have little money. We have always lived by barter and exchange of goods. I have learned it costs a great deal of money to hire surveyors and to go to court. We will need attorneys and translators as well. They all require payment in cash."

Carmen placed her hand on Hernando's arm, "We will find a way. When Carlos comes back with the locations of the landmarks, we will decide what to do then."

* * *

Carlos and Crow rode together across an open field. Carlos brought his mount to a stop. Crow stopped next to him. Carlos pointed with his finger, "See that large rock, the monument should be close by." Carlos and Crow urged their horses in the direction of the rock.

* * *

A day's ride from them at the far end of the rancho, Santiago, and Jed were on foot, leading their horses by the reins as the two searched for a land monument. "It should be right around here," said Santiago. "It will be a large pile of cattle skulls."

Jed moved away from Santiago to search a grassy area. "Over here," Jed called out. "I think I've found it."

Santiago, leading his horse, walked over to where Jed stood in the tall grass. As he approached, he could see a waist-high stack of skulls. "Yes, that is it. So from the monument at the hacienda to here is one day's ride. From here, we must head west using that mountain peak as our guide. We should meet your father and Carlos in one day at the next monument. Let us cut a limb from that tree over there and use it as a marker. I will tie my scarf to it so it will be easier to find."

One day later, in the early morning, Santiago and Jed spotted Crow and Carlos camped under a large tree close to a stream. The two men stood when they saw two horsemen. When Crow recognized his son, he removed his hat and waved it above his head. Jed and Santiago urged their horses into a gallop to join them. "I see you two are working hard," said Santiago, as he and Jed dismounted.

"We have been here for a full day and cannot find the monument," said Carlos. It has must have been destroyed over the years, possibly by animals."

Crow asked, "Did you find yours?"

"Si we found it and have marked it. Carlos, we know the general location of this marker, let us gather rocks and make a new monument. Who is to know? We know it was here. We are not trying to gain land or to lie."

Carlos stood with his hands on his hips thinking. Crow said, "I think that's a good idea, we are not trying to fool anyone. Besides, the markers were laid out by how far a rider rode in a day. We have done the same. Santiago and Jed found us using the other marker as a starting point."

Carlos replied, "I think you are right. We will gather rocks and make a new monument. But first, let us eat, and then we work."

Two days later, Santiago, Jed, Crow, and Carlos returned to the Batista Hacienda. Hernando was pleased with their report and gathered the documents together to present to the court in San Diego.

Carlos came into the dining room where his father was seated at the table the gathered documents in a leather portfolio in front of him. "Papa, you look worried. I thought you had everything you needed."

Fernando looked up at his son. "I am missing one thing. I do not have the money to pay for an attorney or for a surveyor. Don Sanchez has just returned from San Diego. He was unable to pay. He is considering leaving and returning to Mexico. He has family there."

Carlos replied, "Things move slowly within the government. It will take time for them to demand proof of ownership. More and more Americans are coming here. They all want land. Perhaps we can sell some to them. That will give you money to go to court."

Hernando leaned back in his chair thinking. After a moment of thought, he said, "I think you have a good idea. Perhaps you would go and find someone to buy some of our lands. We will want cash or gold. No promissory notes."

"I will leave tomorrow and go to San Diego. I will look for someone who wishes to buy land."

Later, Carlos saw Crow near the corral and called to him, "Crow, wait! I wish to speak to you."

Crow walked over to Carlos, "What is it, amigo?"

"I am leaving for San Diego tomorrow. Would you like to come with me? Perhaps Jed would like to ride along."

"Sure, you have business there?"

"I must sell some of our lands. It will cost a great deal to prove the ownership of our land to the Americans. I will seek buyers in San Diego."

Crow looked at his friend and then clasped him by the shoulder, "I will go with you, my friend. But first I want to meet with you and your father in private. Perhaps you would come to my place, and we can talk."

"I think we can do this; perhaps after dinner?"

"That will do just fine; I'll meet you after dinner."

As Carlos walked back to the hacienda, he heard the hoof beats of a horse. Turning, he saw Crow riding at a gallop, headed west. 'I wonder where he is going?'

After dinner, that evening, Carlos and his father stood at the door of Crow's cabin. Before Carlos could knock, the door opened, and Crow invited the two men inside. "Have a seat at the table. Would you care for a drink?" Both Carlos and Hernando declined the drink as they sat down at the table.

"What is it that I can do for you?" asked Hernando.

Crow went to the corner of the room and retrieved a leather bag. He brought it over and placed it on the table. Crow also took a seat. "Remember the cave where the bandits were camped?"

Both Carlos and Hernando nodded their heads yes, "Si," said Hernando.

"I found this buried in the cave. I hid it thinking someday it would prove useful." With that, Crow tipped the bag and gold coins spilled across the table. Both Carlos and Fernando were astonished by the wealth laid out before them. "I want you to use this to claim your land. There should be more than enough for you to hire the proper people to represent you in court."

Hernando reached across the table and picked up a gold coin. He cupped it in his hand and felt its weight. When he looked at Crow, his eyes glistening, close to tears, "You have saved my family many times. How can we ever repay you?"

"You have more than repaid me over the years. We are family, and we protect our own. I ask only that you not mention where it came from."

"I think I would like that drink you offered," said Hernando.

"Si, I also would like one," said Carlos.

Crow stood and went to a cabinet and got a jug and three cups. Placing the cups on the table, he filled them. The three picked up their drinks, and Hernando said, "Salud!"

* * *

Later, as Hernando and Carlos crossed the yard, Hernando seemed to trip and fall. Carlos dropped to one knee to help his father, but there was no response. "Crow," shouted Carlos, "Crow!"

Crow, hearing his name, rushed from the cabin to Carlos and his stricken father. Crow knelt next to Hernando and felt his neck with his fingers. "I am sorry my friend. Your father has died and is now with God."

A RETURN TO MEXICO

The shock of the sudden death of Don Hernando Batista had delayed any thoughts of going to court about the land. Carlos was afraid that he might lose his mother, but she proved to be much stronger than anyone thought. "I want time to think before you go to court," she told Carlos. Life went on for nearly a year, during which there were reports of gold strikes in the north and that people were pouring into California in the hope of finding riches.

One day, Carmen had Carlos ask Crow to come to the hacienda. When Crow arrived, Carmen asked him and Carlos to join her in the dining room. Carmen sat in her husband's chair as her son and Crow took chairs across from each other. "I have decided to return to Mexico. I have family there and will live with them. Carlos has told me that he will go with me. So, Senor Crow, I will leave the rancho in your hands to do with as you please. I cannot transfer ownership to you as we have no papers showing that we own it. I think it will take a year or more for the new government makes demands as to ownership. During that time the place is yours to do with as you please.

Carlos reached under the table and brought out a bag Crow recognized as the one he had given to Hernando. "My mother wants you to have this back as she will not need it for the courts."

Crow reached across and pushed the bag back toward Carmen. "Señora, I gave this to your husband to use as he saw fit, I want you to do the same. This change you propose will be expensive. As I told Don Hernando, we are family, and we take care of our own.

Carmen looked at the young man who had come into their family. He had saved all of their lives and had loved her daughter and given them a grandson. Carmen reached out and took Crow by both his hands, "You are like a son to me. Hernando loved you like he loved Carlos; you are part of our family. I will ask you now if you think Jedadiah would like to go with us."

Crow was surprised by his emotions in reaction to the question. He had never given any thought to Jed leaving him. But Jed was her grandson. "Jed and LeRue are off hunting and will return in a few days. I will ask him and have an answer for you then."

LeRue and Jed returned earlier than expected. When Jed had settled in Crow told him about his grandmother's request. "No," he said "I don't want to go to Mexico. I want to stay here with you."

"I will let her know," said Crow.

"I think I should tell her. I want her to know that it is my decision and that I love her."

Crow look at his son with admiration, 'I am proud of you. Your mother would have been proud of you too,' he thought. "Yes, I think that it will be better if you tell her."

* * *

It took a month for the Batista's to get ready to leave. When it came time to move, people from the surrounding area came to wish them well. Don Sanchez and his family decided to go with them. Carlos, mounted a horse trained by Crow during better times, removed his sombrero and said, "Adios Amigo, may God be with you!" After they had gone, the rancho seemed to lose its spirit. Work at the rancho went on, as usual. Crow, Jed, and LeRue moved into the hacienda, but the life and the magic that had been the Hacienda Batista was gone.

ENDINGS AND BEGINNINGS

Nearly two years passed since Hernando died and the Batista's left for Mexico. It was on a bright spring morning when LeRue returned from one of his many trips. Crow and Jed were saddling their horses when they saw LeRue ride in.

"Well hello stranger," greeted Crow, "Where have you been off to this time?"

LeRue climbed down from his horse and said, "I found me a job, I have."

"A job!" exclaimed Crow, "You gonna work for someone?"

Jed inched in closer, "He's been drinking," said Jed, "I'm sure of it."

"I ain't been drinking. A man offered me good money to bring a wagon train from Missouri to California. They also want me to teach the greenhorns how to survive out here. He asked me if I knew anyone else that was as knowledgeable as me that might want to come along. I told him I knew one man that was near good as me that might."

Crow looked at his friend with hooded eyes, "You figuring on asking me, LeRue?"

"Sure, why not? Let's be honest Crow, this place ain't the same no more. Besides, I've got the itch."

Jed felt excitement grow within him as he listened to his father and LeRue talk. Maybe he'd get a chance to go someplace new and different. His hopes were dashed when Crow said, "I don't think so, and I don't want to take care of no folks for what... six months on the trail! Hell no, I don't want no part of it."

LeRue winked at Jed, and then with a grin on his face, he said to Crow, "Well you think on it. I hear tell bunches of the Mountain Boys have taken up leading trains. They'll all be there in Saint Louis. I can't wait to see some of them again."

"Yeah, well you go. Me, I'm gonna stay here." With that, Crow mounted up, "You comin' Jed? We've got work to do."

As Jed mounted up and joined his father, he gave LeRue one last look. LeRue was grinning, and he winked again at Jed. "I'll see you when you get back. Gonna get me some sleep."

Jed and his father rode in silence. The creaking leather of their saddles and soft sounds of their horse's hooves on the sandy soil were the only sounds. It was Jed who broke the silence. "I'll miss LeRue."

Crow pulled back on his horse's reins and came to a halt. Jed turned his horse and faced his father. "I have been thinking about something off and on for some time now," said Crow. "I would like you to meet my father and mother; perhaps live with them a spell. What do you think?"

Jed started to answer but thought better of it. "You think on it; no rush. But if you decide to go, LeRue and I will drop you off on our way to Saint Louis."

Jed remembered the wink that LeRue had given him when his father had said no to his proposal. "How long would I be with your father and mother?"

"I'm thinking it'll be over a year. The time it takes us to get to Saint Louis and then to California which will be six months or so. Then the time it will take to get back to get you."

Jed looked at his father. He remembered the many stories of his childhood with the Crow and his father's admiration of his adopted mother and father. "I think I'd like that. From what you've told me, I could learn a lot."

"Well let's get to work. We'll talk to LeRue when we get back."

GOING HOME

Crow, Jed, and LeRue were camped in a valley of the Yellowstone. Jed, like his father and LeRue, was dressed in buckskins; a gift from his father. LeRue had given him two pairs of moccasins. Jed thought he had never seen a place so beautiful and exciting. Wildlife was in abundance, and there were places where steam came out of the ground.

LeRue brought the pack horses around to the camp. The three began loading their kits onto the pack saddles. Crow stopped a moment and said, "I figure about two, maybe three more days, and we can start looking for where my people are camped. They'll more than likely be at a buffalo jump this time of year. We'll head there."

"Buffalo jump?" asked Jed.

Crow replied, "It's a cliff. The warriors will hide close to a herd of buffalo. Near the edge of the cliff, one of the young men of the tribe will wear a buffalo robe. He'll be close enough to the herd so the buffalo will see him. On signal, all the warriors will stand up moving the heard. The boy dressed in the robe will start running towards the cliff. When the herd sees him, they will follow him. Near the edge of the cliff, the boy will dodge to one side and hide in a cleft in the rocks. The buffalo will run past him and go over the cliff. After the last one goes over the edge, another group of warriors down below will finish off the animals still alive."

"The one wearing the robe must be brave to do such a thing," said Jed.

With a smile, Crow replied, "They are all brave, or they wouldn't be called Crow."

* * *

Crow was off a bit on his calculations. It took them four days to find where the tribe was camped. From a hill, Crow and the others looked down on the village. Crow reached up behind his head and removed the binding holding his hair. The long black mane fell past his shoulders. "Something has happened," Crow said. "There aren't as many tipis as there should be. We'll go in slow, let em know we're coming."

THE HOMECOMING

Broken Leg moved through the village. The smell of raw meat and blood from the buffalo kill was thick in the air. The camp dogs growled and fought over scraps thrown to them by the children. The women scraped the buffalo hides while others sliced meat into strips and hung them to dry in the sun. Suddenly the dogs stopped fighting and began barking and then began running.

The warriors took up their weapons when they saw three men riding into camp. Several mounted their war-ponies and raced to meet the strangers.

Crow held up his hand signaling Jed and LeRue to stop. They waited for the warriors to arrive.

Crow stood in his stirrups so the braves could see him. The Crow warriors arrived in a cloud of dust, war-cries and barking dogs. One of the warriors held up his hand halting the others. The warrior urged his pony forward until he was next to Crow. "White Crow, we thought you were dead."

Without another word, he turned his mount and raced back to the camp. Broken Leg stood near his lodge when the warrior rode up and jumped from his mount. "White Crow has returned! Your son is home!"

Broken Leg, without hesitation, mounted the pony and race out of the village. Crow saw him coming and rode out to meet him. Both men dismounted and greeted each other. "I thought you were dead," said Broken Leg. "It has been many seasons since you left."

"I followed the sun to a place called California. I was married, but my wife was killed. I have brought my son, your grandson, to meet my parents.

Broken Leg looked past Crow to the young man in buckskins. Broken Leg left Crow and started towards Jed. Jed watched the old man, who moved with a grace that spoke of his physical strength. Jed dismounted and met the old warrior halfway. Broken Leg eyed the handsome young man before him. 'He is big and strong like his father,' he thought. 'He honors me by dismounting.'

Broken Leg placed his hands on Jed's shoulders, "Welcome, son of White Crow. I am called Broken Leg. I am your grandfather."

"I am Jedadiah Crow; my father has told me much about my grandfather. I am proud to meet you."

"Come, we will go to my lodge, we have much to talk about."

LeRue had already dismounted, when Crow waved him over. "This is LeRue; we have been friends for many seasons and have ridden the warpath together. He has saved my life many times."

"Welcome LeRue, and thank you for making it possible for my son to come home."

"I too have heard the stories of Broken Leg. I am proud to meet you."

Grinning, Broken Leg turned to White Crow and said, "You talk a lot."

Crow laughed along with his father as the others looked on. "Come, we go now," said Broken Leg.

In Broken Leg's tipi, the men sat on leather seats arranged around a fire pit in the center of the floor. Crow asked his father, "Where is my mother, what has happened?"

Broken Leg's face showed no emotion, but his eyes did. "Three seasons ago the white man's disease (smallpox) swept through most of the tribes, killing many. It took your mother and many in our tribe. We are few now compared to when you lived with us."

Broken Leg continued, "We moved many times before we were free from the white man's death."

There was silence as Crow and the others thought about what had been said. Crow broke the silence, "Father, LeRue and I are going to Missouri. We will be gone for at least one season. I would like to leave Jed with you to learn the way of the Crow."

Broken Leg looked at Jed, studying his face. "I am pleased that you have not forgotten us and our ways, White Crow. What does your heart tell you, Jed?"

Jed gathered his thoughts before he spoke and then said, "My father has told me a great deal about his life with the Crow. I have seen how others respect him and I know he is known as a great warrior where we come from. I ask you grandfather, to allow me to live with you and to learn the way of the Crow."

Broken Leg turned to Crow and said, "Your son speaks as a man, he honors you, and he honors me. The tribe and I will teach him what we know until you return."

* * *

LeRue and Crow stayed for a week before they made ready to leave for Missouri. During the week, old friendships within the village were renewed by Crow. Many stories recounted around the campfires as Jed listened intently. Even LeRue, who had been with Crow for years, was impressed by the stories about his friend.

As Crow checked the load on his packhorse, Jed watched. Finished, Crow looked at Jed, "We will return in about a year I figure. I want to know that this is something you really want to do. It will be a way of life different from what you are used to."

"I'm looking forward to it. I like Broken Leg, and I have met two braves that seem to want to be friends."

Crow came around the packhorse and took his son by the shoulders and looked him in the eye. "I have always been proud of you. But I want you to know that your mother and I love you."

'He thinks of my mother as still being alive,' thought Jed. "I love you both also."

Crow dropped his hands from Jed's shoulders. Broken Leg and LeRue rode up leading Jed's horse. "You ready to go?" asked LeRue.

"Yup," said Crow. He went to Joker and mounted up. Jed went to his horse and mounted up. Together, the four men rode out of camp. Soon, warriors from the village joined the group until thirty men rode together in silence. Two miles out of the Crow village, Crow and LeRue rode on alone, as Jed and the Indians watched in silence. A short distance away, Crow and LeRue stopped and turned back to face the group of Crow warriors. Standing in his stirrups, Crow held his rifle above his head. The warriors silently raised their weapons above their heads. Lowering his gun, Crow and LeRue turned around and rode away. The warriors, with Jed riding next to his grandfather, turned their horses and headed back to the Crow encampment.

SAINT LOUIS MISSOURI

It took Crow and LeRue nearly two months to get to Saint Louis, Missouri. They found a city that had grown to almost 80,000. A far cry from the town of 5,000 the last time they had been there. "Jumping-gee-horse-a-fats," exclaimed LeRue. "I ain't never seen so many people!"

Crow craned his neck to gawk at the buildings and then back to the street filled with wagons, carriages, and people on horseback. "Where in the hell did they all come from?" asked Crow, to no one in particular. A short distance away, the high pitched sound of a riverboat whistle made their horses skittish.

With the directions from a helpful pedestrian, Crow and LeRue found Quintin Arsenault, the man they were looking for. Quintin Arsenault was a Frenchman who worked for the Hudson Bay Company. As the trapping business began to wane, the Hudson Bay Company started, for a price, to assist people wanting to go to California. LeRue greeted Quintin in French, "Bonjour Quintin, il a été de nombreuses années depuis notre dernière rencontre (Hello Quintin, it has been many years since we last met)."

"Bonjour LeRue, quand je t'ai entendu venir, je n'ai vraiment pas cru que ça pourrait être toi! (Hello LeRue, when I heard you were coming I truly did not believe it could be you!)"

LeRue turned to Crow, "Quintin, this is my partner, Isaiah Crow. We teamed up shortly after I left Hudson Bay. We have lived the last several years in California."

Quintin stepped up to Crow and offered his hand. Crow took the offered hand and felt the strength in it. Toe to toe, Quintin was as tall as Crow, something Crow didn't experience often. "It is a pleasure to meet you, sir," said Crow.

"Come," said Quintin, "I will take you to the wagon grounds. They are a few miles outside of the city. Our wagon master is Dubois, also from Hudson Bay. I think you know him LeRue."

LeRue nearly stopped his horse when he heard the name, Dubois. 'That son of a bitch,' thought LeRue. 'I cannot wait for Crow to meet him. This should be interesting.'

The three men could hear and smell the wagon grounds. There were twenty Conestoga wagons and over 100 hundred people along with 80 mules and nearly fifty head of cattle. Crow could not believe the stench of human and animal waste. LeRue looked at Crow and saw the anger on his face.

Quintin led the two mountain men to a small building separate from the group of wagons. Knocking on the door, Quintin entered followed by Crow and LeRue. Inside, the smell of sweat and dirty clothes filled the windowless room. Sitting at a table was a man with food and other debris clinging to his thick black beard. His thick hairy fingers held a whiskey bottle in one hand and a glass in the other. Quintin wrinkled his nose at the stench.

Dubois stood up eyeing the two mountain men, "So these must be the so-called scouts we have been waiting for?"

"This is Isaiah Crow and LeRue, who I think you know from our trapping days," said Quintin.

Dubois eyed LeRue. Recognition began to work through the whiskey-induced fog that shrouded his brain. Dubois came around the table. He walked up to LeRue and struck him in the face, knocking him to the floor. Before Quintin could react to the attack, Crow hammered Dubois in the jaw with his fist, dropping him to the ground. Crow drew his Bowie knife and was about to finish Dubois, when LeRue called out, "No Crow, he ain't worth it!"

Crow looked back at LeRue lying on the floor, blood running from his nose. He turned back to Dubois who was beginning to try to stand. Crow returned his knife to its scabbard. Reaching down he grabbed Dubois by the shirt front and jerked him to his feet. "If you want us to work for you," Crow said to Quintin, "you get rid of this man." Crow looked at Quintin waiting for an answer.

Quintin hesitated only a moment and then said, "Dubois, collect your kit and get out. When you sober up, you come and see me for your pay."

Dubois steadied himself on his feet and then said to Crow, "We will meet again, and it will turn out differently."

"You are right," said Crow, "If we meet again, I will kill you. You live only at the request of LeRue."

Crow, still holding the front of Dubois shirt, pushed and then let go, sending Dubois across the room to slam into the wall.

Quintin said, "Let us leave. We will go find the leader of the wagon train, who was elected by the immigrants."

As the three men walked past the wagons, the flies swarmed around them. Crow said to Quintin, "if we don't get these people out of here there will be a cholera epidemic that could easily pass on into the city. I have seen this before but not on this scale."

Just then a small, slender man wearing spectacles approached them and said in a thick accent, "Mr. Arsenault, I must demand that you get our people underway. We cannot stay in this filth!"

Quintin, without blinking an eye replied, "Nowak, I want you to meet your new wagon master, Mr. Crow. As soon as he has a chance to inspect the train and speak to your people, you will be underway."

LeRue looked at his friend with a grin, "You've been promoted before you even started amigo."

Crow looked at the small man standing before him, 'He seems to be intelligent and is concerned for his people. He was elected by them, so he must be respected by them.' Crow offered his hand to Mr. Nowak. "Please tell your people to get ready to move out and then bring them together so I can speak to them."

Nowak took Crow's hand and shook it. "Thank you, Mr. Crow. I will do as you say."

The three men watched as Nowak walked away. Swatting at flies, Quintin said to Crow, "Thank you, something had to be done, and you looked like the solution."

"I understand your man will meet us in San Diego. Before we leave, I want a letter from you telling him of my position and the difference in pay."

Quintin replied, "While you are getting things in motion here, I will go and write the letter and have it here before you leave."

Crow turned to LeRue, "I need you to head out and find us a place to bed down for the night. I figure we won't get far today, but we need a place near water and away from here."

"I'll meet you down the road after I find a place." With that LeRue mounted his horse and galloped away.

* * *

Crow saw a young man walking along the wagons. "Hey there!" Crow called out.

The boy, seeing Crow, walked over to him, "Yes, sir?"

"I need some help. Can you take my two pack horses over there by the other stock? I have to talk with Mr. Nowak."

"Who are you, sir?"

"My name is Crow, and I'm your wagon master." Crow pulled his possibles bag around, opened it and pulled out a coin. "I want you to take this for your trouble, and you have my thanks."

The boy's face lit up at the sight of the coin. "Thank you, Mr. Crow! I'll take care of it for you."

Crow, his rifle in his right hand and Joker's reins in his left, rode down the line of wagons. Some immigrants were hitching their mules to their wagons while others checked the security of items tied to the sides. Crow spotted Nowak and called out to him, "Mr. Nowak?"

Nowak walked over to Crow, "We are nearly ready Mr. Crow."

"Yes, I see that. Your people are well organized."

"I was in the Polish military before I became a teacher. It has helped me in teaching everyone how to get ready."

Crow asked, "Do you have any books with you, Mr. Nowak?"

"Yes, I have several."

"I have a few with me also. Perhaps we can share and read something new while we travel."

Nowak looked at the big man dressed in buckskins and thought, 'Never judge a man by the way he looks.' "I would be happy to do just that. Perhaps tonight when we stop we can talk more."

"I'll look forward to it," replied Crow. "Let me know when you are ready for me to talk to everyone."

An hour later, everyone was gathered in front of the lead wagon. Crow climbed up onto the wagon and stood on the seat so everyone could see and hear him. "My name is Isaiah Crow. I am your wagon master. My scout LeRue and I will take you to your destination, San Diego. We have traveled this trail in the past and lived the last several years in California. I will try to prepare you as we travel for your new life in California. As we travel, there will be hardships and danger that I'm familiar with. I will tell you what to do, and I expect you to do as I say. If any of you think you can't follow my directions, you will be left here. It will save me from telling you to leave the train. Drivers, go to your wagons, and we will get started. Those in charge of stock, get 'em moving."

The sounds of mules, cattle, people and creaking wagons filled the air as the wagon train began to move. Crow, mounted on Joker, rode up and down the line of moving humanity watching for possible problems. All but the drivers walked. The rest, men, women, and children, walked alongside the wagons. Off to one side of the train, herders wielding long staffs moved the cattle while men on horseback watched for strays. Crow, satisfied that all was well, moved to the head of the train. Mr. Nowak arrived on horseback joining Crow. "Thank you, Mr. Crow. I thought we would never get started."

Crow looked back over his shoulder at the wagons and then back to Nowak. "We won't travel far today. LeRue is scouting for a place for us to stop and get to know each other better. I'll want to look at your constitution and your written rules."

"I will have them ready for you when we stop." Nowak touched the brim of his hat with his forefinger in a casual salute. Turning his horse, Nowak rode back to the wagons.

FIRST COUP

From the crest of the hill, Jed and five other Crow youngsters watched a Sioux encampment below them. One of the boys silently pointed to a herd of more than 100 horses. The others nodded their heads in understanding. They then eased down the back side of the hill and disappeared into the woods.

Jed wore traditional Crow clothing: leggings, loincloth, and a leather shirt. On his feet, he wore a pair of the moccasins that LeRue had given him. Each of them was armed with a war-club and a knife. Jed reached for his possibles bag and opened it. From inside the bag, he withdrew a bundle of jerky. Jed offered the jerky to the others. Each took a piece examining it, then smelling it before they tasted it. In a short time, each had a smile on his face as he chewed.

Jed took a bite of his piece remembering the day he and his father had shot the deer. It was the same day his father had taught him how to make jerky.

His reverie was interrupted when a war-cry ripped through the air. An arrow sliced through the shoulder of one of the boys. Jed jumped to his feet as a Sioux warrior charged into the group his raised hand holding a war-hawk. Jed stepped to one side and threw the warrior to the ground then jumped on his back. The Sioux rolled, facing Jed trying to strike him with his axe. Jed grabbed the arm holding the hawk and hit him with his other fist, knocking the warrior unconscious. Jed picked up the weapon and tucked it in his waistband.

Jed signaled to the others that they must leave. Without hesitation, they all followed Jed as he raced through the woods. Behind them, they heard war-whoops which urged them to run faster. Jed signaled them to take cover. The six Crow melted into the undergrowth and waited.

Soon four Sioux warriors came running down the trail. But instead of moving past, one of the sharp-eyed warriors saw that the track had stopped and held up his hand. The Crow youngsters could not believe their eyes. Jed charged into the middle of the Sioux warriors swinging his war-club in one hand and the captured axe in the other. Two of the enemy fell to the ground, their heads cleaved open. Then the rest of the Crow jumped in and finished the fight. Collecting the enemies' weapons, and then their scalps, they turned and raced for home.

Broken Leg was in his lodge when he heard the dogs barking and then whoops and singing from both men and women of the tribe. As he stepped out into the sunlight, he saw his grandson and five other young men coming into the camp. They all were covered in blood, and one was holding his bloody shoulder. Broken Leg watched as the young men approached him. Behind them, their mothers and the Crow warriors followed.

The six stopped in front of Broken Leg. Jed stepped forward and laid an ax, a war-club and two scalps at his feet. The others stepped forward and placed three additional war-clubs and scalps with the others. One of the six spoke. "We planned to take Sioux war-ponies. We were waiting for dark when we were seen by the enemy. One shot an arrow striking Runs Fast. Another charged and your grandson took his weapon away from him but let him live. We ran but were pursued. The young man pointed at Jed and said, "He Who Strikes First told us to hide, which we did until four Sioux warriors stopped to read the sign. He Who Strikes First attacked killing two with an axe in one hand and his war-club in the other. We counted coup on the others, took their weapons and scalps.

There was a murmur of voices until Broken Leg raised his hand for silence. "From this day forward, I will speak of my grandson as 'He Who Strikes First.' Now let us celebrate their safe return."

That night the story was told and retold; sometimes with the boys acting out the action. Later, in Broken Leg's lodge, Jed and his grandfather sat facing each other. "Today, you have counted many coups. You struck an enemy, took an enemy's weapon from him, touched the first enemy to die and led your party back without loss of life. Broken Leg pulled a bag to him and opened it. From it, he withdrew an eagle feather. You may wear this now for all to see, Broken Leg handed it to Jed. You will a make a coup stick and place four notches on its handle. You have been here, but a few moons and have done much. You have the gift of your father. You see quickly and understand. In battle, you do not hesitate. You make this old man's heart sing."

END OF THE TRAIL

LeRue stood on a hill next to his horse, looking down at the trail and the wagon train. They had been traveling for four months now and had just crossed forty miles of salt flats. In the last four months, two wagons had been lost, and ten of the one hundred had perished. All of the deaths were due to accidents or disease. Half of the cattle had been eaten or had died for one reason or another. LeRue mounted his horse and headed for the wagons. 'After days on the flats, the water and pasture I've found will be a welcome sight,' he thought.

Crow rode at the head of the train. 'I hope LeRue has found a good place for us to stop for a couple of days,' he thought. Mr. Nowak rode up and joined Crow, "When do you think LeRue will be back, Mr. Crow?"

Crow pointing to the right replied, "I think he's coming in right now."

Nowak stood in his stirrups to see where Crow was pointing. Seeing nothing, he removed his glasses and then saw a dot on the horizon. 'Incredible!' he thought.

A short time later, LeRue joined them. "I found grass and water; enough for us to rest a few days. At this pace, I figure we'll be there early evening."

"Mr. Nowak, will you pass this on to the others? I'm sure they'll appreciate the good news."

Nowak touched his index finger to the brim of his hat in salute and rode off with the good news on the tip of his tongue.

Crow turned to LeRue, "We all need a rest, that last forty miles were pure hell. I have to give credit to these folks, they're tough. They've walked halfway across this country and still got a couple of months to go."

LeRue looked at his friend, "If anyone needs some rest, it's you. You have been pushing yourself too hard. We get bedded down tonight you have got to get some sleep."

Crow just nodded his head.

'It's that dream he has about Francisca, and he's been shot all to hell by bandits, but here he is. Most men would have given up and died by now,' LeRue thought.

* * *

As LeRue had predicted, it was evening when the smell of water drew the animals to the river and sweet grass. Exhausted, hot and dirty, the people waded out into the water, some just sitting down in the cool running water.

Refreshed, the travelers moved the wagons into a protective circle. The horses and mules were hobbled so they wouldn't wander off. Nowak assigned guards to watch for trouble as the women prepared meals. It was late when everyone that could bedded down for the night.

Crow found a place under a tree near the water. He lay down, his feet pointing east. LeRue watched as his friend of many years fell asleep.

It was early morning when Francisca came to Crow in his dream. Maybe it was because of the running water and the cover of the tree. In his dream, they were by the river next to their hacienda. It seemed so real. Francisca reached out to Crow, but this time it was different. When Isaiah reached out, Francisca took his hand.

The next morning, Mr. Nowak came looking for Crow and found him wrapped in his blanket. He tried to wake him, but Crow did not respond, "LeRue, come quick!"

LeRue knelt next to Crow but knew as soon as he touched him he was gone. Isaiah Crow, the warrior, who fought bandits and the enemies of the Crow. Who fought a grizzly with a knife and won, had died in his sleep.

They buried Crow under the tree with his feet facing east so his spirit would see the sunrise each morning. "Mr. Nowak, I'm gonna be gone for a bit. When you feel it's time, you get the train moving. I'll scout ahead for a place to make our next camp. I'll stay with you till we get to San Diego."

* * *

LeRue rode up into the hills and found a spot where he could see for miles. Dismounting, he hobbled his horse and then went and sat on a flat rock. Without shame, tears rolled down his cheeks. The Mountain Man drew his knife and cut a chunk of his hair in the traditional Crow sign of grief. As if it had been called, a breeze came along as LeRue tossed the hair in the air carrying out across the land. "Well, amigo, we traveled far and have done much. I will miss you like I would my arm. I will fetch your son and return him to California. He too will miss you."

LeRue stood and went to his horse and removed the hobble. Mounting up, he headed west in search of a new campground.

THE RETURN

Jed had been in the Crow village for over a year and a half. His hair had grown long, and he wore it like his father in a net at the nape of his neck. The eagle feather, stuck into the ball of his hair, was worn proudly. He had been on many raiding parties and had earned the respect of the tribe. Though Jed said nothing, he worried that his father and LeRue were late.

It was late spring when LeRue and Santiago found the Crow encampment. Santiago who had never been out of California was amazed by all he had seen on their two-month trek. From their position on some high ground, they looked down at the village. "Sit still and do not touch your weapons," said LeRue in a low voice.

Slowly Santiago became aware that he and LeRue were not alone. From out of the trees, five men wearing wolf hides on their heads appeared. The head of the wolf skin was pulled down over their eyes hiding their faces. Santiago was sure this was to be his last day.

LeRue began signing with his hands to the warriors, "I am a friend of White Crow. I have come for his son."

The Indians stared at the two white men enjoying their nervousness. Then without a word, they turned their war-ponies and disappeared into the woods. "¿Quién diablos eran ellos? (Who the hell were they?)" asked Santiago.

They are called the Wolves; they are the scouts for the Crow. Probably been out all night and came across us. They will let the village know that we are coming."

As LeRue and Santiago neared the village, a lone horseman raced out to meet them. As the horseman drew closer, LeRue saw that it was Jed. 'He has changed so much,' thought LeRue. 'He is heavier and seems taller, and he wears an eagle feather.'

At first, Santiago did not recognize Jed, he had changed so much. As Jed grew closer, for a moment, Santiago thought he was looking at Isaiah Crow.

"LeRue, Santiago!" shouted Jed as he rode up. "Where is my father? Is he coming?"

LeRue rode up close to Jed, "Your father is dead. He died one night as we were headed for San Diego."

Jed sat up straighter on his mount his face like stone. "Was he sick?"

"No, but he was tired. Jed, I think the loss of your mother… He drove himself on the trail. I think that and his wounds from the bandits… well, he went to sleep one night and never woke up."

"Come, we must go and tell Broken Leg."

BROKEN LEG

The death of White Crow brought great sorrow to Broken Leg. In anguish, the old warrior cut off clumps of his hair and cut himself across his chest creating a scar that would remain forever. He then cut off the little finger of his left hand at the first knuckle. These self-inflicted wounds seemed not to cause him as much pain as the loss of his son.

LeRue stopped Jed from following his grandfather's actions. "You are returning to the white man's world. You will need your fingers. Cut your hair. They will understand."

Several days were spent telling and retelling stories about White Crow. Broken Leg and the others asked LeRue, over and over, to talk about the time he spent with White Crow. The stories would influence Jed for the rest of his life.

LeRue had given Jed his father's rifle. Jed had given it to Broken Leg to replace his grandfather's old musket. His grandfather was honored that his grandson would bestow such a precious gift on him. His heart swelled with pride.

The day came when it was time to leave. Jed had conflicting emotions about leaving and told Broken Leg of the pain. "Your father came to me many years ago and told me of the same pain in his heart about leaving. Unlike him, you were first raised in the ways of the white man. You and your father have honored me by his bringing you here to learn our ways. You have proven yourself to be an honorable warrior like your father. Now you must go and find your own way. I think someday you will be a great chief among your people."

Santiago was impressed with the sendoff from the Crow. It was evident that Jed and his father were respected by these amazing people.

NEW BEGINNINGS

Several years passed. The Batista Hacienda was gone, and the land was taken over and sold to new owners by the new American government. The vaqueros had moved on. Only Santiago, LeRue and Jed remained.

The three men were now staying at the mission. It was late in the afternoon, and the three of them were sitting at the table under the tree by the mission cookhouse. "I have decided to head north," said LeRue. "I've never seen that country. I hear there are trees so tall they reach to the heavens."

Santiago stretched out his legs and sat silently examining his hands. Finally, he said, "It is no longer the same. The gringos have taken the land, and our way of life here is over. I have a good horse and enough money to get me to Mexico. I will find Señora Batista, and perhaps she will have a use for me. If not, I have family there."

The two men looked at Jed. "I think I'll head down to San Diego and take a look around; maybe head up to Monterey."

Again, the three sat in quiet contemplation. After a while, LeRue stood up and said, "Santiago, there is one more thing I need to do before you leave. Come with me to my room."

Curious, Jed and Santiago followed LeRue to his room. Once inside, LeRue asked Jed to close the door. With the door closed, LeRue reached under the bed and withdrew a leather sack. He brought it to the table and opened it. He reached inside and pulled out a handful of gold coins. He stacked them on the table and removed the rest, placing them next to the others. "There are one hundred coins here. They are yours," he said to Santiago. "It is the gold Crow and I found buried by the bandits years ago. I know Crow would want you to have this. It will help you get started in Mexico."

His eyes large with surprise, Santiago had trouble finding his voice. "But amigo, what about you and Jed? This is so much oro (gold)!"

"There is more; some for Jed and some for me. Crow gave some to Señora Batista before she left for Mexico. You have been a good friend. We want you to have it."

"Gracious, amigo."

Santiago left the next day. Jed and LeRue watched their friend as he rode out of their lives. "Come, we have one more thing to do." LeRue led Jed back to the room. Once inside, LeRue closed the door and once again reached under his bed. He brought out two bags, both more than twice the size as the one given to Santiago.

"This one is for you, the other for me. Be careful with it, it contains more money than most men will ever see in their lifetime. It could get you killed."

Jed did not open the bag but hefted it in his hand. "I will miss you, LeRue."

AROUND THE HORN

San Diego bustled with activity. The harbor was full of ships from all over the world. The discovery of gold in the north back in '48 had changed California forever. Men of every nation still flocked to the Golden State in hopes of becoming rich. Jed was walking down a street close to the ocean when a voice called out, "Isaiah, Isaiah Crow!"

Jed turned to see a man, short in stature but powerfully built. He was dressed in black and wore a captain's cap. As the man rushed up with his hand extended, he stopped. With a look of surprise on his face, he said, "I apologize, young man, I thought you were someone else."

"You knew Isaiah Crow? He was my father."

"Was?" asked the man.

"My father died a few years ago. I'm Jed, Jedadiah Crow."

"I'm sorry to hear of your father's passing. I'm Captain King. Your father saved me a great deal of money once. We became good friends. I even attended his wedding."

"I'm headed for the cantina down the street. Would you care to join me?" asked Jed.

"Why yes, I feel the need for something to eat. My ship sails tonight and it will be some time before I'll have food from a cantina again."

It was an enjoyable meal. Jed was fascinated by Captain King's stories, and when it came time to go, Jed asked, "I know it's late notice, but could I purchase passage aboard your ship?"

"You want to go to Boston, do you?"

"Yes and no. I have heard about the War of Rebellion (The American Civil War) and thought I would travel overland. I know it would take months. However, if I can get passage with you…"

"You plan on joining the Army, do you?"

"Yes sir, the cavalry if they'll have me. I'm good with horses, and I can read and write."

"Son, you are welcome aboard my ship and to sail for nothing. The money your father saved me paid your passage in advance. Say, you don't happen to own any books do you?"

"I have several of my father's books."

"Yes, it will be a pleasure having you aboard. When we leave here, I'll show you where to be at five this afternoon. I will send a boat to pick you up."

* * *

The sun was setting, and the sky was ablaze with color as **The Boston Queen's** bow sliced through the Pacific waters. Jed stood alone, breathing in the smell of the ocean. They were headed for The Cape of Good Hope, "Around the Horn," as Captain King put it.

Around the Horn and on to a new life.

THE END

About the Author

John was born in February of 1941 and raised in Flint, Michigan. His was a middle-class family. His father was a musician and a radio disk jockey. His mother wrote short stories and radio scripts. His mother and father had a Sunday afternoon radio program. His mother wrote the scripts, and both parents played the different characters.

As a teen, John worked at a gun shop and learned a great deal about weapons, hunting, and shooting. He became an instructor for shooting skeet and trap. John came in second as junior state champion. This training came in handy when he joined the Marines in 1959 after high school.

In the Marines, John graduated boot camp with promotion and sent to Camp Pendleton to work as a small arms repairman. He attended several weapons classes, always finishing in the top ten in his class.

John later was assigned to a guard company in Guam. During this tour, John and another marine were involved in a prolonged gunfight with six intruders in a highly restricted area. They captured five of the intruders and the sixth was arrested the next day. They were given letters of accommodation for "Prompt and heroic action while in a restricted area." John returned to the states just in time to be deployed to Cuba during the Cuban Missile Crisis. Upon his return from Cuba, John was honorably discharged.

John spent the next several years working in law enforcement in California. He was a city officer, federal officer, and a deputy. Police officers did not make a great deal of money back then. By now John was married with two children. He began working in heavy construction as a teamster driving the big heavy trucks you often see in mining. During this time the family decided to move back to Michigan. Unlike California, construction work in Michigan was seasonal, so he sought a more stable job.

John found it in foundry work. He began work as a mold maker and eventually worked his way up to superintendent of a three shift 210 man shop. It was during this time that he saw a business opportunity.

John wrote a business plan for a security patrol. The business started out with three employees and two patrol vehicles. In a short period, it grew to 110 employees, with a superbly trained team of bodyguards. The business expanded into international sales of equipment. During this time John attended schools and became certified as a bodyguard and a security driver. His company protected high profile people from executives to visiting royalty. They also contracted to investigate drugs in the workplace and internal theft, working closely with local and state agencies.

The security business required John to travel across the United States, Europe, Japan, Korea, and the Middle East. He met and worked with men and women of different Special Forces from around the world, and law enforcement. John met and befriended high officials in Eastern Europe many of whom he still communicates.

John sold the business several years ago and retired to Las Vegas, Nevada. He began writing using his experiences and knowledge of the military and police. John has written two novels, "The House of Crow" and "White Crow." John is finishing the third book of The House of Crow trilogy, "The Crow Legacy." A third published book, a novella, "With Deadly Purpose," is published and is also in audio.

Lightning Source UK Ltd.
Milton Keynes UK
UKHW011502041120
372792UK00001B/63